HER BILLIONAIRE BOSS

BLACK TIE BILLIONAIRES, BOOK #1

JO GRAFFORD

Copyright © 2019 by Jo Grafford

All rights reserved.

No part of this book may be reproduced in any form without written permission from the author or publisher, except as permitted by U.S. copyright law.

ISBN: 978-1-944794-22-4

GET A FREE BOOK!

Join my mailing list to be the first to know about new releases, freebies, special discounts, and Bonus Content. Plus, you get a FREE sweet romance book for signing up!

https://BookHip.com/JNNHTK

ACKNOWLEDGMENTS

Many heartfelt thanks to my editor, Cathleen Weaver, for her incredible eye for detail and beta reader J. Sherlock. I also want to give a shout out to my Cuppa Jo Readers on Facebook. Thank you for reading and enjoying my books. I adore our life chats and book chats!

CHAPTER 1: THE INTERVIEW

JACEY

Jacey Maddox didn't bother straightening her navy pencil skirt or smoothing her hand over the sleek lines of her creamy silk blouse. She already knew she looked her best. She knew her makeup was flawless, each dash of color accentuating her sun kissed skin and classical features. She knew this, because she'd spent way too many of her twenty-five years facing the paparazzi; and after her trust fund had run dry, posing for an occasional glossy centerfold — something she wasn't entirely proud of.

Unfortunately, not one drop of that experience lent her any confidence as she mounted the cold, marble stairs of Genesis & Sons. It towered more than twenty stories over the Alaskan Gulf waters, a stalwart high-rise of white and gray stone with tinted windows, a fortress that housed one of the world's most brilliant think tanks. For generations, the sons of Genesis had ridden the cutting edge of industrial design, developing the concepts behind some of the nation's most profitable inventions, products, and manufacturing processes.

It was the one place on earth Jacey was least welcome.

Not just because of how many of her escapades had hit the presses during her rebel teen years. Not just because she'd possessed the audacity to marry their youngest son against their wishes. Not just because she had encouraged him to pursue his dreams instead of their hallowed corporate mission — a decision that had ultimately gotten him killed. No. The biggest reason Genesis & Sons hated her was because of her last name. The one piece of herself she'd refused to give up when she'd married Easton Calcagni.

Maddox.

The name might as well have been stamped across her forehead like the mark of the beast, as she moved into the crosshairs of their first security camera. It flashed an intermittent red warning light and gave a low electronic whirring sound as it swiveled to direct its lens on her.

Her palms grew damp and her breathing quickened as she stepped into the entry foyer of her family's greatest corporate rival.

Recessed mahogany panels lined the walls above

a mosaic tiled floor, and an intricately carved booth anchored the center of the room. A woman with silver hair waving past her shoulders lowered her reading glasses to dangle from a pearlized chain. "May I help you?"

Jacey's heartbeat stuttered and resumed at a much faster pace. The woman was no ordinary receptionist. Her arresting blue gaze and porcelain features had graced the tabloids for years. She was Waverly, matriarch of the Calcagni family, grandmother to the three surviving Calcagni brothers. She was the one who'd voiced the greatest protests to Easton's elopement. She'd also wept in silence throughout his interment into the family mausoleum, while Jacey had stood at the edge of their gathering, dry-eyed and numb of soul behind a lacy veil.

The funeral had taken place exactly two months earlier.

"I have a one o'clock appointment with Mr. Luca Calcagni."

Waverly's gaze narrowed to twin icy points. "Not just any appointment, Ms. Maddox. You are here for an interview, I believe?"

Time to don her boxing gloves. "Yes." She could feel the veins pulsing through her temples now. She'd prepared for a rigorous cross-examination but had not expected it to begin in the entry foyer.

"Why are you really here?"

Five simple words, yet they carried the force of a

full frontal attack. Beneath the myriad of accusations shooting from Waverly's eyes, Jacey wanted to spin on her peep-toe stiletto pumps and run. Instead, she focused on regulating her breathing. It was a fair question. Her late husband's laughing face swam before her, both taunting and encouraging, as her mind ran over all the responses she'd rehearsed. None of them seemed adequate.

"I'm here because of Easton." It was the truth stripped of every excuse. She was here to atone for her debt to the family she'd wronged.

Pain lanced through the aging woman's gaze, twisting her fine-boned features with lines. Raw fury followed. "Do you want something from us, Ms. Maddox?" Condescension infused her drawling alto.

Not what you're thinking, that's for sure. I'm no gold-digger. "Yes. Very much. I want a job at Genesis." She could never restore Easton to his family, but she would offer herself in his place. She would spend the rest of her career serving their company in whatever capacity they would permit. It was the penance she'd chosen for herself.

The muscles around Waverly's mouth tightened a few degrees more. "Why not return to DRAW Corporation? To your own family?"

She refused to drop the elder woman's gaze as she absorbed each question, knowing they were shot like bullets to shatter her resolve, to remind her how unwelcome her presence was. She'd expected no other reception from the Calcagni dynasty; some would even argue she deserved this woman's scorn. However, she'd never been easily intimidated, a trait that was at times a strength and other times a curse. "With all due respect, Mrs. Calcagni, this *is* my family now."

Waverly's lips parted as if she would protest. Something akin to fear joined the choleric emotions churning across her countenance. She clamped her lips together, while her chest rose and fell several times. "You may take a seat now." She waved a heavily be-ringed hand to indicate the lounge area to her right. Lips pursed the skin around her mouth into papery creases, as she punched a few buttons on the call panel. "Ms. Maddox has arrived." Her frigid tone transformed each word into ice picks.

Jacey expelled the two painful clumps of air her lungs had been holding prisoner in a silent, drawn-out whoosh as she eased past the reception booth. She'd survived the first round of interrogations, a small triumph that yielded her no satisfaction. She knew the worst was yet to come. Waverly Calcagni was no more than a guard dog; Luca Calcagni was the one they sent into the boxing ring to finish off their opponents.

Luca apparently saw fit to allow her to marinate in her uneasiness past their appointment time. Not a surprise. He had the upper hand today and would do everything in his power to squash her with it. A full hour cranked away on the complicated maze of copper gears and chains on the wall. There was nothing ordinary about the interior of Genesis & Sons. Even their clocks were remarkable feats of architecture.

"Ms. Maddox? Mr. Calcagni is ready to see you."

She had to remind herself to breathe as she stood. At first she could see nothing but Luca's tall silhouette in the shadowed archway leading to the inner sanctum of Genesis & Sons. Then he took a step forward into a beam of sunlight and beckoned her to follow him. She stopped breathing again but somehow forced her feet to move in his direction.

He was everything she remembered and more from their few brief encounters. Much more. Up close, he seemed taller, broader, infinitely more intimidating, and so wickedly gorgeous it made her dizzy. That her parents had labeled him and his brothers as forbidden fruit made them all the more appealing to her during her teen years. It took her fascinated brain less than five seconds to recognize Luca had lost none of his allure.

The blue-black sheen of his hair, clipped short on the sides and longer on top, lent a deceptive innocence that didn't fool her one bit. Nor did the errant lock slipping to his forehead on one side. The expensive weave of his suit and complex twists of his tie far better illustrated his famed unpredictable temperament. His movements were controlled but fluid, bringing to her mind the restless prowl of a panther as she followed him down the hall and into an elevator. It shimmered with mirrored glass and recessed mahogany panels.

They rode in tense silence to the top floor.

Arrogance rolled off Luca Calcagni from his crisply pressed white shirt, to his winking diamond and white gold cuff links, down to his designer leather shoes. In some ways, his arrogance was understandable. He guided the helm of one of the world's most profitable companies, after all. And his eyes! They were as beautiful and dangerous as the rest of him. Tawny with flecks of gold, they regarded her with open contempt as he ushered her from the elevator.

They entered a room surrounded by glass. One wall of windows overlooked the gulf waters. The other three framed varying angles of the Anchorage skyline. Gone was the old-world elegance of the first floor. This room was all Luca. A statement of power in chrome and glass. Sheer contemporary minimalism with no frills.

"Have a seat." It was an order, not an offer. A call to battle.

It was a battle she planned to win. She didn't want to consider the alternative — slinking back to her humble apartment in defeat.

He flicked one darkly tanned hand at the pair of Chinese Chippendale chairs resting before his expansive chrome desk. The chairs were stained black like the heart of their owner. No cushions. They were not designed for comfort, only as a place to park guests whom the CEO did not intend to linger.

Jacey planned to change his mind on that subject before her allotted hour was up. "Thank you." Without hesitation, she took the chair on the right, making no pretense of being in the driver's seat. This was his domain. Given the chance, she planned to mold herself into the indispensable right hand to whoever in the firm he was willing to assign her. On paper, she might not look like she had much to offer, but there was a whole pack of demons driving her. An asset he wouldn't hesitate to exploit once he recognized its unique value. Or so she hoped.

To her surprise, he didn't seat himself behind his executive throne. Instead, he positioned himself between her and his desk, hiking one hip on the edge and folding his arms. It was a deliberate invasion of her personal space with all six feet two of his darkly arresting half-Hispanic features and commanding presence.

Most women would have swooned.

Jacey wasn't most women. She refused to give him the satisfaction of either fidgeting or being the first to break the silence. Silence was a powerful weapon, something she'd learned at the knees of her parents. Prepared to use whatever it took to get what she'd come for, she allowed it to stretch well past the point of politeness.

Luca finally unfolded his arms and reached for the file sitting on the edge of his desk. "I read your application and resume. It didn't take long."

According to her mental tally, the first point belonged to her. She nodded to acknowledge his insult and await the next.

He dangled her file above the trash canister beside his desk and released it. It dropped and settled with a papery flutter.

"I fail to see how singing in nightclubs the past five years qualifies you for any position at Genesis & Sons."

The attack was so predictable she wanted to smile, but didn't dare. Too much was at stake. She'd made the mistake of taunting him with a smile once before. Nine years earlier. Hopefully, he'd long forgotten the ill-advised lark.

Or not. His golden gaze fixed itself with such intensity on her mouth that her insides quaked with uneasiness. Nine years later, he'd become harder and exponentially more ruthless. She'd be wise to remember it.

"Singing is one of art's most beautiful forms," she countered softly. "According to recent studies, scientists believe it releases endorphins and oxytocin while reducing cortisol." *There.* He wasn't the only one who'd been raised in a tank swimming with intellectual minds.

The tightening of his jaw was the only indication her answer had caught him by surprise. Luca was a man of facts and numbers. Her answer couldn't have possibly displeased him, yet his upper lip curled. "If you came to sing for me, Ms. Maddox, I'm all ears."

The smile burgeoning inside her mouth vanished. Every note of music in her had died with her husband. That part of her life was over. "We both know I did not submit my employment application in the hopes of landing a singing audition." She started to rise, a calculated risk. "If you don't have any interest in conducting the interview you agreed to, I'll just excuse my—"

"Have a seat, Ms. Maddox." Her veiled suggestion of his inability to keep his word clearly stung.

She sat.

"Remind me what other qualifications you disclosed on your application. There were so few, they seem to have slipped my mind."

Nothing slipped his mind. She would bet all the money she no longer possessed on it. "A little forgetfulness is understandable, Mr. Calcagni. You're a very busy man."

Her dig hit home. This time the clench of his jaw was more perceptible.

Now that she had his full attention, she plunged

on. "My strengths are in behind-the-scenes marketing as well as personal presentations. As you are well aware, I cut my teeth on DRAW Corporation's drafting tables. I'm proficient in an exhaustive list of software programs and a whiz at compiling slides, notes, memes, video clips, animated graphics, and most types of printed materials. My family just this morning offered to return me to my former position in marketing."

"Why would they do that?"

"They hoped to crown me Vice President of Communications in the next year or two. I believe their exact words were *it's my rightful place*." As much as she tried to mask it, a hint of derision crept into Jacey's voice. There were plenty of employees on her family's staff who were far more qualified and deserving of the promotion.

Luca Calcagni's lynx eyes narrowed to slits. "You speak in the past tense, Ms. Maddox. After recalling what a flight risk you are, I presume your family withdrew their offer?"

It was a slap at her elopement with his brother. She'd figured he'd work his way around to it, eventually. "No." She deliberately bit her lower lip, testing him with another ploy that rarely failed in her dealings with men. "I turned them down."

His gaze locked on her mouth once more. Male interest flashed across his face and was gone. "Why?"

He was primed for the kill. She spread her hands and went for the money shot. "To throw myself at your complete mercy, Mr. Calcagni." The beauty of it was that the trembling in her voice wasn't faked; the request she was about to make was utterly genuine. "As your sister by marriage, I am not here to debate my qualifications or lack of them. I am begging you to give me a job. I need the income. I need to be busy. I'll take whatever position you are willing to offer, so long as it allows me to come to work in this particular building." She whipped her face aside, no longer able to meet his gaze. "Here," she reiterated fiercely, "where *he* doesn't feel as far away as he does outside these walls."

Because of the number of moments it took to compose herself, she missed his initial reaction to her words. When she tipped her face up to his once more, his expression was unreadable.

"Assuming everything you say is true, Ms. Maddox, and you're not simply up to another one of your games," he paused, his tone indicating he thought she was guilty of the latter, "we do not currently have any job openings."

"That's not what your publicist claims, and it's certainly not what you have posted on your website." She dug through her memory to resurrect a segment of the Genesis creed. "Where innovation and vision collide. Where the world's most introspective minds are ever welcome—"

"Believe me, Ms. Maddox, I am familiar with our corporate creed. There is no need to repeat it. Especially since I have already made my decision concerning your employment."

Fear sliced through her. They were only five minutes into her interview, and he was shutting her down. "Mr. Calcagni, I—"

He stopped her with an upraised hand. "You may start your two-week trial in the morning. Eight o'clock sharp."

He was actually offering her a job? Or, in this case, a ticket to the next round? According to her inner points tally, she hadn't yet accumulated enough to win. It didn't feel like a victory, either. She had either failed to read some of his cues, or he was better at hiding them than anyone else she'd ever encountered. She no longer had any idea where they stood with each other in their banter of words, who was winning and who was losing. It made her insides weaken to the consistency of jelly.

"Since we have no vacancies in the vice presidency category," he infused an ocean-sized dose of sarcasm into his words, "you'll be serving as my personal assistant. Like every other position on our payroll, it amounts to long hours, hard work, and no coddling. You're under no obligation to accept my offer, of course."

"I accept." She couldn't contain her smile this time. She didn't understand his game, but she'd achieved what she'd come for. Employment. No matter how humble the position. Sometimes it was best not to overthink things. "Thank you, Mr. Calcagni."

There was no answering warmth in him. "You won't be thanking me tomorrow."

"A risk I will gladly take." She rose to seal her commitment with a handshake and immediately realized her mistake.

Standing brought her nearly flush with her new boss. Close enough to catch a whiff of his aftershave — a woodsy musk with a hint of cobra slithering her way. Every organ in her body suffered a tremor beneath the full blast of his scrutiny.

When his long fingers closed over hers, her insides radiated with the same intrinsic awareness of him she'd experienced nine years ago — the day they first met.

It was a complication she hadn't counted on.

CHAPTER 2: HASTY BOARD MEETING
LUCA

Luca claimed his office chair for the first time during the interview and rang the Human Resources Department. He resisted the urge to loosen his collar, desperately needing the five feet of distance between him and the delectable Jacey Maddox. "Send someone up to escort Ms. Maddox down. Have her fill out the standard apprentice paperwork and give her the tour." She hadn't moved from where he'd left her standing in front of his desk. "She starts in the morning."

Her slender frame radiated exultation, an emotion he planned to extinguish first thing in the morning. She thought she'd played him. A spoiled rich girl who was way too accustomed to getting her way, she thought she'd outmaneuvered him. *Him!* He hadn't missed the mock lip biting or carefully modulated hand gestures and hated the way the male in him had so eagerly responded.

He worked on his computer, pretending to ignore his newest employee the remaining few minutes it took Human Resources to send up their representative to lead her from his office. But he remained acutely conscious of every inch, every curve that comprised Jacey Maddox. Assuming her curves were even real, not enhanced by cosmetic surgery. Regardless, she was built to entice, from the cascade of her near-white blonde hair to her falsely innocent baby blues to the outrageously expensive navy stilettos encasing her feet. And she knew how to use her attributes to tempt. To ensnare. She'd been honing her skills for years. At least nine years. He could vouch for that.

When the elevator doors closed behind her, leaving the faint trace of her perfume, he lounged deeper in his chair, replaying each sentence of their conversation and dissecting every word. He always studied his opponents. She would return in less than seventeen hours to continue playing her games, and he intended to be ready. He fully planned to parry her next tactic and launch a few of his own. To unveil her true motives and macerate them. To send her running from Genesis so scarred with defeat she would never again present a threat to the family he loved so dearly or the employees he was honor-bound to protect.

It would have helped to extend their interview, to allow her to play out more of her games here and now. Ending it prematurely was a missed opportunity to learn more about her up close and in person, but her tears had eliminated that option.

He'd always been a sucker for a woman in tears, but Jacey in tears? It had almost shattered his composure. Almost, but he was made of stronger stuff.

It was the only part of their meeting that hadn't felt contrived, which meant she'd refined her wiles to deadly levels. She'd managed to stir something deep and elemental inside him. He was going to have to don his thickest emotional chainmail when he faced her tomorrow.

It wasn't the first time she'd practiced her siren charm on him. The difference was this time she wouldn't be the one to walk away laughing.

He'd been twenty-three the last time she'd ensnared him in one of her little games, while he was sunbathing on a secluded stretch of beach at the Gulf Island Country Club. The manmade stream wound its way around and through their award-winning golf course. He'd been alone, emptying his mind of his latest contract negotiations, soaking up the last of the evening's rays when Jacey had strolled across his vision.

AS A RULE, *their families didn't socialize. He nudged his shades higher and settled further behind his book, hoping the youngest of the Maddox offspring wouldn't recognize him if she noticed him at all. He had no trouble recognizing her, the little minx. She couldn't be more than Easton's age, but she was already making headlines. Not the kind most parents wanted, either. She was a hellcat in flip-flops. A spoiled, privileged brat who drifted from one scrape to the next with an occasional run-in with the law. Her list of sins wrapped the perimeter of the city at least twice. Defacing public property, breaking curfews, and getting expelled from her college preparatory high school. A felon in the making if the iron arm of Maddox failed to rein her in.*

Guilt clawed its way around the edges of Luca's mind. He had his hands full trying to curb his youngest brother of some of the same things. He prayed the kid would grow out of it soon. Where was that scamp, anyway? He'd gone on a smoothie run a half hour ago.

Luca squinted at Jacey from behind the corner of his book. Why was she lingering? The few times he'd run into her before, she'd been surrounded by an entourage of friends. Where were they on this unseasonably warm afternoon? It was eighty degrees out, which was almost unheard of in Kodiak — or anywhere else in Alaska, for that matter.

Not only was she alone, she appeared bent on

staying awhile. Gazing over the gulf waters, she slowly peeled down her denim shorts to reveal a hot pink swimsuit.

Luca forced his gaze back to his book, trying to give her some privacy, but Jacey was hard to ignore. She slid to the sand to sit cross-legged facing the water. Her back was to him. If it was solitude she was seeking, maybe he should alert her to his presence. While he debated what he would say, she yanked her swim covering over her head and tossed it aside.

His mouth went dry at the creamy perfection of her skin. There was just enough sun to lend it a faint flush of gold. No freckles. Her lithesome sides curved down to a slender waist and flared over the most beautiful legs God had ever created. Not the most appropriate thoughts for a man several years older than her, but his better judgment seemed to be rolling at a slow pace today. He stared, transfixed, as a hand with silver painted fingernails inched its way across her shoulder blades to the ties of her bright pink bikini top.

Whoa. Stop! No. Luca hastily gathered his few belongings, preparing to exit the beach if necessary, but all she did was push the ties aside to rub on a dollop of sunscreen.

"Heya there, Jace!" Easton jogged across the expanse of the beach toward them, a smoothie in each hand. "Should probably charge my brother, Luc, for

the view. Don't think he's getting much reading done."

Jacey tipped her head to laugh up at Easton. Not a girlish giggle, either, but a full-throated husky sound that made Luca think of rose-petal drenched walkways and candlelit dinners.

The two of them were friends? He shot his brother a what-are-you-thinking-you-moron kind of look and received a shrug in return.

Jacey stood and slowly stooped to retrieve her shorts and swim covering, peeping around her arm at Luca. Her lips curved in an impish, knowing smirk.

He was shocked into immobility. The arms he'd thrown up at his brother remained suspended in midair. She'd staged the pretend strip-down for his benefit?

Her mocking laughter pealed over him again, stoking the tempest she'd stirred in him. Fury laced with desire. The vixen clearly had no idea what a perilous game she played. Eventually, someone was going to teach her a lesson.

He desperately wanted to be that someone, but now was not the time for him to teach Jacey Maddox any lessons. Maybe some day. After she grew up.

Most unfortunately, Luca had never gotten to deliver his lesson. She'd eloped with his youngest brother before he had the chance.

HIS PHONE BUZZED. It was LeAnne.

"It's Rhys on line two, sir." Rhys was one of his brothers, and their shared executive secretary, LeAnne, was efficient and succinct, a woman who didn't waste words. It would be interesting to observe her reaction to Jacey when he introduced them in the morning, once she realized the youngest daughter of their biggest competitor was now employed by Genesis. Not that it mattered. Jacey wasn't going to last long. He would personally see to it.

"Yes?" Rhys never bothered him unless it was important.

"We're assembled in the board room if you can spare a minute." There were questions in his brother's voice. There was concern, too.

Ah. Obviously, his grandmother had seen fit to announce Jacey's arrival to the rest of their clan.

"I'm on my way." Best to face them right away. His family deserved a full and immediate update on Jacey's employment status. As a precaution, he'd alerted their legal council the moment they'd received her application a few days ago.

On the elevator ride down, he carefully formulated what he would tell his family. More than anything, his grandparents and brothers needed reassurance. Reassurance he had this latest crisis under control. Reassurance the Calcagnis hadn't been somehow cursed by the Fates. After the death of his parents two years earlier during a deep sea diving expedition, followed all too soon by Easton's fatal race car crash, they'd suffered enough. More than their share.

He entered the boardroom and scanned the faces of each family member, gauging their expressions and making final tweaks to what he was about to say.

Edric presided at the head of their famed twenty-foot conference table, his hands clasped loosely on the solid slab of white Sylacauga marble. The years were showing in his shock of frosted hair, crepe skin, and hand tremors. Their grandfather only served in an advisory capacity these days, preferring the solid whack of a golf ball most afternoons over the ever-changing screenshots of products in varying stages of design. He'd certainly earned his lighter workload. He also taught Sunday School at the church around the corner. The brothers continued to enjoy his keen and often humorous guidance, dreading the day when they would have to carry on without it.

Rhys, who served as the chief operating officer of Genesis, and Knox, who served as the chief financial officer, were seated opposite each other in the seats closest to Edric. Rhys reclined in his chair, one hand wrapped around a mug of coffee. His knees nudged the cherry wood base of the table with its raised relief carvings of ancient Roman businessmen at work and play. Their youngest brother sat forward in his seat, tapping away on his electronic tablet. Both glanced up expectantly at him.

Waverly was pacing the length of the boardroom. She was past seventy and had never served in any official capacity at Genesis, preferring to leave her handprint on various charities and other worthy causes throughout the city. Now that she was retired, she amused herself by showing up to the office unannounced, flitting from floor to floor, and jumping into whatever project suited her fancy. The employees adored her interest in their work, the bottomless trays of homemade cookies she showered on them, and the impromptu breaks she offered while covering their duty stations. It allowed her to keep a strong finger on the pulse of both official and unofficial company business, an asset the brothers had learned to treasure. It had also allowed her to intercept Jacey Maddox when she'd arrived an hour earlier.

"Oh, Luca!" His grandmother swept his way to clutch his shoulders. "Did that vixen finally spill what she wants? When I asked, all she spouted was some nonsense about how we're her family now. As if!"

He embraced her. When she continued to cling to him, he addressed the occupants of the room over her head. "Ms. Maddox claims the only thing she wants from us is a job."

"Please tell me you said no," his grandmother moaned into his dress shirt.

"I did."

"Thank God. And thank *you*."

"Hang on to that thought." He drew the most beloved woman in his life at an arm's length. "She begged me to reconsider and swore she would take any job we had to offer."

"She actually begged? Lord, have mercy! You didn't fall for that line, did you?"

"She claimed being in the building makes *him* seem less far away."

The color drained from Waverly's face. She sank in the nearest chair and leaned heavily on the table. "You hired her," she whispered. "You already went and hired the hussy."

Luca's chest tightened. He hated being the cause of her misery, but there were certain rules he had to follow as a CEO, certain lines he couldn't cross in the fair treatment of new and potential employees. Jacey would sink her own boat soon enough, giving him reason to fire her. Then his family would be done with her, once and for all.

"What is your theory about her true motives, Luc?" Rhys asked calmly.

Luca didn't know what he'd done to deserve his next younger brother's unshakable trust. It was part of a special bond they'd shared for as long as he could remember. Similar to the bond between twins, though nearly two years separated them.

Rhys's lips twisted in a bitter smile, and he

continued speaking before Luca had a chance to formulate a response. "There are the more obvious explanations, of course. Opportunist. Gold digger. Word on the street is Jacey Maddox is flat broke. Her family disowned her when she left town."

To elope with Easton. The tension in the room swelled to suffocating levels at what Rhys left unsaid.

Knox flung an arm atop the nearest empty chair. "Or corporate spy. It wouldn't be the first time they tried to steal something from us." He waggled his brows, an unconscious imitation of Edric, proof of the bone of humor he'd inherited from their grandfather.

Luca laced his hands together and pointed his two forefingers at Knox while taking his seat. "She claims her family offered to reinstate her marketing position at DRAW, but she turned them down. Sounds like that happened no more than a couple of hours before our interview."

Their grandfather's deep voice boomed across the table. He was hard of hearing and tended to shout when he forgot to turn up his hearing aid. "I met with our attorney over lunch. Easton's wedding was legal and binding, and there's no sign of a prenuptial agreement. If Ms. Maddox wants to pursue a settlement as his widow, the courts may find her entitled to some portion of his estate. However, Easton never got around to making her his beneficiary on his life insurance — no surprise there — so it could take some time for the courts to sort it all out." Easton had possessed no financial management skills and had been content to leave the task to his family.

"We'll fight her every step of the way if she tries to take one cent. She's already taken enough from us." Waverly pressed her lips to steepled fingers. "What are we going to do about her, Luca?"

He waited until all eyes were turned his way. "We're going to give her what she asked for. A job."

"You sure about this, Luc?" Knox straightened his tie. "A Maddox won't exactly be well-received in our marketing department."

"True. That's why she'll be serving as my personal assistant." He offered a humorless smile with the bomb he laid on his family. "Her workload won't leave time for causing trouble. Not that she's going to last long at Genesis."

His grandmother's face brightened.

A knock sounded on the boardroom door. At a nod from Luca, Rhys rose to open it.

The employee they'd been so intensely discussing stood in the doorway, her expression wary.

CHAPTER 3: MEETING THE CLAN
JACEY

It didn't require a degree in psychology for Jacey to deduce the Calcagni clan had been discussing her. She glanced around the room to ensure no one was brandishing weapons in her direction.

"I'm so sorry," Rosa from Human Resources breathed at her side. "I didn't see a meeting on the schedule for this room, and it's the last part of our tour." She raised her voice to address the Calcagnis. "I'm so sorry, ma'am. Sirs." She inclined her head and laid a hand on Jacey's arm, taking a step back.

"Don't be," Rhys assured. "If you're finished with her paperwork, Rosa, one of us can handle the rest of Ms. Maddox's tour." He glanced at Luca. "Unless the Board has any objections?"

"Not at all. Thank you, Rosa. Come in, Ms. Maddox." Luca stood. His family mirrored his movements stiffly, as if pulled by marionette strings.

They beheld her like one would a deadly virus. Under a different set of circumstances, she might have found it humorous. They would soon discover their disapproval didn't phase her. She possessed a thick layer of skin to insulate her from the emotion, which had been doled out in copious amounts her entire life by her parents, grandparents, school officials, the local police department, television reporters, and countless others not worth remembering.

The bruised cast to Waverly's gaze *did* affect her, however. It was the biggest reason Jacey wanted to work for Genesis. She'd witnessed the same deep shadows etched around her own eyes in the mirror each morning, evidence of the incubus who tormented her soul each night. She was simply more skilled than the older woman at hiding her pain beneath makeup and theatrics. Four years of drama class in high school had helped. So had singing in clubs, but not anymore. The only place Jacey sang these days was from the back pew of the church she attended, where no one could hear her.

"I'm looking forward to starting work in the morning, Mr. Calcagni." She graciously inclined her head. "Your job offer was so kind." Now that her atonement had begun, maybe she would find sleep tonight. She was exhausted all the way down to her bone marrow and felt like she was literally tottering in her high-heels.

"My pleasure."

It was anything but. They both knew it.

She shivered at the undercurrent of warning in his tone. Her instincts told her he wasn't envisioning the exchange of niceties over coffee and paperwork. He was more likely mentally roasting her over a spit in some dark corner of the building.

His middle brother held out his hand. "For obvious reasons, we go by first names around here. I'm Rhys. Welcome to the firm, Ms. Maddox."

She shook it. "Thank you. Please call me Jacey."

He nodded gravely and released her hand.

It was the first time they'd ever spoken directly. His impeccable manners didn't extend to his eyes, though. They regarded her with the same shrewdness as his older brother, albeit with a little less ice around the edges.

"I'm Knox." The third brother's handshake was painful.

He was the youngest in the family now, a fact that weighed more heavily on Jacey than his iron hand press. It was largely her fault he no longer had a younger sibling. She wordlessly accepted the black distrust in his gaze, silently endured his attempt to crush her bones, and turned to face his grandparents.

Edric beheld her with a strange mix of suspicion and wistfulness. Instead of shaking her hand, he clasped it between both of his for an extended moment. "You look just like her."

"Who?" She didn't recall reading anything about it in the gossip columns, but maybe the patriarch of Genesis suffered from dementia.

Waverly's fingernails dug into Jacey's other hand. "Iona!" She spat out the name, as if her mouth couldn't get rid of it fast enough.

Ah. She was referring to Jacey's own grandmother, the woman at the root of their family feud. Years ago, Iona had dated Edric but at some point had secretly fallen in love with his best friend and business partner, Jensen Maddox. Jacey's grandfather. Their subsequent marriage had marked the end of a corporate partnership and the beginning of a rival firm.

Though Jacey couldn't be blamed for what had happened before she was born, she had wronged this family deeply of her own accord. It was no wonder everything in their demeanor suggested they wanted her dead or removed to another planet. She'd expected as much and was prepared to fight the long uphill battle toward winning their forgiveness. As much as she wanted to, she knew it would do no good to spell out her true reasons for coming to work for them. It was too soon. They wouldn't believe her. Trust wasn't something a person could buy with a few faint apologies, flowery sentences, or any other words, for that matter. It was something a person had to earn.

"I'll escort you to the door." Luca ushered her

from the boardroom, his serpentine gaze glinting with something she couldn't quite define. Anticipation? Malevolence? Glee?

So her tour was to be cut short. It felt like a bad omen and made Jacey shiver as she glided past him from the room. The sound of her heels clacking down the hallway were amplified by the acoustics of the copper paneled ceiling. It almost sounded like she was running.

Well, maybe she *was* walking a little faster than necessary. Chagrined at what must have looked like a cowardly dash from the boardroom, she abruptly slowed her steps as she neared the front entrance. It was a mistake. Luca, who must have been silently dogging her heels, nearly plowed into her.

His hands clamped her waist, bringing them both to a halt.

There were no apologies for their near collision, no quick unhanding and backing away. His hold on her was unhurried and deliberate. It also forced her to stand much closer to him than she preferred.

His breath stirred a tendril of hair brushing her cheek, unnerving her a few notches more. "Are you running away from something, Ms. Maddox?"

For a handful of heartbeats, she couldn't think, only feel. The awareness she'd experienced in his office earlier charged between them again, more potent than before. An awareness that held not a single ounce of brotherly or sisterly overtones.

"Should I be, Mr. Calcagni?" She wanted to recall the question as soon as it escaped her lips, but it was too late.

"Oh yes, Ms. Maddox. You absolutely should be."

She tipped her chin, lips compressed in determination as she turned around to face him. "Why is that?" She gave herself a mental high-five for her coolly detached voice, despite the scorching heat the imprint of his long fingers had left on her waistline.

The curl of his lips was more of a sneer than a smile. "You've been away from the design industry too long. No doubt you'll find even the most entry-level tasks at Genesis are way over your head."

His taunting only strengthened her resolve. She raised her chin another inch. "I look forward to proving otherwise."

"Until tomorrow then, Ms. Maddox." He neither stepped back nor released her gaze.

Apparently he hadn't received the memo about using first names. Regardless, her knees felt too weak to extend their staring contest a second longer than necessary. Besides, she'd already accomplished what she'd come for. "Until tomorrow, Mr. Calcagni." It was a wonder her voice didn't tremble the way her insides were. She pivoted and exited the building without looking back. Or tripping. Or collapsing.

Her shoulders didn't relax until she rounded the next corner and drew out of sight of Genesis & Sons, Inc. On the short walk to the metro station, she replayed her encounter with the Calcagnis. She weighed each introduction, each handshake, each facial expression. Her conclusion was the tabloids and business rags had been dead wrong on one matter in particular: Luca Calcagni wasn't the only cobra in the building. By coming to work for Genesis, she was climbing into an entire nest of cobras.

CHAPTER 4: FLEUR
JACEY

Jacey rode the bus to the biggest gym in the city where, by some miracle after five years of following her husband on the racing circuit, she remained on the Maddox family gym membership. It was a lucky break, because she needed the locker space to change clothes. There was no way she was wearing her silk blouse, designer pumps, and blood-red lipstick to the far side of town where her studio apartment was located. It was neither prime real estate nor the most secure community, but it was all she could afford on the last few dollars sitting in her bank account.

It was hard to believe how quickly her trust fund had dwindled. Easton's first race car had set them back over a hundred grand, and that didn't count the four hundred dollar tire changes — per tire — or the sixty thousand dollar engine replacement he'd needed halfway through his first season. Or the tens of thousands of other fees incidental to professional racing. And they would have more than made up the difference with his winnings if it wasn't for the fatal pileup that had stolen his rookie lead in the Southern 500 two months ago. He was minutes away from achieving his dreams, only to be cheated by the grim reaper, himself. It was as if fate had been against them from the start.

The tears Jacey had forced herself to swallow during her interview started to flow. She was half numb, emotionally raw, and completely exhausted; so they were tired tears mixed with tears of relief. She knew she was a very lucky young woman to have survived her encounter with the Calcagnis and even more lucky to have secured a job offer.

She emerged from the gym, free of makeup, wearing a pair of gray yoga pants and a faded navy pullover. Her hair was crammed beneath a baseball cap. Wide sunglasses provided another layer of anonymity and hid her red-rimmed eyes. With one arm clamped firmly over her cross body duffle, she returned to the bus and waved her pass at the driver. It was so crowded she rode standing the rest of the way home with one hand on the grab bar above her, making eye contact with no one.

Bouncing in place to keep warm in the frigid autumn breezes, she waited in line at her favorite Turkish sandwich vendor on the street corner. Their döner wraps were enormous and filling. Cut into thirds, it would provide dinner tonight, as well as lunch and dinner for tomorrow.

She jogged up the external black metal stairwell to her third story apartment and bolted herself in for the night. None of the loitering teens outside had ever given her trouble, but she liked to think it was because she minded her own business and didn't go out after dark.

The interior of her small studio apartment was like an icicle. The first thing she did after stepping inside was flip on the switch to her space heater. It was plugged in next to the black card table and folding chairs that served as her dining room furniture. Warm air swirled around her ankles as she ate. Her eyelids were drooping before she polished off her carefully divided sandwich. Next, she rolled the space heater across the room to the double bed she'd picked up second-hand. She tugged back the covers and rolled them around her like a cocoon. If she bundled up enough at night, she could probably hold off another few weeks before turning on the furnace.

For the first time in a month, Jacey's exhaustion was greater than her grief. She nearly overslept. By the time the trill of her alarm invaded her consciousness, it had been sounding off for ten full minutes. With a small shriek of self-recrimination, she hopped out of bed, showered to freshen up, and rode the bus back to the gym to don her black pantsuit and power red heels. Fortunately, she still fit into her premarriage wardrobe, because they were by far the most appropriate outfits she owned for wearing to work. She didn't have the funds at the moment to purchase new clothes.

She arrived at Genesis & Sons a half hour early and mounted the stairs.

Waverly presided over the reception desk again. She lowered her glasses. "You're early, Ms. Maddox."

"Please call me Jacey. And, yes, I'm a few minutes early. I am happy to wait if Mr. Calcagni isn't ready for me."

"Oh, he's ready." The woman punched a few buttons on her keyboard. "Allow me a moment to forward the phones, and I'll take you up myself."

Waverly Calcagni didn't speak a word during their elevator ride, keeping her wide elegant mouth pursed and her hands clasped tightly in front of her.

"I know this is difficult for you," Jacey ventured softly. "Me being here."

The woman's glacial blue gaze clashed with hers.

"It's difficult for me, too." She briefly closed her eyes against the pain radiating from the older woman.

"Coming here won't make it any easier, you know." The same pain Jacey felt was echoed in Waverly's voice.

"No, it won't, but I didn't come here to forget." She opened her eyes and fought to steady her voice.

"I came here to remember." She blinked hard as the elevator doors opened.

Waverly stepped ahead of her into Luca's office. "I doubt you'll find much time for reflection at Genesis," she announced tartly, waving her hand at Luca's empty desk. "My grandson maintains an inhuman pace with his schedule. You're about to become a very busy lady." She threw open the door to a tiny adjoining room.

Jacey was surprised to glimpse a desk filling most of the space. The entire room couldn't be more than a six by six feet square. It was a closet, for crying out loud. They'd probably had to move storage supplies to make room for her inside it.

"This is where you'll be working."

Nice. Jacey wanted to laugh. So the Calcagnis were placing her in an itty bitty room of shame designed to humiliate her. They clearly had no idea the minuscule size of her current living quarters on the far side of the city.

"It's perfect." She offered what she hoped was a brilliant smile. "So close to Mr. Calcagni, too. No doubt it was difficult trying to figure out where to place another new employee in such an antiquated building." She rapped the wall smartly with her palm on her way to her desk, as if testing the soundness of its structure.

Waverly's sharp intake of air was proof the insult had sunk home.

Jacey flipped on the desk lamp and squeezed behind it, dropping her lunch inside one of her new desk drawers. "Lots of companies are pressed for space. DRAW Corporation was, too, before they relocated to their newer, much bigger facility in the Hill district."

Waverly stomped over to Luca's desk, yanked up a thick pile of folders, and stomped back to slam them on Jacey's desk. "Your new boss has an important meeting at 9:00. He needs these notes compiled in a slide show presentation."

"Nine o'clock, as in an hour and a half from now?"

"Yes, and he'll need it fifteen minutes earlier to give him time to review his speaking points."

Nothing like a short suspense project to begin her latest venture. Then again, Jacey had been expecting a curve ball on the first pitch. She flipped open the first file folder and scanned its contents. It appeared to be a standard bid for a general marketing campaign. High-end women's footwear. Her personal specialty — at least from a consumer standpoint. "What audio visual equipment will he be using?"

"His laptop and the big screen in the conference room. If you were paying any attention, you would have noticed it yesterday."

They hadn't kept her in the conference room long enough to notice anything of the sort, but Jacey was familiar enough with most standard equipment to get by sight unseen.

"If you'll excuse me, ma'am." She didn't bother tempering the dismissal from her tone as she booted up her dated-looking desktop computer. The woman had earned herself a swift verbal parry. "I'd best get to work."

With a huff of disapproval, Waverly lingered for several moments as if daring Jacey to say another word. When Jacey started typing without looking up, she finally spun away and slapped at the elevator button.

JACEY WOULD HAVE NEVER BEEN able to compile the presentation in less than an hour without such an exhaustive personal knowledge of ladies shoes. Luca would be making his presentation to a regional fashion boutique that offered an extensive collection of both women's clothing and footwear lines. Display racks and shelves, signage, and lighting. She absorbed the details of his proposal. It was a quickie one-month ad blitz to introduce an all-new summer sandal for next year.

The Fleur-de-Lis. The name of the shoe evoked a myriad of pictures and emotions. Jacey studied the word collage Luca had sketched in royal blue ink on a piece of notepad paper. The name was French.

Delicate. Light. She couldn't agree more when she viewed a photo of the shoe. It was a strappy piece of confection in a champagne-glaze light, beaten leather with a three-inch heel.

With Luca's creative brainstorm of words swirling in Jacey's mind, she combed through the charts displaying each media channel and their respective budgets. His calculations were immaculate, his projected profit margins lofty but attainable, but the name of the product felt too long and a little off. Maybe because of the over usage of the flower in art throughout the years, the term *fleur-de-lis* made her think of carved filigrees and stone tablets. The new line of shoes called for something less cumbersome. Something shorter. Like *Fleur*.

With a chuckle, she deleted the remaining segment of the phrase, leaving *Fleur* to stand on its own merit. It looked right now, stylish and upscale, something a shoe hoarder like herself would purchase.

"Does your new job amuse you, Ms. Maddox?" Luca's voice jolted her from her creative cloud.

"Good morning." She scanned his impassive features. "Your presentation is nearly complete. Would you care to take a peek?"

He swooped down on her desk like a hawk toying with its prey. Too bad the two of them couldn't fit behind her workstation together. He could blame his own lack of generosity in her accommodations for that. She swiveled her monitor around for him to view.

He bent closer, and the woodsy scent of his aftershave slammed into her, more potent and powerful than the day before. Odd how every scent today seemed so pronounced. Come to think of it, everything felt a little *more* today. The lights seemed brighter, everyday sounds more defined, the fall temperatures more biting, and Luca's presence more unsettling, if the increase of her heartbeat was any indication.

Her mouth turned dry as he reached out. But all he did was scoot the flat computer screen a little closer to him. "Take it from the top," he commanded.

Something about his nearness made it harder to breathe. She was going to have to learn how to get by on less air when he was around. She used her mouse to click through the screens.

"Faster, Ms. Maddox. Our guests arrive in twenty minutes."

She clicked faster.

"That's enough." He cut her off before she reached the end of the slide show, straightened, and moved to his desk. "Make the headings bigger. Mr. Sandstone is nearsighted, though he refuses to wear spectacles. And change the slide background to something simpler. It's too busy."

She glared at his retreating shoulders. She'd checked the other files saved to the common drive and used the same size headings and the identical background as his last two presentations. He was asking her to snap her fingers and update more than fifty slides in the space of five minutes. He was being petty, a fact that didn't seem to bother him.

He threw a few folders inside a briefcase and headed for the elevator. "Meet me in the conference room with the presentation on a zip drive. I'll also need a printed copy of the speaker's notes. There's a package of spare drives in your desk."

Since Jacey had nothing pleasant to say in return, she didn't bother responding. Her mind was already working the angles of his ridiculous request. She flipped through the screens one more time to be sure she'd left enough white space in the margins to give the only idea that popped in her mind a shot at actually working. Check. Plan B it was. She changed the slide size from Standard to Wide Screen and selected an option to avoid distorting the photos and graphs. *Voila!* The headings were bigger although no longer a hundred percent uniform. If Mr. Sandstone could read them, though, her mission was accomplished. If Luca Calcagni preferred uniformity and polish, on the other hand, he could hold off on his frivolous last-minute requests next time.

She changed the background to a wall of white marble with three minutes to spare. It left her just enough time to save and print the presentation. It wasn't perfect, but it was the best she could do in such a short period of time — the best anyone could do.

Jacey scooped up the presentation and dashed for the elevator, mashing the down button. *Come on. Come on. Come on.* She tapped the toe of her shoe. And continued to tap her toe. She shifted her weight from one foot to the other and tapped her other toe. Frowning at the flashing panel, she mashed the button a second time. The elevator appeared stuck on the main floor, which was strange since it was Luca's private elevator.

Precious seconds ticked past.

"Oh!" she groaned, whirling to examine the details of her surroundings more closely. Surely, this ancient building had a stairwell or fire exit...or some other way down to the first floor. She yanked open doors, furious to discover two more closets twice the size of the hole the Calcagnis had stuck her in. *That figures!* The last door opened to a stairwell. She bit her lip. It was only twenty flights to the main floor. In heels. Three and a half inch ones, no less. Fortunately, she was young and in top physical shape.

She was also tardy to her first Genesis meeting, arriving a full seven minutes past nine, panting quietly while inwardly groaning over her aching arches. A fine sheen of sweat prickled her hairline and temples.

"You're late." Luca prowled the far end of the

boardroom, irritation radiating from his broad, pinstripe-clad shoulders.

"Oh, dear." Waverly's gracious drawl rang out. "The elevator service man arrived a few minutes ago. It totally slipped my mind we were stranding your new assistant on the top floor."

Save it, lady. A gnat wouldn't drown in such a small drop of remorse. Jacey took the seat Luca pointed to, trying to hide her wince of relief with her best professional smile. "It's alright, ma'am."

"What can I say?" The elder woman shrugged, a twinkle thawing her gaze a few degrees. "Old buildings. They're like old people and their old memories."

Well played. Jacey nodded to acknowledge the hit. She'd done far worse to those who'd crossed her in the past.

Knox breezed through the doorway, a steaming mug in hand. "Mr. Sandstone and his entourage are in the parking lot. Rhys is bringing them in." He sauntered over to claim the chair next to Jacey. While stooping to take his seat, he tipped his mug and spilled his coffee on her knee.

It was scalding. Her lips parted in shock as she absorbed the blinding slice of pain and the pulsing sting that followed.

"The zip drive, Ms. Maddox?" Luca's question seized her from the brink of passing out and brought her back to the boardroom.

Unable to focus just yet, she slid the thin, black drive in the direction of his voice.

Behind her chair, a hubbub of voices announced the entrance of their guest boutique owner and his staff. Jacey fought to focus on the voices instead of her misery. Her hazy vision cleared, and their guests took shape. There were three men and one woman, in addition to Rhys, talking animatedly when they stepped in the room. Luca's voice joined in the greetings and preliminary round of small talk. The group gradually dispersed and took their places around the conference table. At the far end of the room, the big screen flashed on.

Someone pressed a cold pack in Jacey's hand. Waverly's voice sounded low in her ear. "Old eyes don't quite miss everything."

Not yet trusting her voice, Jacey drew a deep breath and nodded her thanks, trying to force another smile. At least she was wearing black. The coffee spill wouldn't show too much, but her knee was smarting so badly she wanted to scream. She pressed the ice pack to it. A gasp of appreciation escaped her.

Luca, now seated on her other side, speared her with a questioning glance. She gave him what she hoped was a nod of confidence. He studied her a moment longer before returning his attention to his notes. His jaw tightened as he read. He produced an executive pen and scrawled a note in the margin, his movements jerky with suppressed anger.

When he moved his hand, she saw what he'd written. *Fleur-de-Lis.* Apparently, he didn't like her shortened version of the proposed shoe line. He shifted in his seat to speak directly in her ear. "We will discuss your attention to detail later, Ms. Maddox."

She didn't doubt it any more than she doubted her grasp of women's shoes. Maybe she should have discussed it with him first before making the change, but she doubted he would have listened to the thoughts of an apprentice. Or an assistant on a two-week trial. Certainly not a Maddox. She shifted away from him, willing the snarling pain in her leg to stand down.

He swiftly rose from his seat, a remote control in hand, and took command of the room. "The *fleur-de-lis*, as many of you know, is widely considered to be a stylized version of the species of flowers knows as the *Iris Florentina.*" With the click of a button, he started the slide show, and a graphic depicting the iris's elegant petals flashed on the big screen. A faint, iridescent white flower that slowly transitioned to a gauzy metallic shade of champagne, the same as the shoe. She hoped he liked the animated meme she'd created, but his expression gave nothing away.

She had to admit he was good. He hadn't paused for lengthy introductions or nauseating preliminaries. He'd jumped right to the heart of the presentation in a compelling manner that grabbed and held the attention of his listeners. He clicked to the second slide, a photo of the shoe with the word *Fleur* emblazoned across the heading in cursive, all lowercase letters. The font she'd chosen was a new one, according to the site she'd downloaded it from. It exuded casual elegance, bringing to mind half-filled glasses of wine and garden parties in full swing.

"*Fleur*." Mr. Sandstone spread his hands. "It's genius. With a single word, you captured the essence of our product. Lush. Feminine. Upscale."

"You asked for branding, sir. It's what we do." Luca's dark gaze flickered briefly to Jacey and returned to his prospective client.

"I like it. I like it well enough to skip ahead to the terms of the contract and get an early start to the golf course. I promised Edric lunch and a game if you sold me a marketing plan this morning. Where is that old codger, anyway?" The deal was done. The rest was just details, nothing more than a formality.

The meeting didn't last more than ten minutes. Rhys escorted their satisfied customer and his staffers from the room.

"Nailed it." Knox raised his mug, grinning, while Jacey edged as far away from him as possible until he set it down.

"Old codger indeed," Waverly chuckled. "Wait

until Mr. Sandstone discovers Edric's been warming up the greens since dawn."

Luca flipped off the big screen. "If you'll excuse us a few minutes, I need to speak with Ms. Maddox about the presentation. Alone."

From his tone of voice, his displeasure had to be clear to everyone listening. Knox smirked at her and took his leave. To her credit, Waverly cast a doubtful look at Jacey's leg, which was still hurting like crazy. Jacey waved her on, heartbeat thudding in anticipation at facing Luca alone. She should have known a successful contract wouldn't be enough to appease him for her audacity in altering his proposal.

The moment the door clicked shut behind Waverly, he rounded on her. "Why did you do it?"

She shook her head. "Do what, Mr Calcagni?"

"Pretending to misunderstand is pointless. You changed my presentation without my authorization."

"We landed the contract."

"I would have landed it without your interference. Just so you know, I've fired people for less."

"Oh?"

"Why did you do it?" he asked again.

"I read every inch of your notes." She paused, seeking the right words. "*Fleur* was right there in the middle of your word collage on page five, flashing neon lights up at me. It was the right name for the product. The right branding."

"Was it now, Ms. Maddox?" His voice was

dangerously low. He stepped closer, looking angry enough to strangle her.

Her chin came up. "I know shoes, Mr. Calcagni."

"As well as you know the ones torturing your feet right now, I suppose?"

"They were never meant for hiking down twenty flights of stairs. I'll keep a more practical pair on hand in the event of future elevator malfunctions."

He blinked. "You truly expect to continue working for me after altering a key presentation without my permission?"

"Yes." She folded her copy of his speaker notes and started to stuff them in her purse.

His hand closed around the other end of the papers, halting her movement. Her breath caught at the sight of his long, bronzed fingers resting so closely to her much lighter ones, so close his fingertips brushed the edge of her hand. For a moment, Easton was in the room again, holding her hand, making one of his ridiculous statements that made her laugh.

"I don't believe you understand the magnitude of what you did. Had you been wrong, you could have cost Genesis & Sons up to seven figures in long-term revenue."

His deeper voice snapped her out of her daydream. Definitely not Easton's. It resonated through her in ways his never had. "I wasn't wrong."

She held his gaze, knowing she'd correctly named the new shoe line, and wished her heart wouldn't thud so crazily around in her chest each time they crossed verbal swords. She couldn't recall ever being this jumpy around another person before. It was a terribly inconvenient reaction to Luca Calcagni, considering how closely they would be working together.

"Not this time, Ms. Maddox, but I can't afford the risk of a repeat performance. Sabotage is a serious crime."

"Sabotage!" Thanks to her, they'd just landed a major contract. She yanked her hand away, leaving him holding the folded papers. The rapid movement made her wince at the pain shooting through her arches as well as her burnt knee. The ice pack slipped from her hand and thunked to the floor. "In case you've forgotten, I work for you now, Mr. Calcagni. I am on your team."

"Are we on the same team, Ms. Maddox? Or do you have an ulterior motive for coming to work at Genesis & Sons?"

Her chest heaved at the implication. *Now I'm a corporate spy, eh?* She'd anticipated the Calcagnis presuming the worst about her intentions, but she couldn't fathom how helping them land such a profitable contract contributed to the problem. "Fine!" she snapped. "I won't make any further changes to your precious notes without first discussing them with you." *I'm sorry I tried to help you, you low-down rat of a...*

"Good. Otherwise, there won't be a next time." Luca bent over the table to return the Sandstone file to his briefcase along with her folded copy of his notes. "The next project awaits us upstairs." He cocked his head at the door, indicating she should walk ahead of him.

She took a few hobbling steps and gave up the fight, knowing she wouldn't make it to the elevators in her current state, much less up twenty flights of stairs. Kicking off her heels, she bent to retrieve them and stormed ahead of him from the room with them dangling from two fingers. Or would have if her knee hadn't been hurting so badly. The coffee-dampened fabric chaffed her scalded patch of skin so much that her barefoot limping was hardly much of an improvement over her high-heeled hobble.

"Are you injured, Ms. Maddox?"

"I'm fine." She laid a hand on the wall for support, feeling lightheaded.

With a sound of irritation, he reached for her. "Here. Take my arm," he commanded harshly.

"No, thank you. I am fine." Jacey limped a few steps farther down the hallway, her hand never straying from the wall. They were still a healthy distance from the elevator.

AS LUCA WATCHED his new assistant, his instincts told him something was wrong. It crossed his mind that she might actually be faking an injury so she could file a workman's compensation claim; but he quickly dismissed the idea. Playing the part of a victim wasn't her style.

"We have more work to do, Ms. Maddox, and it won't get done at that pace."

"Oh, for pity's sake!" she rounded on him, with a furious hissing sound, and promptly lost her balance. She pitched forward.

He lunged to catch her. When she sagged against him, he lifted her in his arms and was immediately shocked at how effortless it felt to do so. She was willowy and a good inch or so above average height, even without her signature heels. He'd not expected her to feel so light, her bone structure so delicate.

Looks could be so deceiving! He stood there, wondering if he should call an ambulance.

"Put me down!" she hissed through clenched teeth, her face as red as cherries.

Then again, maybe she wasn't ready for a 911 call just yet. "Happy to," he growled, irritated at how defensive she sounded when he was only trying to help, "but are you sure you can walk?" He was trying to do the right thing here, to be a gentleman as much as it killed him, in her case. He spun around with her in his arms, searching for a bench to place her on, anything to get his hands off the poisonous creature as soon as possible. Unfortunately, it was an old building and they'd cut through a private, narrow hallway in the back. It had none of the client lounges and sofas their main walkways boasted.

"Good point!" She averted her face and relented in a knock-yourself-out voice, "by all means, carry me up all twenty flights of stairs, if you wish."

He snorted, even more incensed by her sarcasm. Perhaps, he should have just let her take the tumble. "I imagine the elevator is back in service. I can at least get you that far."

"Of course it is," she snapped, still not looking his way. It was clear she blamed him for her earlier trek down so many flights of stairs, or at least she blamed his family, and she had every right to.

Truth be told, Luca felt a little guilty about Waverly's treatment of his new assistant. He seriously doubted his grandmother's story about a service call on the elevator, since no one had reported a break-down to him. If she'd pulled a fast one on Jacey, it was beneath her. It was beneath all of them. He'd always taken great pride in his family's name, reputation, and impeccable professionalism. He hated to think they were failing to live up to their own standards where Jacey Maddox was concerned.

Clenching his jaw, Luca returned his attention to the immediate problem — the woman he was carrying to the elevator. Even if his grandmother *had* stooped so low as to pull a fast one, Jacy's current condition seemed a little exaggerated for simply being forced to walk down a bunch of stairs. Had she pulled a muscle? Sprained an ankle? Or was it something else, altogether?

It was clear she was medically underweight. Must be one of those women who starved herself down to centerfold size. His upper lip curled. She'd certainly posed for enough of them in the past few years. Because of her family name, the gossip columns had their heyday with the photos, but he doubted she cared. She'd never concerned herself with anything more than living in the moment. Unfortunately, her penchant for thrill-seeking had set his youngest brother on a course that had cost him his life.

A fresh burst of anger coursed through Luca's veins as he reached the elevator. When he was through with his newest employee, she certainly would not look back on her short stint at Genesis as one of her many larks. His arms tightened in an unconscious reflection of his thoughts. At Jacey's quick gasp of surprise, he forced them to relax, which had the unfortunate effect of returning his attentions to her delectable person.

His assistant was turning out to be one big mixed signal. For starters, she was authentic. Every attribute he'd suspected was fake during their interview wasn't. Up close, her hair was shiny and supple, not fried from hair straighteners and other chemicals. Her lush lips were twisted with irritation, not frozen in place by Botox.

Even her heartbeat was very, very real.

Though her expression was bland, her heart rate was anything but. It raced erratically against the fabric of his shirt, which both surprised and stoked him. She was skilled at hiding her inner emotions from her facial expressions, better than most people of his acquaintance, but she was undeniably nervous around him. *Excellent.* For some reason, the discovery gave him more satisfaction than the ink drying on the Sandstone contract. He'd be sure to remember that glorious fact the next time she raised her saucy chin at him or bit down on one of those pouty lips.

By some miracle, they'd made it to the elevator without running into any other employees. Luca was monumentally grateful, because he wasn't in the mood to explain why he was man-hauling his new assistant around the building.

Thankfully, there was no wait, either. The elevator door opened, then slid shut behind them. Almost immediately, the small enclosed space felt too intimate. Luca started to lower Jacey to her feet, but her fingers clenched on his shoulder when the elevator started to move. It elicited a jolt of awareness that shot straight from her fingertips to his heart. He glared at her, wondering what sort of game she was up to this time, but she was still looking away from him, tight-lipped and angry, as far as he could tell. *Good.*

She was pale, too. *Not good.* His concern revived in full force. Something about her current demeanor was off. Way off. Her grip on his shoulder lent a certain vulnerability to her normally aloof and uncaring attitude. And, unless he was mistaken, there was a bruising cast to her gaze this close up. Either that, or he was completely losing his mind.

It seemed like an hour before the elevator door opened. Luca stepped inside his office, and his sense of reason returned. He was immediately furious for allowing himself — even for a few moments — to view Jacey Maddox as anything other than the troublesome vixen that she was.

It was only her first day on the job, and already she'd gotten under his skin. Grimacing, he carefully set her on her feet hating himself a little for missing the warmth and essence of her in his arms. To his unholy satisfaction, he was rewarded with a faint whimper as she landed on her tiptoes and hobbled back to her desk. He'd waited a long time to teach Jacey Maddox a lesson. It was way too bad the opportunity had come too late to save Easton from her wiles.

He'd best remember how dangerous she was every time he looked at her. Any man who had the misfortune to fall beneath her enchantment...

Stop. Just stop. He forced his thoughts back to work.

"Check your inbox." His voice was louder than necessary, but it helped to pull his brain out of the quicksand where it had sunk. "Our next presentation is 11:30 at the Four Seasons. We'll be needing slides, speaker's notes, twelve copies of the handouts, table favors, and all the necessary audiovisual equipment."

He should have enjoyed the way his orders made Jacey's shoulders stiffen. Instead, sympathy twisted his gut, and he had visions of walking across the room to gently massage the kinks from them.

Oh, yeah. He was in trouble working this close to Jacey Maddox. Deep trouble.

CHAPTER 5: ALMOST FIRED
JACEY

Jacey wasn't sure how she survived the first day working for Luca Calcagni, or the second, or the third. He was a relentless taskmaster, driving her like a musher in the snow, holding the reins to a team of northern race dogs. Except she was a lone dog pulling a very large sled. In the few days she'd worked at Genesis and Sons, she'd put some serious miles on the spare, low-heeled pumps she'd tucked in her lower desk drawer. Luca certainly didn't hesitate to run her all over the building on his endless lists of errands.

There were mailroom runs, inventory checks, and impromptu dashes to the drafting tables to update him on the stages of each ongoing design project. Updates which, most of the time, could more easily have been made over the phone or by email.

Though pressed for time, Jacey tried to turn all

the tedious busy work into opportunities. She introduced herself to as many employees as possible and made an effort to learn their names, titles, job descriptions, and something personal about each of them. By the end of her first week on the job, her reports back to Luca grew more specific in employee names and details.

She breezed off the elevator mid-day Friday, announcing as she headed to her desk, "Tineel on the Harbinger account says there will be a twenty-four-hour delay on their newest thirty-second spot package." It was a television marketing campaign. "One of the actresses called in sick to the first shoot."

Luca didn't glance up from his computer. "Why haven't they replaced her?"

"They tried. Harbinger won't budge on the casting. It's his granddaughter."

"He will when he sees the projected loss of revenue. Get him on the phone."

She turned away and rolled her eyes. It was time for her lunch break, and her stomach was protesting its emptiness. Playing cat and mouse with a temperamental restaurant chain owner could literally take hours.

It ended up taking two hours and forty-five minutes to connect the difficult-to-pin-down Mr. Harbinger with her equally difficult boss. While they were speaking, she forwarded her phone to voicemail and took the elevator downstairs without looking back. She knew if she caught Luca's eye, he wouldn't hesitate to send her on some other fool's errand.

When she arrived at the employee lounge on the basement level, it was nearly three o'clock. The room was empty, which didn't bother her at all. She welcomed the break from all humanity and noise.

She plopped her brown bag sandwich on the nearest bistro table and went to fill her empty travel mug with ice and water. The lounge was set up diner style with chrome and glass tables, leather bar stools, old movie signs and posters, and a retro countertop displaying every beverage dispenser imaginable — coffees, teas, soft drinks, flavored waters, juices, smoothies, and shakes.

Jacey caught a whiff of the last coffee or latte someone had brewed, and it brought on a wave of nausea. She dashed for the Authorized Personnel Only restroom and slammed the door. Leaning over the sink, she gripped its sides and forced herself to draw in a few deep, steadying breaths. *What is wrong with me?*

She was sleeping at night again. *Finally!* It had taken an entire two months after Easton's death for her to do so. She had no doubt her newfound ability to sleep was due to utter exhaustion brought on by working for Luca Slave-Driver Calcagni. He hadn't been kidding about the no-coddling part of her work schedule.

What was strange about the return of her ability

to sleep, though, was her simultaneous loss of appetite. She'd experienced trouble eating since the funeral, but she'd managed. As of the last two days, she'd found herself having to forcibly choke down every bite. Nothing smelled or tasted right, anymore. Probably something best discussed with a pastor or shrink, but she didn't have the time to spare a trip to go see one. Or the money. Maybe when her two-week trial was over and her benefits kicked in, she'd look into an evening or weekend appointment.

Jacey dampened a paper towel and dabbed at her temples, trying to lessen the sick feeling in her midsection without ruining her makeup. It helped, and her breathing soon returned to normal. She dried her hands and stepped back inside the employee lounge.

Waverly was waiting for her, perched on one of the barstools at the table where her brown bag rested.

The woman had an uncanny way of popping up where she was the least expected.

"Good afternoon, ma'am." Jacey had learned it was impossible to avoid the woman. Waverly had her finger in every pie at Genesis.

"You don't have to do this, you know."

"Do what, ma'am?" Jacey unrolled her brown bag and withdrew her sandwich. She took a bite and labored to chew it.

"Working for Genesis won't bring your husband back."

Jacey choked and reached for her bottle of water, washing the bite down whole. "I'm not trying to do that." *Or am I?* She couldn't quite bring herself to meet the woman's gaze.

Waverly waited until Jacey set down her water to reach across the table and grasp her hands. "Look at me, Jacey Maddox."

She blew out a slow breath and tipped her head up. It took every ounce of her willpower to face the woman squarely without squirming.

"I've watched you a solid week. I'll admit I had my suspicions about you when you came on board. I still do. But you've worked hard. Harder than I expected. And you've taken every punishment without complaint that my grandsons have seen fit to dole out. They're angry about their brother's death, you know, and they blame you."

"*I* blame me!" The words tore themselves from Jacey's chest and shattered on the table between them.

Waverly's eyes widened, and her gnarled grip tightened. "I see." But her voice sounded puzzled. "Then consider this. My grandsons are good men, every one of them, but they are grieving their hearts out. We all are, and your presence isn't helping. Every time we have to look at you, it's like having a scab ripped off all over again."

Jacey closed her eyes to suppress the sting behind her lids. She felt the same way every time she looked at each of the Calcagnis. "I'm sorry. More sorry than words can express. I wish there was something I could do to make you believe that, but there's not."

"Sure there is. If you are truly sorry, then leave. Leave this building, and never come back."

Jacey's eyes flew open at Waverly's vehemence. "I can't." Alarm gripped her chest. She had no other job. No place else to go. Her own family had washed their hands of her for the last time once they learned of her employment at Genesis & Sons.

The grandmother sighed. "Of course you can. Unless..." Her lips thinned to a determined line. "Hear me well, child. If someone forced you to come here for the interview, or if someone is forcing you to stay and work for us—"

"No! I am here by my own choice. I swear it." Jacey crossed her heart.

"That doesn't explain—"

"I am no corporate spy, if that's what you're implying, Mrs. Calcagni. I have no hidden agenda. Well, not all the ones you're worried about, anyway."

"Do tell. Then why are you here?"

It was way too early to admit the truth, but Waverly wasn't exactly giving Jacey much breathing room on the matter. "To atone," she sighed.

At the elder woman's snort of disdain, Lacey shrugged. "I knew you wouldn't believe me, and I don't blame you. If you don't mind, I'll just get back to eating my lunch."

"At least tell me what you're atoning for."

You're relentless, you know? Not unlike another family member of yours who reins from the top floor of this blasted building. Jacey rolled her neck around in a full circle to loosen a cramp. "I was the one who encouraged Easton to pursue his dream of racing. When you froze his assets and refused to fund his campaign, I purchased his first car. I paid to rebuild the engine. I lost count of the tires I replaced. Dozens. And that makes me completely and utterly responsible for . . . what happened next." Her voice broke.

Misery and dull acceptance flashed across the woman's face. "I suspected as much about the funding, but you didn't cause the crash, child."

"No, but I'm the reason he was out there in the first place. I was the one who encouraged him to race." It was a relief for Jacey to vent her spleen at long last to the matriarch of the family she'd wronged. She expected no rapid-fire forgiveness, but it felt good, nevertheless.

"You could be saying these things merely to inspire my sympathy." This was said through white lips.

Jacey tugged her hands from the woman's grasp, close to losing control and dissolving in a fit of weeping. She rolled up her sandwich and returned it to her bag. With her stomach churning so disturbingly, there was no way she would be able to force down another bite. Besides, the end of her half-hour break was fast approaching. "You can believe whatever you want. It won't change my decision to stay. I can't bring Easton back, but I will lend myself to Genesis & Sons for as long as your family will have me here." Her voice shook. "It's what he would have wanted, I think. Everything considered."

The quiet sobbing on the other side of the table crushed something in Jacey's chest. She paused in the act of gathering her things, wishing there was something she could do to comfort her grandmother-in-law. Unfortunately, the only thing the woman wanted at the moment was for her to be gone.

Waverly seemed to be struggling to compose herself. "Luca's not going to make things easy on you. You know that."

"Yes. I know." Jacey headed for the door, paused, and returned to snatch up her bottle of water.

"Oh, child!" There was a world of heartache in Waverly's voice.

It echoed in Jacey's chest cavity throughout her entire elevator ride to the top floor.

When the elevator door slid open, Luca was lounged against the front of his desk, arms crossed. "You're late, Ms. Maddox. Again."

THE SECOND WEEK of Jacey's trial at Genesis & Sons rumbled along at the same relentless pace as the first. It came with a gruesome workload and few breaks. It also came with an ever-more-critical boss who was literally impossible to please.

He greeted her on Friday morning by dumping a stack of folders in her arms the moment she stepped from the elevator. "The Pillmeyer account is threatening to jump ship to DRAW Corporation. I don't suppose you knew anything about this?"

Jacey shot him an are-you-crazy look and swiftly juggled the folders to keep from dropping any of them. "I haven't worked for DRAW for over five years." She marched to her desk to deposit them.

"Not directly, no, but there are other ways of communicating with our competitors."

Inwardly rolling her eyes, Jacey sauntered over to the coffee maker on the side bar and brewed two servings in a pair of foam cups. She presented one of them to her boss.

"What's this?" He stared at the cup in her hand.

"Coffee. For you." *In the hopes of earning at least half of a brownie point. I could desperately use one.*

He surveyed it like it was a scorpion ready to strike.

Jacey bit her lower lip and set the cup down on his desk. What she wouldn't give for a simple good morning once in a while from the man, anything other than his constant harping and barking and not-so-thinly veiled insults. Or this morning's persistence in presuming she was here to sabotage his precious company. Or poison him with a simple cup of coffee.

Perhaps a change of subject was in order.

"What's their beef against us?" She moved back behind her desk to boot up her computer system. Watching him from beneath her lashes, she gave an inward sigh of defeat when he ignored her offer of peace, leaving the foam cup and its steaming contents untouched.

"Apparently DRAW criticized their lineup of autumn blends." Pillmeyer Bakery & Brews offered danishes, pastries, muffins, petit fours, a small selection of hot breakfast items, and a much broader selection of coffees, lattes, and teas. "Said it was too predictable. That we aren't giving their account the attention it deserves."

"Their revenue streams say otherwise," she pointed out. "They've enjoyed above-average growth across their product lines for three straight years."

"They're giving us until our meeting at 2:00 this afternoon to come up with a quick marketing gimmick."

"A gimmick! Who's idea was that?" She chuckled at the ludicrous suggestion. "Pillmeyer's is too classy for gimmicks."

His caramel gaze hardened. "Mine, Ms. Maddox. Something quick and easy to satisfy their need for attention without disturbing their solid revenue streams."

"Oh." She bit her lip, wishing mightily that she'd kept her thoughts to herself. "Well, lay it on me, Mr. Calcagni. My typing fingers are all limbered up." She wiggled them playfully at him.

"I have a better idea, Ms. Maddox. You lay it on me."

She blinked at the snarl in his voice. *Okay, then.* "What do you want?"

"The concept and a mock up of your idea by 1:00. Feel free to make full use of all our resources at Genesis." He yanked open his middle desk drawer and pulled out a pen. "Time to start earning your keep, or I'll have no reason to keep you on the payroll at the end of business today."

Start earning my keep? Start earning! Start? Outrage filled Jacey's mouth, tangy and bitter. She'd earned her pay at least fifty times over. They'd closed three new contracts together and expanded the scope of nearly a dozen more. And she was totally taking credit for *Fleur*, whether he ever recognized her contribution or not! Not to mention all she'd endured from *his truly* with the occasional crush, burn, or jab from Knox.

Luca's insulting tone ended up being more than Jacey could take sitting down. She shot to her feet and moved to stand in front of his desk, tamping down on her temper to the best of her ability. "We've covered an incredible amount of ground in two weeks, Mr. Calcagni, and we're just getting started. There's no limit to what we might accomplish, given more time together."

He tipped his head against the back of his chair, fixing his beautiful, hateful dark eyes on hers. "Believe me, Ms. Maddox, there are dozens of other interns waiting to take your place. Many of them with advanced degrees and far better ideas than yours."

He had a waiting list for his interns? How in all creation had she ever gotten hired, then? It made no sense. Unless — a fresh wave of nausea clenched her midsection — unless his whole offer of employment had been a setup from the beginning. A setup to watch her fail.

Jacey absorbed the feeling of shell-shock in her chest without any change of expression, though it was difficult. She glanced away, shaking her head. "You're going to fire me no matter what I do today, aren't you? That was your plan all along." It made sense. She should have expected no less. What didn't make sense was her brain-numbing sense of disappointment. Any normal person would be turning cartwheels. Like a convict receiving an unexpected pardon and being set free. They'd go find another job with more money and less stress. But not her. For no easily explainable reason, she wanted this job. *Really* wanted it.

"Save the theatrics, Ms. Maddox." Luca sounded bored. "We both knew this wasn't a partnership forged in heaven."

She'd never asked for a partnership, only a job. It was his choice to stick her in this particular role, and she'd done a decent job of it despite every roadblock he'd thrown in her path. Despite every pothole he'd dug overnight to trip her up the next morning. Despite every rug he'd ripped out from beneath her heels.

"You're wrong," Jacey snapped, no longer able to hold back.

His brows rose to twin dark arches of hauteur. "Come again?"

"I said you're wrong, Mr. Calcagni. Wrong, as in dead wrong about me. I bet that's something you don't hear very often, because people are too afraid to speak up around you. Well, I'm as right for this job as I was about *Fleur*, and I'm going to prove it."

"Are you now, Ms. Maddox?" He sounded amused now.

She planted her palms flat on his desk, bringing them eye-to-eye. "You're going to eat your words this afternoon in front of Mr. Pillmeyer. Correction. You're going to drink them."

His gaze flickered lower and returned to her face but not before she caught the glint of disappointment in his eyes.

She glanced down and flushed to realize the shirt

she'd unbuttoned earlier during a hot-flash was gaping a little wider than she intended from this vantage point. *Good gracious!* It was an accident, not some ploy to wage a war of feminine wiles against him. She quickly straightened, face flaming, but remained where she was standing. No doubt he was thinking the worst of her right now.

Again.

She drew a deep breath and finished venting her spleen. "After our next appointment, you're going to change your mind about firing me."

"Your presentation isn't going to write itself, Ms. Maddox. Tick tock." He smiled. Not a charmed smile or a conciliatory smile. Not even a challenging smile. It was one hundred percent smug — the leer of a man who had the power and position to annihilate her and knew it.

Jacey's heart sank as the precariousness of her position skidded into place like a baseball player sliding across second base, dusty scraped knees and all. To Luca Calcagni, her apprenticeship had never been about giving his sister-in-law a chance, about offering her a job, or testing her talents. He'd only intended to punish her. To crush her. To break her.

She spun away from his desk, glancing at her watch. Well, he didn't quite hold all the cards in the deck. Not yet. She still had a few connections and resources. Powerful ones. Ones that she preferred not to use for pride's sake. Unfortunately, it looked like she was going to have to swallow a bit of said pride if she wanted to keep her job at Genesis & Sons. Which she did. Very much.

Jacey returned to her desk, staring blindly at her screen for several minutes, tapping aimlessly on the keys and biding her time. When Luca stepped away for his 9:00 meeting, she would make her move. Until then, she had a holiday gimmick to pull out of thin air.

She flipped through the pages of the Pillmeyer account, immersing herself in their tried-and-true autumn brews. Autumn Spice. Pumpkin Cheesecake. Cinnamon Apple Latte. Cinnamon and Waffles Latte. She picked up the first scent sample stick and slid it from its plastic casing. The cloying scent of cinnamon and apples was so strong it rendered her dizzy. *Ugh.* She slid it back inside its casing. Apparently, her olfactory senses weren't going to provide any inspiration today. She returned to studying the Pillmeyer list of flavors. Their autumn list provided a seamless flow into their winter one. Eggnog Latte. Peppermint Spice Latte. Mint and Fudge Mocha.

An idea came out of nowhere in particular. It simply popped into her head. She opened her email and shot an urgent message to their testing and experimenting division. *Please tell me you have a bottle of Candy Corn syrup on hand.*

One of the apprentices wrote back almost immediately. *Sorry. Will anything else work? We have about everything other than Candy Corn. —Byron*

No, she needed candy corn. *If I bring you a bag of candy corn, can you mock up a bottle of syrup for me by noon today? We can engineer the real thing later.*

His response flashed across her screen. *Sure can, sweet stuff.*

So far, so good. Jacey quickly sketched out the rest of her idea for the gimmick. It would be a Mystery Mix. Instead of the clear, tall-necked glass bottles they normally poured their syrups from, it would be encased in a dark-tinted bulbous container that resembled a magic potion, and it would bear an enormous white question mark on the label. They could play it up as a Halloween prank. A drink-this-if-you-dare sort of thing and offer some sort of customer loyalty incentive for those who purchased the flavor. Or the first one hundred patrons who guessed the flavor.

There were a bunch of directions they could go with this. The reward could be a coupon, perhaps, or an entry into a drawing for free coffee for a year. They could do as many Mystery Mixes as Pillmeyer cared to invest in. Peanut Brittle. Carmel Apple. Roasted Marshmallow. She made a list of as many fall favorite flavors as she could think of.

Luca shifted in his chair, alerting her to his approaching departure. He rose and slung his blazer on, leaning forward to log off his system like he normally did.

"Wait!" Jacey said quickly. She needed to distract him before he logged off his computer. Her plan was wholly dependent on it.

His head swung in her direction.

She slipped out from behind her desk and hurried his way so swiftly, she didn't see the pile of folders resting on the floor next to his desk. She tripped over them with a yelp of surprise and literally went flying in his direction.

CHAPTER 6: IRRESISTABLE

LUCA

Luca kicked his briefcase out of the way to catch her. Her chin collided smartly with his chest.

"Ow!" She struggled to stand upright, clapping a hand to her jaw with a grimace.

"Are you okay?" He'd be lying if he didn't admit he liked the way her heart had momentarily pounded against his chest. His own heart rate had accelerated in response.

"Everything but my pride," she grumbled, swaying a little on her feet.

He found himself reluctant to leave the office. He should be asking what it was she needed to tell him so urgently, but all he could think of was how alive and vibrant she looked and how good her perfume smelled. Something faint and flowery.

Lord help him, but he was attracted to this capricious, maddening woman. Seriously attracted! His fingers tightened on her upper arms.

"You can let me go now." Her voice sounded breathless and uncertain as she pressed one palm to his lapel to regain her footing.

His own breathing became uneven as her slender fingers tightened on the suit fabric. He made the gigantic mistake of glancing down at her. One look at her parted lips only inches from his own and her blue eyes regarding him with such dazed absorption, and all rational thought escaped him.

He wasn't sure who made the first move. All he knew was his mouth found hers, and his brain nearly exploded from the wonder of finally living out the fantasy that had been tormenting him for days. The touch of her lips against his was everything he'd imagined, both intoxicating and breath-stealing, but sweeter. Far sweeter.

Two weeks of pent up anger and frustration erupted inside him, but he fought to tamp down on it — hard. Jacey's overly thin frame was far too fragile, too delicate for brutishness. He found himself cradling her against him, savoring the scent of her berry flavored lip gloss, along with her softness, warmth, and vitality, like a man dying of thirst.

Her response to his kiss made the floor shake beneath his feet. His heart thundered at the way she kissed him back, twining her slender arms around his neck and clinging to him like a lifeline. Somewhere in his distant hold on his sanity, Luca perceived he hadn't felt this out-of-control in any situation since high school. Make that junior high. Every touch, every small sound Jacey made drove him closer to the brink of utter madness.

He was supposed to be firing the woman. Instead, his crazed brain was protesting all the reasons he wanted to keep her in his life. He wanted to get to know her better, wanted to date her, wanted to be with her more than he'd ever wanted to be with another woman. He was a man accustomed to pursing and getting what he wanted; but with Jacey, he wasn't sure about anything. Wasn't sure what he wanted from her, and still had no earthly idea what she ultimately wanted from him or why she'd come to work for him in the first place.

Regardless, what was happening between them right now wasn't supposed to be happening. Certainly not with a woman in his employ, and certainly not with her of all people.

"You drive me crazy," he muttered against her lips, forcing himself to break off the kiss.

"Me?" she gasped, pulling back a fraction and tipping her face up to stare at him in incredulity. "You're the one who's been acting like an insufferable beast the past two weeks!"

"While you've tried every second of every day to crawl under my skin," he shot back.

"Fine! But it's only because you make me so

angry." This time he was very sure she made the first move. With a sound of frustration and a glare that would melt the paint off his Porsche, she tugged his head back down to hers.

Their next kiss was more intense, each of them demanding answers the other wasn't yet prepared to give.

He abruptly broke off the kiss and pulled away from her. He jammed his hands in his trouser pockets and stared blindly out the glass wall overlooking the city.

"Mr. Calcagni," she whispered, sounding appalled. "I, er..."

He was equally appalled and unsettled about what had just happened between them, but her insistence on using his last name afterward was utterly ludicrous. "Luca," he corrected harshly. They were well beyond using titles at this point.

"Luca, I—" she choked.

"What, Jacey?" He rounded on her, needing to look into her eyes to make some sense out of what had transpired, and to beg her forgiveness. He'd never before behaved so unprofessionally with another employee.

"We should talk about this." Her voice shook, making his jaw clench in response.

Yes. They most certainly should. His lawyer was going to have a hey-day with this one. It was probably going to take a sizable settlement to make this problem go away.

She promptly burst into tears and not just a bit of mist. Fat tears rolled down her cheeks and splashed on her collar, dampening the fabric.

"Talk to me, *chica*!" Shocked, he took a step in her direction, raising and lowering his hands helplessly, not quite daring to touch her again. "Did I hurt you in any way? Please assure me—"

"No! Kissing you was wonderful."

It was? Luca should have been focusing on the coming harassment lawsuit. Instead, he was ridiculously pleased to hear her describe his kisses in such a complimentary light.

But the sob in her voice wasn't at all reassuring. "I'm sorry." She sounded like she was cracking from the inside out. "I don't feel so well today. I really don't know what's wrong with me."

He watched in agony as her face crumpled. Feeling helpless, he watched her while she wept. Every tear she shed, every gasping breath she took weighed on his conscience. He'd spent the past couple of weeks trying to break her, but this? This is not what he'd wanted. Lord, have mercy! It was the exact opposite of what he wanted.

He'd been too hard on her. Pushed her in ways he'd never pushed another employee before and for what? To vent his own anger and assuage his own grief and guilt? She was his brother's widow, which meant she was grieving, too. She deserved better, so much better than the way he'd treated her. She was family, for crying out loud! *Family.* The one thing he'd always sworn to protect.

Luca couldn't have been more staggered at the realization. Despite the fact that Jacey had refused to take on the Calcagni name when she'd married his youngest brother, she was one of them. His family. His responsibility. He'd spend the rest of his days, if that's what it took, to make it up to her. The problem was, he had no idea what to do to mend the long stretch of broken fence between them, or where to even start.

Throwing all caution to the wind, he closed the distance between them and took her in his arms again. "I'll do anything, *princesa,*" he murmured against her temple. "Anything you ask to make this right. Just tell me what you want."

At the moment, he realized there was nothing in the world he wouldn't do to bring back the sassy, vibrant version of her. No effort or expense would be too much.

"If you don't want to work for me any longer, I'll transfer you to another department. I'll give you any job at Genesis you want to tackle. You've more than proven what you're capable of."

She raised her head at last, and her puffy, tear-streaked cheeks ripped his already aching heart open wider. "That's been your go-to solution for everything lately, hasn't it? To get rid of me."

Maybe, but that's not what I said, and it's most definitely not what I meant. "No, I—" he protested.

She gripped his lapels. "You're a lot of things, Luca Calcagni, and not all of them are nice, but I never pegged you for a quitter. And I sure as heck am not a quitter, either. Surely, you've figured that out by now."

"Okay, then." Her swing in emotions was starting to give him whiplash. He lowered his arms to give her space but kept her hands clasped tightly in his. "Tell me, *princesa*. What do you want from me?"

Say you want to be with me. To date me. Luca had no idea where those thoughts came from, only that they were true. Sure, there would be the devil to pay with his family, but he was willing to pay whatever price it took to keep Jacey in his life. The air between them practically sparked with the intensity of their feelings for each other.

"Nothing has changed," Jacey said firmly, letting go of his blazer and stepping away from him.

Nothing? "What!" He was astounded. She'd responded to his kisses. No, she'd more than responded. She'd kissed him back. He was sure of it. Of course, that changed things between them! It's not like he made a habit of necking with his employees. Everything in his world had changed the moment her lips touched his!

Jacey moved to stand behind her desk, not quite meeting his gaze. "You offered me an apprenticeship, and I accepted. That's what I want from you. To continue being your assistant. No more, no less."

"Too late," he growled. "You're a lot more than my apprentice now. If you didn't want to be, you might have considered that a little more carefully before you kissed me."

The minx actually shrugged at him. Shrugged! "Listen, Mr. Calcagni." The gaze she raised to his was still red-rimmed, but her expression was unreadable.

No way! They were back to surnames now? After what they'd just shared? Anger seared through his internal organs.

"I haven't been myself lately, and I apologize for it. The kisses are as much my fault as yours, so all your talk about making things right is entirely unnecessary." She shook her head. "Clearly, I've been exhausted and run-down, grieving and overly emotional. Not to mention worked to death by an impossible-to-please, slave-driving—"

"I hear you," he interrupted with deadly calm, snatching up his briefcase. "Loud and clear." He wanted to go crawl in a hole somewhere like an injured dog to lick his wounds. He needed time to process her rejection. It made little sense. She'd enjoyed his kisses as much as he'd enjoyed hers, and she'd melted all over him when she cried, letting him hold her and comfort her like a real boyfriend. Unfortunately, he suddenly wanted to be exactly that. He wanted to spoil her and look after her. He had the resources to give her everything — the whole world if she'd but let him!

They glared at each other in heated silence for several long moments. She smoothed her hair and skirts and drew a deep breath, eyeing him defiantly.

Luca's heart sank, realizing Jacey apparently meant what she said. He shook his head in disbelief. *You're a heartless tease, Jacey Maddox!* His heart felt cold, and he was back to wanting to strangle her.

"You promised me no coddling," she reminded with the hint of an impish grin, "and I'm holding you to it." She tilted her head at him. "It's just my opinion, something I know you've never welcomed, but you might want to change your dress shirt before your next meeting. You look all wrinkly and…" She let her words dwindle as she surveyed him with a careless arch to her blonde brows.

"Not another word," he snarled and headed for the restroom. He already knew how he looked, like he'd been cutting the fool with his personal assistant. Lucky for him, he kept a spare suit in his locker, because he didn't have time to drive home and change before his next meeting.

Five minutes later, he re-entered his office in a

fresh shirt, suit, and tie. Without looking Jacey's way, he snatched up his briefcase and made a straight line for the elevator.

CHAPTER 7: FAILING

JACEY

The breath Jacey had been holding eased out as she sat behind Luca's desk. *Well!* Making out with her boss wasn't at all how she'd originally planned to distract him, but she couldn't help feeling a wee bit exultant at her success. The almighty Luca Calcagni had been distracted, indeed — so much so that he'd utterly forgotten to log off his computer system.

She picked up his private line and dialed the Vice President of Operations at DRAW Corporation, the only person in her family who was still speaking to her.

A musical female voice trilled across the line. "Alora Maddox speaking."

"Hello, Alora." Jacey blinked back a fresh sting of tears. It was so good to hear her older sister's voice.

"Well, well, well. If it isn't my favorite little black sheep. How are you holding up, dear?"

She was referring, of course, to Jacey's stint at Genesis & Sons. "I survived the first two weeks, thank you, but I need a favor."

"I suspected at much, chickadee." Alora didn't sound the least bit surprised. She didn't sound affronted, either, though it had been nearly a month since they'd last spoken. "What's it going to be this time?"

Jacey hated to be in the position of asking yet another favor, but it couldn't be helped. "A bit of insurance in the form of a press release." Sure, she and Luca had kissed, and maybe that would give her some measure of job security, but she preferred something more ironclad.

"I smell a story. Details, details!"

"Actually, there's no story." At least, not one Jacey was ready to tell yet. "It's just that I'm up to my neck in Calcagnis, and you can only imagine what that feels like."

"I'd prefer not to," Alora returned dryly.

"So I'd like a little something to pressure them into keeping me on board." Jacey hastily explained what she wanted the press release to say. "Is that something you can do for me?

"Is my name Alora Maddox?"

It sure was. All day long. Her sister had the press release written and texted to her in ten minutes, quick enough for her to retype it and send it to the paparazzi from Luca's own computer before he returned to his office.

◊

JACEY COULDN'T WAIT to show off the new syrup flavoring the Genesis testing team had developed with such haste. She hoped when Luca saw it, he would finally recognize her contribution to his firm despite their rough start working together.

As it turned out, Byron had pulled together a team of apprentices over his lunch break and really come through for her. He assured her it was little more than melted-down Candy Corn suspended in water in its current state, but it would serve its purpose during the upcoming client appointment. The real kicker was the bulbous black bottle Byron and his team had unearthed with the beauteous white question mark emblazoned across its label.

One o'clock ticked past. Jacey tapped the toe of her shoe against the chrome leg of Luca's desk. She'd set everything out for him to review — speaker's notes, handouts, tiny party favors of candy corn wrapped in black lace and tied with translucent webbing, and the Mystery Mix itself. She was neither a statistician nor a strategist. However, creativity was the one thing she did have to offer, and she was pretty sure she'd outdone herself this time.

There was a small risk her burst of creative energy might have something to do with the way Luca had kissed her earlier. She blushed at the memory. His kisses had invigorated her beyond belief. She almost felt like her old self again. However, the feel-good vibe was punctuated with a sliver of guilt at the way Luca had acted afterward, as if he thought she'd used him or something. All they'd done was share a few kisses. She bit her lower lip. Okay, so maybe kissing Luca Calcagni had felt a little more monumental than that, but they were two consenting adults. There was no crime in kissing. Sure, it was a little awkward that it happened with her boss, but . . .

Jacey examined a small chip in her nail polish, flicking at it with a sudden spurt of edginess. Luca's kisses had been pretty amazing, actually. No, they were more than that. If she was being honest with herself, they were mind-blowingly wonderful! He'd been gentler than she imagined he would be, too. His touch had been cherishing, bordering on worshipful. She sighed out loud and smoothed a hand over her hair. Easton had never been so polished or so classy. So utterly dreamy.

She gave herself a fierce mental shake. It was wildly wrong on every level to compare the two brothers. Still, her brain slipped stubbornly back to her previous line of thought. It had come as a surprise to find out how well Luca could treat a woman after he had pretty much convinced her he despised her. Which meant he should have been relieved to discover she wanted to walk away from their kisses with no strings attached. Instead, he'd been as growly as ever, as if she'd offended him, somehow. Or hurt his feelings. Was such a thing even possible? That would require the man to possess feelings, which she highly doubted. Or did he?

She smoothed the side darts of her navy pencil skirt, wondering what cues she'd missed with him. He clearly was attracted to her — against his better judgement, no less — but could it be something more than that? Did he truly want to be with her, as in date her?

The thought made her dizzy. What an uproar that would cause in his family, given her regrettable and short-lived marriage to their youngest son. Just thinking about it made her stomach hurt all over again. Or feel weird. Something was definitely off with her stomach. Even though Jacey was positive she hadn't gained an ounce in recent weeks, her suit felt tighter today. Maybe it was just her imagination...or all the zinging nerves at the thought of facing Luca again.

She tried to shake off the unsettling mood, trying to find comfort in the fact she could probably quit worrying about Luca's threat of firing her this afternoon. Kiss or no kiss, the fact remained he was a businessman. He'd be a fool to let her go after she single-handedly salvaged the Pillmeyer contract during their upcoming meeting. However, if Luca so much as attempted to follow through with his threat, the press release Alora had composed would serve as Jacey's back-up plan. Her safety net, one that would force the Calcagnis to reconsider keeping her on their payroll, at least for a few more weeks. The press release was on its way now to Alora's long list of local media contacts.

The best part of the sisters' plan was how they'd made it look like Luca himself had sent the press release from his own email account. Mercy, but he was going to be furious when he found out! It would be too late, of course, for him to do anything about it, other than keep her employed. Or so Jacey hoped...

One fifteen rolled around, and it finally dawned on her that Luca wasn't going to make it back to the office to review the presentation she'd put together for the Pillmeyer account. It was the first time he'd completely stood her up. Was he avoiding her on purpose?

Whorls of fear cramped Jacey's stomach. Their presentation was in less than forty-five minutes. As much as she dreaded his criticism of her work, she was learning to respect it in a completely twisted sort of way. He was the king of last-minute demands, but his instincts were rarely wrong. He forced her to dot every *i* and cross every *t*. His arrogant input made her insanely angry at times but kept her razor sharp. She would have very much appreciated his input on the first solo assignment he'd given her.

Where are you? At a quarter 'til two, she gave up all hope of a preparatory hazing from her boss. With a sigh, she transferred her presentation to a zip drive and moved all her props from his desk to a wire basket. There was a tiny part of her that was fearful on Luca's behalf, too. She hoped he was alright. His last meeting had been halfway across town, and city traffic could be treacherous on Friday afternoons.

Jacey descended the elevator to the first floor and hurried to the main conference room. The familiar clack of her heels resounded down the long hallway. In an unexpected way, the maze of hallways at Genesis & Sons was starting to feel like her home away from home. An employee crossed the hall in front of her and waved before turning a corner. She smiled and waved back. After five years on the road with Easton, mostly in the southern states, it was nice to finally be back in Alaska. To be home.

Jacey sailed through the conference room door and stopped at the sight of Luca dropping his briefcase on the table.

"Mr. Calcagni! Where have you been?" She set her wire basket in the chair next to his, fearing the wire mesh might leave a scratch mark if she set it on the white marble tabletop.

"Working," he informed her coldly, piercing her with a harder look than usual.

"You don't write. You don't call," she teased. "I've been worried about you."

"Have you, now?" His tone was clipped and impersonal. He took his seat and hunched over his electronic notebook.

He was still mad at her. Either that, or something else was wrong.

"Of course I have. There was no one to take a bite out of my backside the past several hours." *Or help me prepare for this appointment.* "Here are your speaker notes."

He spared little attention to the stapled packet she slid across the table to him. He pushed it back in her direction. "I don't have time to review it. This one's on you, Ms. Maddox."

She frowned at the dull tenor to his voice and the tiredness in his features. In that moment, he didn't look or sound anything like the Luca Calcagni she knew. "You want *me* to give the presentation? Alone?" When he didn't answer, she swallowed hard and hurried to the side cabinet to pour herself a bracing cup of coffee. She took a gulp, scalded her tongue, and coughed. *I can do this. I have to do this. He's not giving me a choice.*

She poured a second cup for her irascible boss. He liked his black and strong. She returned to the table and set both their mugs on felt-bottomed coasters.

"What's this?" he growled.

"A peace offering. You resemble a bear ready to maul something. I'd prefer it not be me."

To her increasing despair, he ignored the cup and continued working on his tablet. Her inner sense that something was wrong increased several notches.

Frank Pillmeyer arrived with his secretary, forming a much smaller entourage than she'd been expecting. Where was their marketing manager? Their sales team?

Luca rose long enough to give the two a cursory greeting then returned to his seat.

Jacey set her notes on the table in front of her and lifted the bottle of Mystery Mix, hissing to her boss, "If you need to be somewhere else, I can handle this." She preferred him to stay, of course.

"Just get on with it, Jacey."

It was the first time he'd ever used her first name in public. She almost dropped the bottle. They shared a long look. His unguarded expression wrenched her heart. It contained so much bleak acceptance and bitterness, she wanted to beg him to tell her what was wrong. Right this second!

But as quickly as it had appeared, his bitterness vanished. Like turning off a switch, he schooled his features to their usual hard, enigmatic lines.

She sighed and stood, clicking the remote control in her hand to display the first slide of her presentation. "The flavors and scents of autumn add up to one of the most captivating times of year. Cinnamon spice. Pumpkin. Nutmeg. Eggnog. Peppermint. They stir old memories and inspire us to create new ones, while the crisper temperatures bustle us ever closer to the holidays, our families, and our cultural traditions. But you want to spice it up a little more this year, Mr. Pillmeyer." She pivoted dramatically in his direction to gauge his reaction to her presentation so far.

He smiled benignly at her, his body language urging her to get to the point. Neither he nor his secretary had touched their candy corn favors.

This is not going as well as I hoped. Jacey flipped to the next screen. "And what better way to spice up the holidays than by adding a little mystery?" She flew through the rest of her presentation, sticking to the highlights. The last part of her pitch included pouring a fresh round of coffee and inviting their guests to try the mystery flavor that Byron's team had developed.

They did, and their faces brightened. "It's good." Mr. Pillmeyer nodded, sounding surprised. "Really good, Ms. Maddox. Which makes what I'm about to say that much harder. Mr. Calcagni?" He stood and pushed his chair away from the table. "The only reason I kept our appointment was to thank you for three straight years of profit across every one of our product lines. We've had a good run together, and I hope we find ourselves working together at some point again in the future."

Jacey gripped the back of the nearest conference chair while her insides deflated like a popped balloon. They'd lost the contract? *No-o-o!* Sickness twisted its way painfully through her gut at the knowledge that her first solo mission had been a complete bust. Even worse, it sounded as if Genesis & Sons had lost the contract before the appointment ever began, a fact that wouldn't likely carry any weight with Luca when it came to pointing fingers later on. He would blame her for failing to win the account back. *Sheesh!* Jacey raised a shaking hand to tuck a loose strand of hair behind one ear. She couldn't catch a break with the guy.

Jacey forced her smile to remain in place while numbly watching Luca rise for the final round of handshakes.

Mr. Pillmeyer glanced her way from the door. "You have some real talent in Ms. Maddox. No doubt her family was devastated to lose her."

The door shut behind their guests, and she was alone again with Luca.

"I'm sorry," she whispered. "I'm so sorry." It was their first defeat together. No, it was her defeat. Hers alone. She wished he'd say something. Criticize her. Blame her. She preferred just about anything other than his stoic silence.

"Meet me in my office, Ms. Maddox. I'll be needing you to sign a few forms before you leave our firm."

What? She stared numbly at him. So that was it. He was firing her, after all. She pressed a hand to her stomach. He was giving her no anger. No emotion at all. Just a pink slip. Oh, this was harsh! Even for him. The man who'd kissed her so passionately earlier in the day was long gone. Jacey had never felt so defeated in all her life.

So what if her insurance policy was blaring across every major news station in town? She shouldn't have bothered. Luca's total censure, his absolute rejection of her despite all her hard work on his behalf, had finally worn her down beyond her endurance. She couldn't wait to sign his blasted papers and leave his miserable company behind, once and for all.

CHAPTER 8: WAR
LUCA

Luca didn't wait for Jacey to walk beside him to the elevator. He couldn't take another moment of her falsely innocent features or her enticing navy suit that did nothing to hide her siren curves — a soft, feminine frame that he'd had the pleasure of holding in his arms earlier in the day. What was wrong with his traitorous heart for still wanting the hateful creature? One taste of forbidden fruit was all it had taken, and now he feared he would never be able to get her out of his system.

He strode ahead of her, inwardly cursing her every step of the way, and was relieved when she didn't join him in the elevator. He didn't trust himself in such proximity with her at the moment. He might do something he regretted, like strangle her.

On the short ride to the top floor, he mulled over

the last two weeks and could come up with only one conclusion. He was the one to blame for her treachery today. He'd let his guard down and allowed her to get too close. He'd all but forgotten his family's decades-old mantra: *Never trust a Maddox.*

They'd lost an enormous account as a result. They might have lost it, anyway. Accounts come and go. But they'd lost it for sure with her behind-the-scenes interference. The printout of her two calls to DRAW Corporation earlier, compliments of his attorney, were burning a hole in the pocket of his slacks. He was not sure why he'd expected anything better from her, but he had.

Her betrayal stung. The fact she'd used her widowed status to wheedle her way inside Genesis & Sons stung almost more than he could bear. The fact she'd used his own grief against him stung, too. She'd nearly succeeded in convincing him he was wrong about her. He'd wanted to believe her. Oh, how he'd wanted to believe her!

His phone was ringing before he stepped from the elevator.

"Luca Calcagni speaking."

"Oh, Luca! I heard." Waverly sounded tremulous and confused. "I'm sure you have your reasons, but—"

"It's okay." He threw his briefcase down on his desk and dragged a hand through his hair. "There was nothing we could do to save the account. It was an inside hack. Ms. Maddox placed two calls to DRAW Corporation from my office earlier today."

"What calls? Are we talking about the same thing, love?"

"I'm talking about Jacey Maddox and my plans to fire her as soon as she returns to her desk."

"Oh, dear!" his grandmother sighed. "That might not be the best idea, given the current media attention directed at Genesis and Sons."

"What are you talking about?" He was fresh out of patience for riddles.

"I thought you already knew." At his silence, she sighed again. "Maybe you should turn on the evening news, sweetheart."

He snatched the remote from his center drawer and flipped on the flat screen mounted to the wall across from his desk. The announcement ribbon scrolled across the bottom of the screen. He frowned and looked again. *Breaking News: CEO of industrial design giant Genesis & Sons hires daughter of rival DRAW Corporation as Personal Assistant.*

He turned up the volume. The animated voice of the news anchor rang across the room. "In a startlingly aggressive move, CEO Luca Calcagni snapped up the youngest Maddox daughter two weeks ago, signing her on as an apprentice to their world-famous think tank."

Her fellow anchor laughed. "And that's just the beginning of this delicious story. Ms. Maddox happens to be his grieving sister-in-law, the widow of Easton Calcagni, who died a few months ago in a tragic NASCAR pileup in southern Florida. What an all-around altruistic move! It certainly begs the question we're all wondering about. Does Mr. Calcagni's decision mark the end of one of the greatest corporate rivalries in history, or the beginning of a whole new feud? Stay tuned for more details after this commercial break."

Luca flipped off the TV, unable to listen to another word. Neither of the news anchor's speculations was correct. This whole debacle was nothing more than yet another one of Jacey's games. Her audacity apparently had no boundaries. She and her family had gone to unimaginable and unconscionable lengths to prevent him from firing her this evening. Was that the only reason she had kissed him this afternoon? To distract him from logging out of his computer, so she could access his email account?

He could barely see past the blood in his eyes. She'd played him for a fool, and he'd fallen for it — hook, line, and sinker. For real. He'd allowed his foolish feelings to get all tangled up in knots over her.

Well, she'd won this round. Far too much media attention was focused on Genesis & Sons at the moment to fire her, and the attention would continue to be on them for days. Maybe weeks.

He tossed his remote control on his desk and folded his arms. The movement was the only thing keeping him from pounding something. He, Luca Calcagni, CEO of Genesis & Sons, had actually gone and hired a corporate spy for his personal assistant.

He clenched his teeth. If the heartless woman thought he'd been tough on her the first two weeks of her employment, she was about to find out what it felt like to work in a gloves-off, bloody, winner-take-all kind of environment.

This was no longer about families, businesses, or feuds. No! This was personal.

CHAPTER 9: SERVING THE COBRA

JACEY

Jacey remained standing in the conference room, alone, head bent and palms resting on the Sylacauga marble conference table. She refused to look at her watch. It really didn't matter how long she took to return to her desk. Luca was upstairs preparing to fire her the moment she stepped inside his office. She'd failed in her mission to atone for her past sins against his family. Woefully and miserably failed.

She was torn. Should she even attempt to wheedle him into giving her another chance? Or, should she hurry upstairs and get the inevitable over with? Maybe it was time to admit defeat, take her marching orders, and run.

More than anything, she wished she could take back the news release she'd talked Alora into sending on her behalf. It was the first thing she'd done since Luca had hired her that smacked of outright dishonesty. It was exactly the sort of behavior he'd been expecting from her. Duplicitous and manipulative. Any progress she'd gained in the last two weeks toward securing his trust would be lost the moment he watched the news announcement.

The fact that he'd been the one to goad her into sending it to the media didn't make her feel any better. He'd backed her into a corner and left her with no choice but to come out fighting if she wanted to keep her job. Unfortunately, going to battle with the Calcagni family sort of defeated the whole purpose of coming to work for them — to atone for her past mistakes and make things right between them.

Her pulse pounded between her temples, and her face burned so feverishly that she finally gave in to the temptation to take a seat. She laid her cheek against the stone tabletop and let its cool surface soothe her aching head.

Through the cold stone, she also absorbed the harsh truth of what was really at stake here. At some point in the last two weeks, Luca's thoughts and opinions had become important to her. She'd crossed the line of trying to secure his good opinion and had crossed a totally different line in her endless attempts to impress him. Mercy, she cared for the man and wanted him to care for her in return!

I'm such a fool. She slowly turned her head and pressed her other cheek against the table.

It wasn't because he was a nice person or an easy person to converse with, nor was he comfortable to be around. He was none of those things. Yet she'd found herself taking more care picking out her clothes each morning before coming to work than she had for any other dates she'd been on — to include those she'd gone on with her husband.

The truth was so simple it hurt. Luca was a brilliant human being. Arrogant and autocratic, yes, but he also challenged and stimulated her. And somehow in the midst of all his intense scrutiny, criticism, and demands during business hours, he'd managed to also make her feel like a beautiful and desirable woman again.

He wanted to be with her, and she wanted to be with him. They'd proven it to each other this afternoon, before she'd gone and ruined things between them like a silly high school girl. For the first time in her life, she'd exercised a caution she didn't know she possessed. She'd been too afraid to take the next step, too afraid of ruining things like she always did.

Jacey moaned and threw a hand over her eyes. She had to be the worst sort of person. Crushing on the older brother of her husband so soon after his death. He was still grieving, and she was, too. In a manner of speaking. Was it truly grieving to be mourning over what might have been if Easton had lived longer? To be sighing over the missed opportunity to attend marriage counseling to try to save their dying relationship?

Her failed marriage was the one dark and dirty secret she would carry to her grave, one secret she'd never shared with anyone. Not even Alora.

She'd endured five years of being invisible. Five long years of taking second place to one tricked-out race car after another. Or third or fourth place. Which had made it feel unbelievably nice to feel appreciated again this afternoon in Luca's arms. To be noticed again. To matter to someone.

Luca had never once told her she mattered, not in words. He didn't have to. All the subtle tells over the past two weeks had given away his true feelings on the subject. The way his broad shoulders stiffened ever so slightly when she entered the room. The deliberate hard tenor of his voice when he was barking orders, all the while caressing her with his eyes. The way he looked at her when he thought she wasn't looking. The way he'd kissed her. And held her. And begged for her to tell him how to make things right between them.

She moaned again. In the deepest recesses of her mind, she inherently knew Luca would never *ever* be more interested in his car or career or anything else, for that matter, while she was in the room. He was too aware of her as a person, as a woman. He just was.

"Jacey?"

Rhys's voice jerked her from her pool of self-pity and recrimination.

"Are you alright?" He touched her shoulder, and she flinched. She preferred to wallow alone in her misery, but it probably wasn't wise to tell the Chief Operating Officer of Genesis & Sons to go away and leave her be.

She raised her pounding head and focused blearily on his features. It was difficult to scrape together her usual poise, but she was done playing games. She opted for full-out honesty, instead. "Haven't you heard? I failed my first solo presentation today. I lost the contract."

His face was slightly narrower than Luca's, his nose more aquiline though his jaw was equally heavy. He usually emanated the energy of a man in the middle of considering some monumental decision. At the moment, however, he looked more concerned than contemplative.

"You can't win them all, Jacey."

She stood, wincing at the pain knifing through her temples. "My boss doesn't agree. I'm pretty sure he's going to hand me a pink slip over it."

She had no idea why she was confiding this in his brother, his partner in crime. There was simply something about Rhys that inspired confidences. *Darn him for looking all grave and attentive in his designer dark chocolate suit and mahogany-colored wingtips!*

She tossed the remnants of her failed presentation in her wire basket.

"Here. I'll carry that for you." Rhys reached for the handles of the basket, but she shook her head. Then she had to breathe through the fresh wave of pain created by the jarring movement before she could speak again.

"Thank you, but I can handle it." If she brought an audience with her, Luca would see it as a weakness. Another attempt to manipulate him. She'd rather face him alone and look him in the eye while he said his piece. She was done with summoning outside assistance to sway his decisions where she was concerned.

She quickly moved toward the door with the basket clutched in front of her, but Rhys was quicker. He didn't immediately open the door as she expected. "I really hope to see you back at work on Monday."

It was the nicest thing anyone in his family had ever said to her. Why, oh why, did her heart skip with hope at his words when she knew there was no more reason to hope? Jacey drew a long, shuddery breath. "I didn't just lose an account. I lost it to DRAW Corporation. Now, can you see the problem?"

Rhys raised a single eyebrow. "A few weeks ago I might have answered yes. Correction. I *would* have answered yes, but that was before you told my grandmother something we don't take lightly around here. I believe your exact words were, 'This is my family now.' If you truly consider us to be your family, Jacey Maddox, then I have no reason to want you gone. Not anymore."

Wow! Maybe Jacey had managed to do a little atoning, after all, before their CEO gave her the boot. With one member of their family, at least.

She tried to smile her gratitude and couldn't quite make her lips stretch that far. Her headache was blooming in too many directions. Instead, she gave Rhys a vague nod that required little movement and swept past him through the door he opened for her.

WAVERLY WAS WAITING for her at the elevator. A silky blue-gray shawl draped her thin shoulders and did nothing to soften her folded-arms stance or the determined set to her wide, elegant mouth. She tapped the long, pointed toe of one gleaming black leather pump.

"I don't suppose you know anything about the news release Luca supposedly sent out this afternoon? The one eulogizing his offer to apprentice you."

There wasn't any point in denying it. "Yes. I sent it." *And regret it.* Unsure how long she would be detained, Jacey set her wire basket on the floor and braced herself for the scorching of her life.

"Of course you did. My grandson was going to fire you this afternoon, and now he can't. At least not immediately. It would be a PR nightmare for our firm."

"If anyone can find their way around it, Mr. Calcagni can." Jacey was too close to tears to say more.

Waverly's lids constricted to slits. "I'm not sure if that's a compliment or an insult."

Jacey resisted the urge to fidget. "It's a true statement either way. The fact that he despises me doesn't make him any less brilliant. If he truly wants to fire me this afternoon, he will find a way to do it while insulating his family from the worst part of any public backlash."

"Yes, he will." The elderly woman cocked her head a fraction to the right, mouth pinched in concentration as she scoured Jacey's soul with her eyes. "Why do you persist in remaining at a company where you clearly aren't wanted?"

"Not everyone wants me gone. Byron in the lab called me sweet in an email this morning."

The lines around Waverly's mouth twitched as if she was fighting a smile. "Boy, do you have him fooled!"

"True. Then there's Rhys. He stopped by the conference room a few minutes ago to say he hoped to see me on Monday."

Waverly's smile flat-lined, transforming all the papery lines around the edges of her mouth to rigid creases. "Point taken. I may not like what I'm hearing, but I'll be the first to admit Rhys is nobody's fool."

"What about you, Mrs. Calcagni?" Every cell in Jacey yearned to know where she stood with the indomitable matriarch of the stalwart sons of Genesis. She was starting to like the woman. "A week ago you asked me to leave this building and never come back. I've thought a lot about what you said. And if you ask me again to leave — right now, in fact — I think I could finally do it." Despite her efforts to the contrary, some of Jacey's inner weariness crept into her voice.

The straight line of Waverly's lips disintegrated into a dozen or more spidery downward creases of disapproval. "Don't you dare walk out on us now, Jacey Maddox! You started this infernal media nightmare, and you will stay and help us fix it."

It was the last thing on earth Jacey had expected to hear. In her own crusty, hard-edged way, the woman wanted her to stay employed with them.

Jacey gave the elder woman what she intended to be a mocking smile, but it ended up feeling one thread short of tremulous. "How could I do otherwise? This makes you the third person today who insisted I continue working here."

"You think I *want* you to stay?" A gallon of incredulity dripped from the elder woman's words. "Oh, child! Don't press your luck."

Ha! Jacey had been pressing her luck since the moment she'd filed her job application at Genesis & Sons. "If you'll excuse me, ma'am?" She picked up her basket, encouraged to have learned the heart and soul of the Calcagni clan was no longer gunning for her dismissal. At least not tonight. "I probably shouldn't keep my boss waiting any longer."

"If I were in your shoes, I'd pray all your stalling down here has given him time to harness some of his temper."

My stalling? You're the one who waylaid me, woman. But that didn't keep Jacey from shivering at her warning. She tried to cover her apprehension by jiggling the wire basket. Better to come across as impatient than fearful.

Waverly turned to press the elevator button for her. Giving Jacey another hard once-over, she clicked away in her low heels, every clack resounding down the hall like a death knell.

THE ELEVATOR DOOR rolled open to the top floor all too soon, and Jacey stepped out to face her nemesis. Luca was seated at his desk, but he didn't look up. She wasn't a hundred percent sure what to expect, but it certainly wasn't to be deliberately and completely ignored by him. There was none of the usual stiffening of his shoulders when she walked in the room. No flicker of increased awareness in his expression. Nothing at all. She would have preferred his indignation. His fury. Anything but his indifference.

She opted to keep silent, practically tiptoeing past his desk on the way to her own. She was anxious to set down the wire basket which was growing heavier with each step.

He allowed her to round the corner of his desk before speaking. "Where are you going, Ms. Maddox?"

She sucked in a breath and froze mid-step. *So we're back to addressing each other by our last names even in private?* It was way too bad, because she really, really liked the sound of her first name spoken in his faint Spanish accent.

"To my desk, Mr. Calcagni."

He swiveled his leather chair around, confronting her at last with a gaze as frosty as frozen caramel pie. Accustomed to his quick mercurial outbursts, she found the glacial version of him far more disturbing.

"Before you get too comfortable over there, I'd

like to discuss your two phone calls to DRAW Corporation today."

Jacey doubted it was possible for him to infuse any more derision or sarcasm into his voice.

"The ones you placed *before* you lost the Pillmeyer account for us," he continued.

Okay, I get it. You're never going to let me live this one down. "I spoke to my sister, Alora. Why?" She tried, but failed, to muffle the defensive ring to her voice.

He pounced on her words, his expression hardening further. "Everything that happens at Genesis & Sons is my business. What were you discussing?"

She shrugged as well as she could with the wire basket remaining in her arms. "I'm surprised you have to ask. Aren't my calls recorded?"

"Answer the question, Ms. Maddox."

"It was personal." *As if you don't already know the topic we discussed.*

"Well, then." He rose and rounded his desk to tower over her.

She was suddenly thankful for the basket between them. It provided a few precious inches of breathing room he would have otherwise snuffed out with his breadth and height and overwhelming presence.

"I must not be keeping you busy enough if you have so much time left to indulge in personal phone calls." Some of the ice thawed in his eyes, but behind it seethed a raw fury that made Jacey desperate to avert her gaze.

She managed to hold her ground, though she wasn't sure how much longer she would be able to hang on to the wire basket. Her arms were starting to tremble from the weight of its contents. "I don't see how any of this matters since you plan to fire me today," she countered quietly.

"Oh no, Ms. Maddox. I don't plan to let you go. Not any more." His leer caused a thrill of razor fear to scrape its way around the base of her throat. "I've come up with a better idea. You mentioned you needed the income, so I'm putting you in for overtime pay, instead. How does that sound?"

Dizziness gripped Jacey, and the basket dropped from her nerveless fingers. Whatever Luca was up to couldn't be good. Not for her, by any stretch.

He caught the basket neatly with one hand, swiveled, and transferred it to his desk.

"You're too kind," she said cautiously.

"Don't worry. You'll be earning every minute of it."

I never doubted it.

"Starting tomorrow morning."

His announcement sucked the rest of the wind from her lungs. Tomorrow was Saturday, and she'd been wildly looking forward to sleeping in. Her energy level had dropped well off its peak the last few days. She was operating on little more than coffee fumes.

"What time would you like me to come in, Mr. Calcagni?"

"We'll get an early start. How does seven o'clock sound?"

Seven in the morning? That would require getting up earlier than usual. Too discouraged to respond, Jacey stepped around him and dragged her feet to her desk.

"I emailed you the first set of files for the accounts we'll be working on tomorrow, so you can get a head start before you go home tonight."

So he expected her to stay late, as well. *Your generosity knows no bounds.*

"Don't forget your first two weeks of employment were merely a trial period. We'll be stepping up the pace from now on."

Stepping up the pace? Such a thing wasn't humanly possible unless Jacey set up a cot behind her desk and worked around the clock. Even then, what Luca was proposing still sounded, tasted, and felt impossible. She took a seat, staring blindly at her computer screen. So this was to be her punishment for crossing him. Luca intended to work her into the ground.

CHAPTER 10: PANG OF GUILT
LUCA

A pang of guilt twanged its way across Luca's conscience at the small choking sound Jacey made when he unveiled her new work schedule, but he ignored it. She deserved everything she had coming after sabotaging a major client account. This was how things worked in the professional arena. She'd thrown herself in the ring, however unwisely, and he planned do his part to deliver a full knockout. But it would have been more pleasurable to throw his last verbal punch if she hadn't looked so tired. And pale — *her* fault, of course, for continuously interjecting herself into places she wasn't welcome. Like Genesis & Sons.

Eventually, she would pack up her bag of tricks and leave. No one could keep the schedule he'd specifically tailored for her over the next few weeks, not even himself. He was wagering she would quit in under a week.

Luca rubbed a hand over his jaw and moved out of Jacey's line of vision to stand in front of the wall of windows. Jamming his hands in the pockets of his slacks, he stared unseeing across the bustling waterfront.

Unfortunately, watching Jacey leave his family's firm wasn't something he would relish. It should have been, but it wasn't. The truth was, he was going to miss her. He was going to miss every inch of her slender, willowy frame and traitorous heart. And thanks to one ill advised tryst in his arms, he was also going to miss her scent and touch, her embrace and her kisses.

The truth of how Luca felt about Jacey Maddox rocked his carefully planned career, his brutally organized world, his formerly well-insulated heart. He wanted her, despite all she'd done to hurt him and his family. He wanted her in his arms and in his life.

It was the private little hell he would get to suffer through in the coming days. Thank God no one ever needed to find out!

CHAPTER 11: WEEKEND DUTY

JACEY

It was every bit as difficult as Jacey imagined it would be to awaken when her alarm went off at six the following morning. She was way too tired to eat, and her crabby boss could forget about her dressing up. Saturdays weren't meant to be spent in suits and stilettos. She'd be earning her overtime in something comfortable, or he could finish firing her. At the moment, she didn't care. With the last tendrils of sleep still hazing her vision, she dragged on a comfortable pair of jeans and soft camisole. She threw a pink button-up shirt over it, snagged a water bottle, and stumbled her way to the bus stop.

Luca was waiting for her in his office, one hip hiked against the edge of his desk. He was tossing a zip drive in the air repeatedly and catching it. She hated to admit it, but he looked incredible in his gray polo shirt and black slacks. Incredibly good looking and incredibly well rested. Nobody had the right to look that good so early in the morning. She resented it on principle.

His gaze raked over her skinny jeans and untucked, candy-pink oxford shirt and settled on the two undone buttons at her neck.

She raised her chin, daring him to say something. The crisp, autumn weather outside hadn't been enough to cool her. She was several weeks overdue for her monthly cycle and a raging rollercoaster of hormones, as a result of it. *It's all your fault my health is so screwed up. You and your stupid work schedule, so deal with it, Mr. Calcagni.*

The answering smolder in his eyes made her temperature spike a few more degrees.

She resisted the urge to curl her shoulders forward, wishing the shirt wasn't such a snug fit. She could have sworn it wasn't this tight the last time she wore it, but that was months ago. She was a little foggy on the details. Oxford shirts weren't exactly standard wear for wives of NASCAR drivers. Or centerfold models, for that matter. She'd spent far more time in sundresses and swimsuits in recent years than business or casual wear.

A faint sneer curled Luca's upper lip as he tossed her the zip drive. She managed to catch it even though she hadn't anticipated the impulsive gesture. Her jerky movements awakened the first twinges of a headache. *Great. It's going to be another one of those days.*

"Everything you need to get started is in the file marked *Pending*." Unlike the heat of his gaze, his tone was clipped and impersonal. "I have a reservation at the Legends, but I'll check on your progress in a few hours."

He was headed to a country club while she worked her fingers to the bone? "You're leaving?" She'd fully expected him to stay and crack the proverbial whip over her head. How dare he pull her out of bed on a Saturday if he didn't plan to stay and work alongside her? She clamped her teeth together. He dared, of course, because he was the CEO of Genesis & Sons and could do anything he wanted.

"I promised to meet a friend for breakfast. She'd never forgive me if I cancelled."

His reservation wasn't even business related, which made the insult sting all the more.

With that, Luca strode around Jacey so quickly all she could do was glare at his retreating shoulders. The elevator door closed behind him, leaving her in the aromatic cloud of his aftershave. It was a heavenly, expensive-smelling scent that made her think of snowy mountains covered in pines.

She clenched her hands at her sides. Who was going to answer her questions about the account while he schmoozed the morning away? On a date, no less! Heaven knew he would make her redo her work in a heartbeat if it didn't please him. Which it most surely wouldn't without his input. She was the world's biggest fool for not calling his bluff and walking out. Right now.

Unfortunately, she needed the money too much to walk out. After refusing her parents' offer to reinstate her position at DRAW Corporation a few weeks ago, she was pretty sure she'd burnt her last bridge there — for good. If things failed to work out at Genesis & Sons, she was going to be job hunting or standing in line at one of the local soup kitchens. Amazing how quickly and how far a girl could fall after walking away from her family's billionaire lifestyle and squandering her entire trust fund shortly thereafter.

C'est la vie. Dwelling in the past wouldn't propel her forward. Mechanically, Jacey took her seat and forced herself to get to work. She was less than inspired this morning. Her creative spark seemed to have gone into hibernation. Either that or it was too tired to work properly.

As it turned out, her creative streak wasn't needed. Luca's Pending file consisted of multiple audio recordings of a series of meetings over the past several months with a potential client. She hastily added up the times. There were more than six hours of meetings, and her first task was to transcribe them to a single document. *Ouch!* That was *before* compiling the usual slide presentation, meeting notes, handouts, sketches, and story boards. It was a good two days' worth of work, which probably meant he expected her to work on Sunday, too.

On a growl of frustration, she went to work. As always, there was something a little hypnotic about listening to Luca in action. He was a natural-born negotiator. With his voice resounding through her headset, the morning flew by more quickly than she anticipated. By noon, however, the buzz of his various conversations with the prospective client were starting to run together. She needed a break.

Feeling dizzy, Jacey pulled her headset down around her neck, shoved away her keyboard, and dropped her head on her arms. The dizziness increased and morphed into full-blown nausea. *Not good.* She yanked off her headset and dashed for Luca's private bathroom, barely making it in time. Gagging, she emptied what few contents were in her stomach into the toilet. Afterward, she leaned on the sink, hands shaking and insides quaking. The suffocating heat was gone, and a chill shook her. If she was falling ill, it was Luca's fault. Him and the stupidly insane work schedule he'd created for her.

Voices in the office on the other side of the door made her stiffen. It sounded like the monster himself was back, and he'd brought company. A woman. *Just great!* Jacey turned on the faucet and bent to swish and spit out a mouthful of water. She wished she had a toothbrush on hand, but the stash of gum and breath mints in her top desk drawer would have to do.

Curious about the identity of her boss's guest, she opened the bathroom door and stood riveted. A brunette in a tangerine jacket and white golf slacks was standing on her tiptoes, plastered against Luca in full lip-lock. They were only a few steps inside the room as if they'd barely made it from the elevator before pouncing on each other.

Jacey's heart wrenched painfully in her chest. Luca had kissed her like that only a day earlier. Not that it mattered. He and she meant nothing to each other.

Outrage replaced her initial shock. Luca knew she was working in his office today. He could have at least had the decency to curb his romantic flings in her presence. But that wasn't the only reason she was angry. Or even the main reason. She gritted her teeth. She was jealous, though she had no right to be. She was the one who'd insisted their make-out session had changed nothing between them. Well, she was wrong. She couldn't stand the sight of him kissing another woman, a fact that made her unaccountably furious with herself.

Jacey debated her two choices: Quietly slip out the stairwell door without being noticed; or she could get back to work, make a little noise, and create an awkward moment for them all.

Unfortunately, for Luca's guest, Jacey hadn't had

a bite to eat all day, so her malicious side was the one that kicked in.

She quietly returned to her desk, unbuttoning another button of her shirt to reveal more of her lacy camisole as she walked. She reclaimed her seat and deliberately unplugged her headset. Taking another swig of water and popping in two breath mints — she really hoped the peppermint would settle her stomach — she pushed the button on her screen to restart the audio. The recording of Luca's voice, in the middle of his client presentation, blared across the room.

From the corner of her eye, she watched the brunette flinch and break off the kiss. "Who is that woman?" she asked in cool, indignant tones. "I thought we were alone."

"One of my new apprentices." Luca's voice was dismissive. Though he spared a mocking look in Jacey's direction, he didn't bother introducing the two women. "I thought she was out to lunch."

Really? They hadn't discussed break times. He had to at least have an inkling his necking session was at risk of being witnessed by his assistant.

"Oh. My. Lands!" the woman hissed. "That's Jacey Maddox, isn't it? I heard all about what you did for her in the news."

Jacey offered a smile infused with false apology, one she'd perfected with years of practice. "I'm so sorry about the transcription recording, ma'am. I forgot to plug in my headset."

"I see." The woman's head tilted to one side as she took in the open bathroom door and the overhead light Jacey had left on. Her gaze traveled the length of the distance Jacey had walked to her desk. A flush of angry embarrassment tinted her perfectly sculpted cheeks and plump lips, both of which were enhanced by surgery. Jacey knew all there was to know about cosmetic procedures, having attended dozens of consultations with friends. After learning the shocking list of risks and side effects, she'd been extra careful to keep her own figure in shape in the hopes of avoiding the scalpel, herself.

"Mr. Calcagni." She made a show of plugging in her headset once more before laying it carefully in the center of her desk. "If you'll just take a peek at what I've done so far and let me know whether you're happy with it." She allowed a bit of a simper to creep in her voice and was rewarded with a tightening of his features.

He strode to her desk, jaw rigid and a warning light in his eyes.

She waited until his large frame blocked his date from view. Then she batted her lashes a few times as she pivoted her monitor around for him to view her work. The warning in his eyes morphed to cynicism and something else as he watched her. Bitterness.

So much for teasing him. Apparently, he still

hadn't forgiven her for the press release. Jacey's stomach pitched sickeningly. Swallowing hard, she pressed a fist to her mouth while she pointed with her other hand to direct Luca's attention to the screen.

His gaze never left her face. "Ms. Maddox?" A scowl settled across his brow.

She shot to her feet with a moaning sound and tried to push past him. He gripped her shoulders for a moment, warm fingers burning through the thin cotton of her shirt, but she shook her head wildly. He let her go, and she sprinted to the bathroom, slamming the door and emptying her few swigs of water and breath mints in the toilet. *I want to die. I want to curl up in a corner of the floor and absolutely die!*

She was on the brink of tears, which was even more humiliating. She rarely cried, and she wasn't about to give her boss and his guest the pleasure of seeing her do so. She'd stay locked in the bathroom all day if she had to.

Fortunately, the muffled voices on the other side of the door faded after a few minutes. Jacey washed her mouth out a second time and took a stroll around the room, which was laughably quite a bit bigger than her tiny excuse of an office. The bathroom possessed the usual facilities, in a statement of marble tile and black granite counters, but it also boasted a small lounge area plus a changing room with a pair of lockers. Luca's spare suit was hanging from a hook on one of them. She moved to examine the label, suddenly curious about where he bought his clothing. It was a label she didn't recognize that read Black Tie, emblazoned in metallic gold threads on a black shield.

She sniffed in disdain. *Wow!* His choice of clothing lines was certainly a bit on the nose. Surprisingly, it was a brand she'd never heard of. Probably something custom tailored, which was technically none of her business.

Jacey moved back to the enormous mirror over the vanity and rinsed her mouth out a third time. Whatever the sick feeling was seemed to be passing. Taking a deep, bracing breath, she cracked open the bathroom door. When silence greeted her, she stepped inside the room with an expulsion of relief and nearly choked.

Luca was seated at his desk. Alone. "Are you sick, Ms. Maddox?"

She tested her voice with a single word and prayed it wouldn't bring on another attack of the dry heaves. "Yes." The word came out sounding thin and breathless.

"I believe I gave you fair warning about the long hours that would be required by this job."

"That you did, Mr. Calcagni. And out of respect to you and your guest, I will take my flu bug home immediately and pray I didn't share it with either of you."

"Are you running a fever?" He swiveled his chair around so quickly that she jumped.

"Maybe. I've been hot all day."

At her use of the word *hot*, his gaze dipped briefly to the open neck of her shirt. "Maybe you should see a doctor. I know of a few acute care centers open on Saturdays. Can't afford to have you out of work for long."

Oh, for heaven's sake! She could be dying, and all he cared about was how far she'd gotten on transcribing his precious meeting notes. She stormed to her desk, saved her work, and emailed it to herself. Then she swiped the zip drive from its plug without bothering to eject it properly and held it out to him.

"If you still think I'm a corporate spy, take it. If not, I'll go suffer in silence at home and keep working. Your choice, boss." She was too miserable to bother hiding her sarcasm.

"That's the kind of work ethic I'm talking about. Document your hours, and I'll make sure you're fairly compensated." He offered a smile so grim it hardly qualified as a smile. She hoped his face broke from the effort.

CHAPTER 12: PUSHING JACEY
LUCA

Luca stared after his maddening personal assistant until the elevator door snapped closed. He fisted his hands on his desktop, denying himself the urge to go after her. His gut said she had no intention of visiting a doctor. He wished he was in the position to make her. Unfortunately, anything involving her outside the scope of office work was none of his concern. She'd made that clear enough.

Then again, she could be faking the whole illness thing. He'd always been a good judge of character, a quick study of the vast range of human emotions, but never before had anyone puzzled him as much as Jacey Maddox. Or challenged him. Or so thoroughly captivated and bewitched him.

He shook his head.

She was a born flirt, so it was unwise to read anything into her latest escapade. All the eyelash batting, as well as her purposeful blaring of the audio recording to interrupt his and Katarina's kiss. He knew this, yet he'd been fool enough to try to goad a reaction from her by bringing the snobbish Katarina to his office. He'd wanted Jacey to see him with another woman, though he hadn't counted on Katarina turning it into a make-out session. Either way, it was a petty move that should have been beneath him. He wasn't sure what he'd hoped to achieve. To make Jacey angry? To spark a bit of jealousy? Instead, in true Jacey style, she had turned the tables and created a humorously uncomfortable situation for Katarina, rendering him all the more entranced by his personal assistant.

When she'd offered him the zip drive and turned the word *boss* into an insult, he'd wanted to haul her into his arms and claim her sassy mouth right then and there, flu bug and all.

His breakfast date had been none too happy when she left, demanding to know if there was anything between him and his new "secretary." He wanted to shake Jacey for her shenanigans, but he was still too busy catching his breath from his quick and searing response to them.

He pushed to his feet, swinging away from his desk to pace his office suite. What was it about the woman that climbed under his skin and shot through his veins every time they got near each other? He didn't know how much longer he could fight it, whatever *it* was. Attraction? Lust? Something else? Best to stick to his original plan. The sooner he drove her away from Genesis & Sons for good, the sooner he could regain his peace of mind.

A slow grin worked its way to the surface and tugged his mouth at the thought of what she would do when she found out LeAnne had already transcribed the meeting notes. He'd still pay Jacey for the overtime, of course, but she would have wasted hours of her weekend. He'd be sure to blame her for not checking the other folders, including the one he'd purposefully mislabeled that contained LeAnne's notes.

Eventually, he was going to find the right button, push it, and watch Jacey Maddox explode.

CHAPTER 13: LATE BOARD MEETING
JACEY

Jacey was so ill during the bus ride back to her apartment that she had to hop off midway to dry heave over a public trashcan. Which meant she had to wait a full twenty minutes for the next bus. By then, her overheated state was dissipating, and she was freezing again. Wishing she'd brought a jacket, she buttoned her shirt all the way to her throat and crossed her arms to hold in as much body heat as possible.

Oddly enough, she no longer felt like vomiting by the time she arrived home. *Quickest flu in the world.* Or maybe she was just too tired to feel the symptoms any longer. She heated a cup of tea in the microwave and sipped on it while munching a few salty crackers. The tea warmed her insides, and the crackers finished settling her stomach. *Forget work!*

She needed a nap, though a short power nap was all she had time for.

She set her alarm and forced her groggy self out of bed a half-hour later. She succeeded in making several more hours of progress on her laptop before bedtime. She turned in early and picked up where she left off first thing in the morning, plowing through one recording after another while perched at her tiny breakfast bar in the kitchenette. The sickness slammed into her again mid-morning, making her glad she'd decided to work from home.

It wasn't until just before bedtime that she discovered the notes LeAnne had typed and saved in another folder on the hard drive. For a moment, Jacey couldn't believe what she was looking at. She clicked open the first file and scrolled through a few pages.

No. Way. Heat flooded her cheeks.

Luca had purposefully wasted her weekend. Not only had LeAnne already transcribed all the meeting notes, she'd already plugged the basic information into his presentation slides. All Jacey really needed to do was add a few charts and graphs, jazz it up, and make it beautiful.

A scream worked its way up her throat as she slapped her laptop closed. She hadn't felt so humiliated, so invalidated, in years. Not since the day she'd finally worked up the courage to walk away from her family and their stifling expectations of her. She'd grown tired of their constant criticism and their conviction she'd been born broken because she wasn't like the rest of her siblings. She'd never been content to walk in her parents' shadows and patsy up to their every whim in order to keep the funds flowing freely through her trust account.

In all Luca's arrogance and lofty expectations of her up to this point, it was the first time he'd treated her like she was completely worthless. Like her contribution didn't matter. Like she, herself, didn't matter. And it hurt — deeply.

Before this weekend, he had driven her mercilessly but had always included her work in his presentations, kept her present during his client meetings, and briefed and debriefed her.

This was a side of him she absolutely and utterly hated discovering. He was acting just like her parents. Grasping and ambitious, willing to run over anyone or anything that stood in the way of their mighty corporate machine. Why, oh why, oh why, had she expected more of him?

Something in her snapped. To heck with subjecting herself daily to the impenetrable and unforgiving Luca Calcagni. She would find some other way to wrestle her inner demons. Some other way to atone for all past crimes, sins, and mistakes.

She was done trying to please Luca. She was quitting Genesis & Sons. *Bye bye, suckers!* The good Lord, Himself, couldn't expect any more from her.

She'd begged His forgiveness again and again. She'd started attending church again. She'd truly attempted to turn over a new leaf and tried to be a better person, but the Calcagnis had refused to let her.

She no longer cared about the PR nightmare it would create for their family when she walked out on her job. That was their problem. In the morning, she would march up those stony stairs one last time and toss her resignation in their CEO's smug face.

JACEY'S DECISION didn't help her sleep. She stared at the ceiling all Sunday night, mulling over her resignation speech and coming up with nothing satisfying. She rose early and, on an angry whim, tucked a black leather skirt in her duffle, a daringly high set of red stilettos, and a creamy lace blouse with a waterfall of ruffles that accentuated her ample assets even more. There was no way she was passing up the opportunity to torment Luca one last time. Might as well give him a full taste of what he'd be missing when she was gone.

She arrived forty-five minutes early, loving how the extra-high heels made her hips swing. Her outfit wasn't the most professional, but she wasn't gunning for professional today. The leather and lace ensemble showcased her height, slenderness, and curves to perfection. She was the full embodiment of the bad girl Luca had written her off as. He certainly wouldn't be able to ignore this version of her today, and she greedily anticipated the advantage it would give her over him.

For once, the front desk of Genesis & Sons was empty. *Excellent.* She didn't need Waverly trying to guilt her out of resigning again. Unfortunately, the woman had worked her way into Jacey's affections. Thus, avoiding her would make it easier to walk away.

Jacey debated and discarded the idea of using Luca's private elevator. Preferring to catch him off guard, she rode the main elevator to the fifteenth floor and walked the final five flights of stairs to give her time to finish composing her coming tirade. By now, she knew the layout of the building. Every elevator. Every stairwell. Every side hallway.

It gave her time to finish deciding the exact angle of her exit speech. Luca probably wouldn't believe her, but she was going to confess her real reason for coming to work for his family. She was also going to tell him she'd finally discovered why Easton had found it so easy to leave the hallowed halls of Genesis & Sons. She would point out how the Calcagnis' refusal to properly fund and train him made every surviving Calcagni as much to blame for his death as she was. All Jacey had done was encourage him to follow his dreams and pick up the tab when they had refused to finance them. She would toss her brief exit speech in Luca's lap like a dirty bomb and make her grand exit before he had the chance to regroup.

Reaching the top floor, she tiptoed her way across the landing and quietly let herself through the side entrance into Luca's office. Her chest leaped at the sight of him at his desk. He was present. *Perfect!* That would allow her to get her rapid-fire resignation speech over with and be gone before the other employees arrived.

A fierce sniffling sound assailed her ears. Luca Calcagni lounged deep in his chair, facing away from her, a large ragged square of paper clutched between his thumb and forefinger. She crept closer and stopped mid-stride.

It was a photo, a much faded and dog-eared one, of him and Easton. They were younger. She'd known Easton most of her life, so she guessed he was no more than fourteen or fifteen in the picture, a good ten years ago. The two brothers had their arms slung around each other, holding up an enormous string of bass between them. They were grinning straight at the camera, the kind of goofy pride reserved for fishermen and their whopping fishing stories. A pride Jacey couldn't relate to. She'd never seen anything exciting about men holding up a bunch of icky, smelly dead fish.

Luca reached up and pinched a hand over his

eyes. His long fingers came away wet at the pads, and Jacey's breath shuddered out of her. Only one other time had she ached so profusely on behalf of another human being. It had been for the inconsolable Waverly at Easton's funeral.

At the sound, Luca spun his chair around, staring at Jacey in confusion for one tortured, unguarded moment.

"Luca?" she whispered, unable to bear the sight of him so agonized.

Though his eyes were red-rimmed, his mouth immediately tightened in anger. He stood and yanked open a desk drawer. Tossing in the photo, he slammed it shut.

"What are you doing here so early, Ms. Maddox? I expected you to call in sick."

It suddenly seemed like an awful time to turn in her resignation. In the midst of his grief, Luca no longer came across as the unfeeling monster she'd made him out to be. Like herself, he was hurting, and hurting people did stupid things like lashing out at the nearest person. In this case, her.

She raised and lowered her hands. The zip drive containing the phony work assignments was clasped in her palm. "I wanted to get an early start. Seems like LeAnne already transcribed your meeting notes. I'm afraid I wasted a lot of time re-transcribing them when I should have been building the presentation. My mistake." *With a not-so-helpful nudge from you to set me in the wrong direction.* "For this reason, I won't be turning in a timecard for my work this weekend."

His lips thinned. "Exactly how many hours did you waste reinventing the proverbial wheel, Ms. Maddox?"

She stared at him, incredulous. How dare he try to pin this mistake on her! He'd set her up; she was sure of it. "Twelve, Mr. Calcagni." Her voice grew brittle as she studied him for a reaction. *Twelve hours of honest effort despite how ill I was, because I can really use the income.* "But I refuse to accept a penny of what isn't due me. I should have checked all the files on the disk." *Not just the one you mentioned on Friday afternoon.* She'd fallen for his trick way too easily. Normally she was more on top of her game.

His expression didn't change. Disappointed at his lack of remorse, she swayed to her desk in her dangerously high heels. Not the best choice of footwear after a weekend punctuated by acute bouts of dizziness and nausea. She was fortunate she had a spare pair of more practical shoes in her desk to change into.

She sat and yanked her lower desk drawer open to swap out her shoes. So much for her rush of empathy for Luca Calcagni. Apparently, her brief glimpse at his human side was over. The monster in him had returned and was raring for a fight. Her brain gave a mental shiver. She really didn't feel well enough to spar with him, but she was no longer in the mood to resign, either. He was like a wounded bear in his grief, swinging and dangerous. She would just have to stay out of striking range.

Now that she was seated, she might as well put in another day's work. At least she'd get paid for this one.

A tall shadow fell over her desk. "You will receive two full days of overtime pay, Ms. Maddox. We do not take advantage of sick employees at Genesis & Sons."

Her head jerked up in surprise. His gesture was better than an apology, both generous and unexpected. Maybe there was hope for the man, after all.

He dropped a stack of files on her desk with a resounding slap. "As soon as you decide which pair of shoes you're going to wear for the day, here's another pile of presentations that aren't going to prepare themselves."

Nope. There was no hope for the man. None whatsoever.

He turned away abruptly, or she might have thrown something at him.

IT WAS like attending boot camp beneath the never-wavering stare of a raging drill sergeant. That was the only way to describe Jacey's next five days.

Despite working through her lunches and taking files home each night, she couldn't seem to fall into a new rhythm, couldn't get caught up with her new workload. She waffled between blaming her rusty office skills and blaming Luca for the unreasonable increase in his demands.

Every day he handed her a new mountain of work. There were no smiles. No thank you's at the end of any project. Just more work. Her energy level continued to drop. She knew she couldn't maintain her current pace much longer on the rat wheel Luca had crafted for her. Not even with the carrot of a bigger paycheck dangling in front of her.

She squinted at the time stamp on her monitor. Less than an hour from closing time. By some miracle, she'd made it to another Friday. She rubbed her eyes and tried to stifle a yawn. Hibernation was sounding very attractive right now. She could easily sleep through the coming winter months and not return to work until next spring.

"Tired, Ms. Maddox?" Luca's mocking voice sliced through her thoughts.

Jacey lowered her hands, too exhausted to work up any more anger at his utter lack of compassion. Or his unwillingness to recognize her endless efforts to please him with her performance. *Bed.* It was the only thing she needed right now. *And sleep.*

"Do you need my assistance with something, Mr. Calcagni?"

Irritation flashed across his dark features. Not the personal kind. More of a distant, distracted kind. By now, she knew the difference. "Our board meeting starts in ten minutes. I'd like you to attend it with me."

She winced and scanned his face. Surely he was joking. Some of their board meetings lasted for hours, and she didn't have that kind of steam left in her. No amount of coffee would keep her eyelids open for several more hours.

He was no longer looking at her, his movements jerky and impatient as he tossed paperwork inside his briefcase. "Bring the Pillmeyer file. During his golf outing today, Edric claims he learned something new about their account transfer that might prove significant."

Dread coursed through Jacey's limbs. She drew on the small burst of negative energy to mobilize herself to retrieve the requested file. What could there possibly be to rehash about the account they'd lost to DRAW Corporation, unless, of course, Luca planned to humiliate her all over again? If that was the case, this time it would be in front of his entire family.

CHAPTER 14: COLLAPSE

LUCA

Needing to work off some of his rapidly escalating edginess, Luca took the stairs. His grandfather was acting mysterious over whatever information he'd learned about the Pillmeyer account, refusing to share even a hint of it before their meeting. He was also insisting Jacey had to be present when he made his big announcement.

Luca couldn't think of many good reasons for Jacey to be present. He would have preferred Edric to be more forthcoming about whatever information he'd uncovered. Whether his family liked it or not, Jacey was his personal assistant. She was his business. He was dealing with her in his own way, though he was beginning to worry about the wisdom of pushing her so hard during and after her illness.

She'd been visibly sick all week, though she denied it profusely the few times he'd tried to bring it up. She'd taken it the wrong way, of course — as a personal criticism — and stepped up her pace even more. It had been a busier week than he expected, so he hadn't needed to fabricate any more fool's errands to keep her busy. As long as whatever Edric had to say didn't involve firing Jacey on the spot, he was going to insist she take the weekend off. No overtime. No exceptions. He needed her to get well.

Man! Luca rubbed a hand over his face as he bounded down the final flight of stairs, briefcase swinging at his side. He just needed her. Period. A need he had no hope of assuaging anytime soon. Ever since she'd caught him mourning over Easton's photo, she'd stopped. Stopped mouthing off at him. Stopped flirting with him. She'd pretty much stopped talking to him, altogether.

Her pale silence was wearing on him. The old Jacey had her issues, but he missed her — all the way down to her sass and insubordination.

He strode through the conference room door, hardly hearing the greetings of his family as he awaited Jacey's arrival. She was only seconds behind him, looking way too pale and thin in her simple black sheath dress. She'd lost weight since she'd come to work for him. Everywhere, that is, except on top. He was sure of it. Due to the nature of their business, he knew everything there was to know about the clothing, shapes, and sizes of women. If he hadn't been working her such long hours, he would have suspected plastic surgery, but that wasn't possible given the hours she'd put in. Maybe she'd invested in new push-up lingerie. He could only hope she wasn't planning another round of centerfold photo shoots. Genesis & Sons didn't need *that* kind of publicity!

She stumbled on her way to the conference table, and he lurched in his seat, leaning in her direction. However, she righted herself with an angry glance at him. *Great.* On top of being ill, she was in one of her poisonous moods.

He frowned across the table at his grandfather. *Let's just get this over with, shall we?* "What do you have for us, sir?"

Edric shot him a gleeful grin. "Well, son? You were right about the sabotage of the Pillmeyer account."

His heart sank as all eyes turned toward Jacey. Her face jerked to his. Bewilderment stained her features. She paled another few degrees, shaking her head slightly at him with a beseeching expression.

He wanted to throw himself bodily between her and whatever else his grandfather had to say, to protect her from any more grief over the Pillmeyer account. Whatever part she had played in that mess, she was clearly sorry for it, and that was good enough for him.

"It was the Maddoxes alright. Up to their old tricks."

Jacey made a choking sound. Luca half-rose from

his seat in concern. She seemed to be having trouble breathing. Waverly leaned across the table to clasp Jacey's hands, but Jacey moved them out of reach. She pushed her chair back and stood, gripping the edge of the table. She swayed slightly, her chest heaving.

"Stop." Luca couldn't tear his gaze away from Jacey but didn't dare approach her. She wouldn't welcome his help.

Edric continued as if he hadn't heard him, chortling so loud it made them all jump. He must have turned down his hearing aid again. "We weren't supposed to find out, but ol' Jensen couldn't resist bragging to a golf buddy. They were upset with Jacey for putting in her application with us after turning down their offer to make her a VP. They'd already cut off her funds. What else could they do but set her up to get fired from her new job? It must chaff their backsides to see how well she's performing at our firm."

Luca hated how chalky Jacey's face had become. "Sir, I'm not sure this is a topic for boardroom discussion." Why in heaven's name couldn't his grandfather have broken the news to him one-on-one?

Edric ignored him and spread his hands wide. "Ms. Maddox, I'm of a mind to make it up to you with a sizable bonus. I'm as sorry as I can be that you took the heat last week over something that was no fault of yours."

Jacey's mouth moved, but no sound came out. A deep flush replaced her paleness and just as quickly evaporated. She stood, slowly turned away from the conference table, and pitched forward.

Luca stopped thinking and simply moved. He pushed his chair back so hard it went flying, but he was too far away to reach her in time. She crumpled like an old building falling in on itself. She would have smacked the merciless tile floor but for Rhys's swift intervention. Fortunately, his brother was sitting much closer to her. He caught her limp frame and lowered her to the floor.

"Jacey!" Her name tore from Luca's lips as he flew across the room to crouch on the floor beside her. "Somebody, call an ambulance!" He pressed two fingers to her wrist. *Thank God she has a pulse!* It was a wildly erratic one, however.

Her face pinched in concern, Waverly eased herself down on the floor on the other side of Jacey and gently cradled her face in her wrinkled hands. "Remove my shawl," she instructed sharply. "Put it under her head."

Luca rapidly complied. "I'll ride with her in the ambulance to the E.R. Someone else needs to inform her family."

"What?" His grandmother looked outraged. "After all they've done to her? That's the last thing she needs right now. Why, those hooligans—"

"Ask for Alora. Her sister." His voice was firm.

He'd begun to suspect the older Maddox sister had something to do with the press release that had made it difficult to fire her younger sister. Since Jacey was innocent of sabotage, it was the only other logical explanation for her calls to Alora hours before losing the Pillmeyer account. He sincerely hoped it meant Jacey had at least one ally left in her family.

Rhys laid a hand on his shoulder. "You don't have to go to the E.R., Luca. I know things haven't been easy between the two of you. I don't mind being the one to accompany her."

"Yes, I do. This is my fault." Raw guilt tore through Luca's gut. "I was angry about a lot of things, and I pushed her too hard."

"Yes, you did," Rhys didn't bother to sugar-coat his tone, "so how about we put a different face in front of her, besides yours, when she wakes up?"

"Thank you, but no." Luca was beyond reason on the topic. He wasn't leaving her side, and that was final. "I'll fix this. I owe it to Easton." He couldn't roll back the years or undo the distance that had sprung between him and his youngest brother before his death, but it was past time to quit punishing Easton's widow for things outside her control. He'd make it up to her. Somehow. When she woke up, things were going to be different between them. They were going to start over.

Something in Luca's face made Rhys lower his hand. "If you're sure about this, brother."

"I'm sure. Just try to reach her sister. I really think Jacey would want her to know about this."

"I don't think Alora Maddox cares too much for any of us, especially me, but I'll do what I can."

Especially you, eh? Luca frowned up at him, sensing a story, but it wasn't the time to pursue it.

One thing for sure, the idea of reaching out to Alora Maddox had his calm, unshakable brother looking worried.

CHAPTER 15: HOSPITAL

JACEY

Jacey awoke to a world of muted sounds and blackness since her eyelids refused to open. She willed the sounds to go away again, so she could sleep.

Then again, maybe she was still asleep and dreaming, because Luca was present. He wasn't snarling at her any longer, though. Or angry. Or disapproving. Or criticizing. She couldn't understand what he was saying, only that he sounded worried. Anxious, even. His thumb was tracing circles on the top of her hand, and his touch felt amazing.

This was the Luca she'd fantasized about. The Luca who cared. The warmth of his fingers seeped through her hand and did crazy things to her heart. She wanted to sit up and assure him everything was okay, but she only managed a fragile-sounding moan.

"Jacey? Can you hear me?" His voice was thicker than usual, rough with concern. It resonated through her and nestled in her chest, warming the coldest parts of her.

Something sharp pricked her wrist, and a sliver of coolness traveled up her vein. She shivered.

"Here." Luca's voice cracked as he tucked something around her shoulders. It was smooth and silky, and it smelled like him.

She shivered again, this time in delight.

"If you'll just sit back, sir. We have heated blankets." To Jacey's intense disappointment, someone removed the silky fabric with Luca's scent. She quickly forgave them when the toasty blankets they replaced it with put an end to her shivering. It was sheer heaven. It was also the last thing she remembered.

JACEY AWOKE a second time to muted voices, a distant wail, and electronic beeping noises. Swiveling her head, she groaned at the ache between her temples.

"Jacey!" Luca's head was inclined in her direction. He was perched on a swivel stool, his forearms resting on his knees. White floor-to-ceiling curtains surrounded them.

She hated how ravaged he looked, wishing she

had the strength to reach over and brush the tousled lock of hair from his forehead, wishing she had the right to.

"Where am I?"

She loved the way he raised one brow at her question in that half incredulous, half challenging way of his. "At the medical center. You passed out during our board meeting."

The memory of Edric's shocking announcement made Jacey's stomach pitch dizzily. She swallowed.

"I'm sorry you had to find out about the Pillmeyer account sabotage that way. Sometimes Grandfather gets carried away. He was so tickled to learn you were innocent of any wrongdoing, he didn't stop to consider how upsetting the news might be for you."

Jacey's brain must be addled from her collapse, because she could have sworn Luca was apologizing. *To her!* "I already forgave him. He offered me a bonus."

His brows shot up in surprise at her attempted joke.

The curtains brushed aside, and Alora Maddox faced them, clapping softly. "Congratulations on the bonus, darling. Hopefully, your hard work at Genesis & Sons will come with more than a bonus, though. You're way over-qualified. I'm thinking a pay raise and promotion are warranted soon." Her voice was taunting, her words clearly directed at Luca.

She was an inch and a half shorter than Jacey, a fact that had irritated her for years as the older sister. She more than made up for it with the twist of red-gold hair atop her head and queenly presence. She looked immaculate this evening in her charcoal pinstripe suit, minty green shirt, and silver jewelry.

Luca stood and held out a hand. "It's been awhile, Alora."

"That it has, Luca."

They knew each other. Personally or just professionally? Either way it was news to Jacey, but she couldn't sense any major undercurrents of animosity beneath their mutually chilly greetings.

Alora stood at the end of her hospital bed and squeezed her foot through the blankets. "You don't look so good, little sis. What gives?"

"Who knows? I was thinking a flu bug, but it lasted all week." Jacey yawned. "If it's something deadlier, you've all been exposed. That means I'm taking you down with me."

Luca laughed. It was such a beautiful, unexpected sound, Jacey's heart raced. She gazed up at him in awe.

He gave her a slow, deliberate wink that made her stop breathing.

"Well, isn't that precious of you?" Alora's voice was dry. "Greyson is on his way. Thought I'd warn you."

"Why would he bother?" Jacey's gaze returned

to her sister's while her chest clenched in apprehension. He was the oldest of their siblings, and they hadn't spoken in over five years. Not since the day she'd eloped with Easton.

"He caught me on the phone with Rhys and overheard enough to guess something was wrong. It's kind of hard to explain, but Greyson still cares about you. In his own way."

Could have fooled me.

Alora's head swiveled to the curtain which was opening, and her voice hardened. "He just isn't good at showing it."

Greyson walked in, shrugging the shoulders of his dark, navy suit. He sported a moronic but endearing red bowtie that shouted nerd even louder than his short, spiky auburn hair flying in all directions. His ridiculous lack of style suited him, though, and he managed to look good despite it. "You know what they say about eavesdroppers."

"Nothing good," Alora snapped.

"Thank you for coming," Jacey interrupted, sensing an argument brewing. "It's good to see you." *Finally, albeit a few years late.*

He nodded and moved to stand beside her older sister. "So what happened? Someone try to poison you?" There was no mistaking the meaning of the dark look he sent in Luca's direction.

"Greyson!" Alora hissed.

"It's a fair question," he muttered.

Luca hadn't bothered rising to greet him as he had Alora.

Interesting.

"No, not poison, though a lot of women claim that's what it feels like." Dark eyes snapping with humor, a slender Asian woman in a white coat bustled in, a stethoscope draped from her neck. "Hi, there," she trilled cheerfully at Jacey. "I'm Dr. Shu. You weren't awake the first time I examined you. How are you feeling now that you have a few extra pints of fluid in your system?"

"Much better, thank you. Just tired."

"Well, that's to be expected for a woman in your condition, Ms. Maddox."

Jacey stared. "My condition?"

"Uh-oh! You mean, you don't know?" The woman's dark, pencil-thin brows rose. "You're expecting a baby, Ms. Maddox. Allow me to be the first to congratulate you."

"I'm pregnant?" Jacey whispered. *I can't be.* How was it even possible? Her hand crept to her mid-section. Easton was dead, and they hadn't exactly been intimate very often during the past year. His schedule had been too consumed by the whirl of the racing circuit. Except for the night of their five-year anniversary. About thirteen weeks ago.

Mercy! I'm pregnant. It would certainly explain

the sickness, the exhaustion, the clawing edginess, and her late monthly cycle.

What in the world am I going to do with a baby? I can barely support myself. Jacey slumped against her pillows, wanting to howl her frustration at the ceiling. "How far along am I?"

Dr. Shu shook her head, her smile wry. "I'm going to have to defer to your OB-GYN to answer that question. You can't be very far along if you didn't even know you were in the family way."

Greyson, who'd been gulping like a fish for several seconds, finally found his voice. He swung in Luca's direction. "You sick, filthy—!" He stubbed the toe of his shoe on the edge of the bed in his effort to launch himself at the other man.

Greyson's fists made a pummeling motion, but Luca easily held him off.

Dr. Shu hastily shoved aside the curtain. "Security! We have a situation!"

"Stop it!" Jacey's voice cut through the chaos. She was surprised at how calm she felt and how firm her voice sounded. "It's Easton's baby, if you insist on knowing. And mine. It's my baby." Her breath hitched with embarrassment as all eyes turned in her direction. There had never been anyone else. Despite her wild teen years. Despite her dubious reputation. Despite what everyone thought of her. She might be a tease and a flirt — even a liar in the past — but she'd not been unfaithful to her husband or his memories. At his death, she'd promised God she was going to clean up her act, and she had.

Or had she? Kissing Luca hadn't exactly been part of her plan to remain faithful to her dead husband. However, being in his arms had felt so special after five years of being married to a man who hadn't made a habit of coming home most nights. Easton had preferred to hang out with his friends and party until the wee hours of the morning. He was quite simply a guy who'd refused to grow up.

And I'm doing it again. Comparing the two brothers. Guilt stabbed Jacey in a dozen places.

She couldn't bring herself to meet Luca's gaze, though she felt it on her. She was dying inside at what he must be thinking of her, with the way she'd practically gobbled him up with her kisses, all while being pregnant with another man's son. His own niece or nephew, no less!

Greyson dropped his fists, and Luca took the opportunity to shove him a few feet away. Alora caught their brother's arm and gave it a yank. "I can't believe you. Brawling in the middle of an E.R. We better bounce, before they arrest you for disturbing the peace." She shot a frustrated look at Jacey. "I'm so sorry about this. Call me. Please?"

Don't go, please. Don't leave me alone with Luca. "I will." Jacey stared after them, too distraught to say anything else. *I'm pregnant. Heaven help me, I'm pregnant!* She was in no way qualified to be a parent.

Not on any level — financially, emotionally, or otherwise.

Dr. Shu ducked back on their side of the curtains, smoothing her white jacket. "Alrighty then. Looks like our crisis is averted." She clasped her hands in front of her. "My nurse will be paying you a visit shortly to give you some pamphlets about prenatal care. She can help you set up your first OB appointment, too, if you'd like. Do you have any questions before I leave, Ms. Maddox?"

"When may I go home?" Jacey had no idea what time it was, but it had to be getting late and she hated traveling to her apartment after dark. It was a part of the city that could quickly turn ominous at night.

Her doctor smiled in understanding. "It's no fun being in a hospital bed, I know, Ms. Maddox, but you were pretty dehydrated when you came in. I'd like to keep you awhile longer for observation and get another sack or two of fluid in your system before you go."

"Ah, okay. Thank you." Jacey watched her go, tiredness seeping over her once more. Maybe she would call Alora for a ride or try to get a cheap motel room nearby. She didn't feel up to a lengthy bus trip tonight with a stopover at the gym. She turned drearily back to Luca, who remained in the curtained off area with her.

His mouth still looked pinched around the edges, even though Greyson was out of sight.

"I'm sorry about my brother. What an awful conclusion for him to make!"

"How long have you known?" he growled.

"What?" Every muscle in Jacey's body tensed at the ferocity in his voice.

"About the baby. How long have you known?"

The breath left her with a huffing sound. "Five minutes, maybe? Same as you." She searched his face, thoroughly puzzled. Having a baby wasn't a crime, was it?

"You had to have known something!" he exploded. "It's your body."

She felt a flush burn its way across her face. "My monthly cycle has been late before. *Not* that it's any of your business."

"Not my business! You're carrying my brother's child. When were you planning on telling my family?"

She blinked. "We can call them right now, if you want." She sat up in bed, scanning the room for her handbag.

"I can't believe what a fool you've made of us!" He leaned closer, his face reddening. "This is the real reason you came to work for Genesis & Sons, isn't it? It was your end game all along. Why you've been slowly worming your way into my grandmother's good graces. You nearly had Rhys fooled, too. They wanted so badly to believe in you, Jacey. You have no idea how much." His voice grew so hoarse, he had to stop and clear his throat.

"M-my end game?" she spluttered.

"What exactly do you want from us, Jacey? I think it's finally time to come clean. You owe us that much, at least."

Realization splashed over her like icy rain. "You think I want money." She fisted the blankets with both hands as pain skidded through her chest. It had been foolish of her to hope Luca was ever going to change his opinion of her. His mind always jumped to the worst possible conclusions, no matter what she did.

"Everyone has a price, *chica*. What kind of price tag have you put on your baby's head?"

She couldn't bear his sneering any longer. It hurt too much. "Get out." Her voice was shrill but firm with finality. It was her own fault for crushing on a man who despised her. It was her fault for wanting and expecting anything other than his never-ending disdain.

"Nice try, Ms. Maddox, but we're not even close to being finished with this discussion."

She held his gaze, her own fury mounting. Whatever he saw there made his lips curl in derision.

Jacey's heart twisted in response. "Yes, we are." Her voice grew calmer. "I don't want anything from you, Mr. Calcagni. I never wanted anything but a chance to atone for the way I wronged your family. A chance to say I'm sorry for encouraging Easton to pursue a career that ultimately got him killed." She moistened her lips, too angry to stop her tirade. "You would have never listened to the words of a Maddox, so I came to work for you, instead. I hoped in time I could win your forgiveness through my service to your company. But you know what? I'm not half as sorry as I was the day I first walked into your office, because now I understand why Easton left."

"By all means, enlighten me," he commanded coldly.

"None of you were willing to listen to him, were you? None of you were willing to let him be what he was meant to be. That makes you as much to blame for his death as I am. Maybe if you had been willing to properly fund and train him, his attempt to race cars wouldn't have ended so tragically."

Luca turned red, then white. She'd never seen him so furious, but she was far from finished. She'd held back speaking her mind for too long. It was his turn to listen.

"This past Monday, the real reason I came to work early was to turn in my resignation. Your grief was the only thing that made me decide to stick it out another week under your hateful iron fist. I felt you deserved another chance, because I realized you were hurting as badly as I was. Unfortunately, you have the most unkind and spiteful way of showing it, so I've decided you don't deserve one thing more from me. You've made it clear over and over and over again how unwelcome I am at Genesis & Sons. I get it now, and I am resigning. That's all I have to say. You can leave now."

His mouth parted as if he was debating what to say next.

"That means get out." She gritted her teeth to keep them from chattering against the chill radiating from her heart.

His lips clamped, and his eyes burned into hers, a kaleidoscope of fury, hurt and accusation whirling in their depths. Without another word, he turned and slapped his way past the curtains.

Her chest heaved at the cloying emptiness his absence left in the emergency bay. She sank against the mattress, closing her eyes. It had felt so good to have him holding her hand while she dozed. So incredibly good for her soul to come into contact, however briefly, with his humanity. His compassion. She had not mistaken his concern for her. It was real.

But it was over. Luca couldn't have humiliated her more than he already had with his assumption that she would use her baby to squeeze money from his family's coffers. The very thought made her ill. Hadn't she just spent the past several weeks proving she was willing to work for a paycheck? And work hard?

The truth made her sink farther down in the hospital bed linens. Luca was never going to accept her for who she was any more than her parents had. And why should they? She was but a twenty-five-year-old woman with a handful of unrealized dreams that didn't fit into any of their corporate missions or personal agendas.

She'd dreamed for years of a career in music, and now her dreams were over. She was widowed with a baby on the way and no contingency plan. There was no new job lined up to replace the one she'd given up this evening. No strong ties to any of the friends she'd left behind five years ago or the ones she'd met on the racing circuit. The only thing going in her favor was the fact that Luca had paid her far more than she expected, so she had a few thousand dollars saved in the bank again. If Edric Calcagni kept his word, she also had a bonus on the way.

An idea gripped her and took root. She could leave this God-forsaken city. Tonight, if she wanted. There was no law keeping her here. She'd done it before when she'd eloped with Easton. If she asked nicely, Alora would probably grant her one last favor and empty out her apartment for her and toss her few belongings into storage. Or just toss them out, altogether. Jacey owned very little of value these days.

If she was going to endure an unplanned pregnancy, she might as well endure it in peace somewhere far beyond the reaches of both the Calcagnis and Maddoxes. She could sing and wait tables for a living. It wouldn't be a fancy life, but it would be hers and hers alone. She would not be beholden to anyone.

The idea grew more appealing by the second. Jacey would head straight to the airport after leaving the hospital and purchase a one-way ticket to somewhere. It didn't matter where so long as it was far from Luca's sneering face, which was still burning a hole in her heart.

CHAPTER 16: ATTEMPTED ESCAPE

LUCA

Luca strode unseeing to the parking lot, then remembered he'd arrived by ambulance with Jacey. He whipped out his phone and called his chauffeur.

Don Kappelman picked up right away. "Yes, sir?"

"Pick me up at the medical center, in front of the emergency entrance."

"On my way, sir."

Luca shoved his phone back in his pocket and crossed his arms, too agitated to remain still. He paced the sidewalk while the twilight deepened to night.

How dare Jacey try to pin Easton's death on him! Or anyone else in his family! That was low, even for her. Rage simmered in his chest, mingling with the pain over the unfairness of her accusations.

He'd always loved his brothers. He'd looked out for every one of them his entire life. Maybe he hadn't been as attentive to the wayward Easton right after their parents' deaths, but Luca had staggered around for a few months — they all had — trying to come to terms with such a tremendous loss while still running a mega corporation. Who on earth could blame him for a bit of inattention during a time like that?

Apparently Jacey did. The thought infuriated him further. He normally paid no attention to criticism. It was part of being a CEO. Part of being in the constant crosshairs of the media, their competitors, and anyone else who wanted to voice a dissenting opinion or took exception to his corporate decisions. But Jacey's criticism was personal. A direct attack on his character, it rankled deeply and heavily.

The fact that her disapproval mattered to him at all at this point bothered him, too. He'd never met a more maddening woman. He'd never met anyone who'd crawled so thoroughly beneath his skin and stayed there. To desire her good opinion after all she'd done to him was inexplicable.

He hoped she wasn't serious about her resignation tonight. If she was, Waverly was going to shoot him in the knees when she found out about the baby. Her first great-grandchild. It had nearly killed Waverly to lose Easton. He didn't want to think of how she would react when she learned he'd personally and single-handedly alienated the mother of her first great-grandchild from their family — forever.

Don cruised up to the curb in Luca's sleek black limousine and leaped out to open the door. He was a hulk of a man, tall and broad with blonde hair and a slightly darker goatee. He'd served in the Special Forces until a near-fatal helicopter crash had broken his back, crushed his legs, and left him with a permanent limp.

"Thanks, Don." Luca slid his long frame into the passenger seat.

"Where to, sir?"

"Home." *I suppose.*

Don firmly shut the door. He'd come highly recommended a few years earlier, and Luca found his loyalty and commitment to be irreplaceable. Don was more than a driver. He also served as Luca's co-pilot during their semi-frequent helicopter trips, bodyguard, and whatever else Luca needed him for. In his spare time, which wasn't often, Don pulled guard shifts at celebrity events.

Luca buckled himself in but couldn't relax. He was still too shocked about Jacey's pregnancy. He had experienced a moment of unholy thrill when Greyson had assumed the baby was his. *Man!* A crazy part of him wished it was. He wished Jacey had never eloped with his brother, that she'd married him, instead.

But when Greyson had left the hospital with

Alora, all Luca's previous suspicions about Jacey had come crashing back. It simply wasn't logical to assume she hadn't known about the pregnancy. There would have been signs. More than a missed monthly cycle or two. There would have been any number of other symptoms. Morning sickness, exhaustion, swollen breasts, raging hormones, edginess.

He leaned forward to grip the edge of his seat as guilt slammed into him. *How could I have missed so many clues?* Jacey had been showing every one of those symptoms for the past week and *only* for the past week. His mind weighed and dissected each detail. He recalled how she had gone home sick the previous Saturday, claiming a flu bug. She hadn't known. She couldn't have. *God, forgive me! What have I done?*

"Everything okay back there, sir?" Don asked.

"No! Not even close." Luca whipped out his phone and dialed Jacey. He was drowning in guilt, choking and gagging on it, suffocating in it. He'd driven her mercilessly at work, acted like a world-class jerk every time they were in the room together, punished her for a thousand things outside her control, and all that time she'd been pregnant. He hated himself for what he'd done to her. Absolutely hated who he'd become ever since Jacey had sauntered back into his life. He was capable of being a much better man than this. Instead, he'd allowed his grief and anger to spill all over an innocent woman like poison.

"I'm sorry," he muttered under his breath. "God, forgive me. I know I don't deserve it, but..." The phone continued to ring.

Please pick up the phone, Jacey. He didn't know what he was going to say to her, but he would start with an apology. A whole string of apologies. More than anything, he needed to hear her voice to make sure she was okay. He would offer her a ride home if she'd let him. Promise her she didn't have to look at him or speak to him if she didn't want to. It would serve him right if she never spoke to him again.

The call went to voicemail.

Growing more frantic by the second, Luca dialed Dr. Shu's office number next. Thankfully, someone picked up right away, but he was put on hold for several minutes. Each minute felt like a year. A woman's voice finally sounded across the line. "Dr. Shu's nurse speaking."

"Hi. This is Luca Calcagni. I'm the one who rode to the hospital in the ambulance with Jacey Maddox. I had to take off in a hurry, but I'm calling to check on her. I can't seem to reach her on the phone."

"I'm sorry, sir, but she's gone."

"Gone?"

"She checked out against doctor's orders a few minutes ago."

"Thank you for letting me know." He disconnected the line and turned to Don, sick with worry.

"Yes, sir?"

"Pull over somewhere. Anywhere."

"Roger that, sir." Don pulled into the nearest parking lot and awaited his next order.

Luca dialed Alora Maddox.

"Well, well," she drawled. "To what do I owe the honor of receiving calls from not one but two Calcagni brothers in the same evening?"

"Where is Jacey?"

She drew a rapid breath. "Isn't she at the hospital? I just took Greyson home. I'm on my way back there now."

"I just called Dr. Shu's nurse. She checked herself out. I'm not proud to admit this, but we exchanged a few words. I owe her an apology as soon as we find her."

Alora screamed something into the mouthpiece. He had to hold the phone away from his ear.

"Men! Who needs any of you?" she finally snapped. "Hang on. I'll call her." She put him on hold.

He anxiously watched the seconds tick away on his watch.

Alora abruptly clicked back to their call. "I don't know what you said or what you did, because she's not telling me. All I know is she's leaving town.

Asked me to clear out her rat hole of an apartment and put her things in storage."

His ears twitched at her description of Jacey's living arrangements. "What's this about a rat hole?"

"Wow! You don't seem to know much about your personal assistant, Luca Calcagni." Alora's voice was brittle and impatient. "She lives in one of the seediest sections of the city."

"No!" His blood congealed in his veins. "Why would she do a fool thing like that?"

"Because she's broke and too proud to accept any help. Believe me, I offered. She takes the bus every morning to the gym to change into her office clothes. Says it's too risky to ride all the way to her apartment in a skirt and makeup."

Especially for a centerfold beauty like her. His blood chilled a few degrees further, icing around the edges of his heart. At least Jacey had the sense to take a few precautions though it wasn't enough — not near enough. Every organ in his body shuddered at what he'd just learned about her.

He'd long suspected she was hiding things from him, but this was far from what he expected. Every detail he was finding out about her pointed to one thing and one thing only: Jacey Maddox was a good person.

"Please, Alora. Just tell me where she is." He wouldn't be able to sleep tonight until he laid eyes on her and saw for himself she was okay.

"She'll never forgive me if I do."

"Neither of us will ever forgive ourselves if something bad happens to her. Or her baby." He was ill to the deepest pit of his belly just thinking about it.

"Fine. She wouldn't tell me when I asked, but I'm pretty sure I heard her asking her cab driver to drop her off at Terminal One. I might have heard an airplane taking off in the background."

Luca rapped on the window again to get Don's attention. "Take me to the airport. Terminal One."

"Roger that, sir." Don nosed the long black car back on the freeway and picked up speed.

"I'll meet you there." Alora's voice was terse.

Tires squealed in the background, and her voice grew muffled. She didn't return to the line for a full minute. "Looks like I'll be running late. There's a multi-car pileup in front of me."

There was more screeching of tires and a crashing sound followed by a muttered expulsion from Alora.

"Are you okay?" he cried.

"I'm fine. I whipped off the road on to the shoulder in time to avoid it. Just get to my sister before she does anything stupid. Anything *else* stupid," she corrected, "and call me as soon as you find her."

"Count on it."

DON CRUISED up to the long line of cars waiting to let out and pick up passengers from the Terminal One entrance doors. He managed to squeeze his way to the curb, where he left the motor idling. He hurried around the hood of the car to open Luca's door, but Luca was already flinging it wide. He sprinted across the long entranceway leading into the terminal.

"I'll circle around, sir," Don called after his boss.

Luca waved two fingers without turning and dashed through the nearest set of glass entrance doors. He paused to survey the long lines of humanity snaking out from the endless stretch of ticket counters. Jacey could be anywhere in this crowd or behind security already.

Where are you, princesa?

He started at one end of the room and painstakingly scanned each of the zigzagging roped-off lines of people, praying to catch a glimpse of her.

He found her halfway down the enormous span of ticket counters. She was wearing her much-crumpled black sheath dress from work and those favorite red heels of hers. Not exactly appropriate footwear for a woman on a trip, certainly not for one in her extra delicate condition.

His kneecaps felt strange. Must be that whole weak-with-relief thing hitting him.

Her elbows were propped on the counter, and she appeared to be arguing with the attendant. As he drew closer, it sounded more like pleading. "I don't know what happened to my driver's license. It probably slipped between the couch cushions or something. But here's my employee badge for Genesis & Sons and my gym card. Surely, you can accept some other form of I.D."

"Jacey!" Luca cut across the front of the line and moved to stand beside her. "Don't leave." He spoke low in her ear. "All those things I said in the hospital were unpardonable. I wasn't thinking straight, something that's becoming a habit of mine around you."

"Luca?" She dropped the pen she was holding, spinning to face him. The movement put her off balance, and she reached wildly for the cabinet to regain it. "What are you doing here? How did you find me?"

"It wasn't easy." He caught her waist to steady her. "Don't go, *carina*," he repeated softly, pleadingly. "We need to talk. We can still work this out."

"There's nothing to work out, Mr. Calcagni. I'm leaving town." She turned back to the ticket counter, leaving him clenching and unclenching his hands helplessly.

He did the only thing he could think of to draw her attention back to him. He purposefully needled her. "It's the one thing you're good at doing, isn't it, Jacey Maddox? Running away." It pained him physically to use such a sarcastic tone of voice with her. He would have preferred to haul her into his arms and kiss her until she couldn't think straight, but desperate times called for desperate measures.

"How dare you!" she gasped, spinning to face him again.

That's right, beautiful. Get mad at me. I deserve it. "To borrow your own words from a few days ago, I never pegged you for a quitter."

"This isn't quitting." She jerked her gaze away from his to address the open-mouthed attendant. "Are you sure there isn't a way you can sell me a ticket without a drivers license or passport?"

"Do you have a military ID or Permanent Resident Card?"

"No."

"Then I'm sorry, ma'am." The airline worker shook his head regretfully. "I'll be glad to sell you a ticket when you find your driver's license. In the meantime, if you'll please step aside, so I can help the next passenger in line."

Jacey eased away from the counter and took a few swaying steps toward the exit. The lost look on her face and the exhaustion pinching her eyes shifted something heavy in Luca's heart.

He followed, remaining within reaching distance should she require his assistance. "At least allow me to give you a ride home."

She glanced up at him, frowning as if surprised he was still there. "No, thank you," she said firmly.

"Please?"

"Did you just say please? What's the world coming to?" There was a glazed cast to her blue eyes that spiked a new layer of worry deep in Luca's gut. Something was wrong.

"Jacey, are you okay?"

She shook her head slowly. "I don't feel so well."

Call him a cad for taking advantage of the moment, but he stepped in her path and settled his hands on her waist, blocking her progress. "Then don't wait for a taxi." Or try walking all the way to the bus terminal, which was apparently her preferred method of travel. How had he failed to notice she'd not once driven a personal vehicle to work? "My driver is waiting at the curb."

"You have a driver?" There was no mistaking the envy in her voice. "But of course, you do!"

His main goal at the moment was to keep her talking. "His name is Don. Wounded warrior, veteran, really great guy. You'll like him."

She wrinkled her nose at him. "Fine. I'll accept your ride."

Thank you, God! Relief coursed through his chest.

"But I still hate you." She slurred the last few words as she swayed in his direction, making them hard to understand though he got the gist of them.

He could live with her hate for now. It was better than her indifference. A lot of medical professionals these days claimed there was a thin line between love and hate, anyway. As long as he could keep Jacey in town, he could work on nudging her back over that line.

Whoa! Love? Where had that thought come from?

Luca bent his head next to her ear. "May I carry you?" he asked softly. *Please say yes.*

For an answer, she slid her arms around his neck.

Grateful beyond words, he lifted her gently in his arms, and she burrowed her face against his neck like a broken doll. Her quick acquiescence on the issue of transportation alarmed him even more than her slurred speech. He wanted Jacey, but he wanted her whole. Not this beaten-down version of her. He'd nurse her around the clock, whatever it took, to get her sass back.

Because I'm falling in love with her. The realization staggered Luca. He could think of a thousand reasons why they weren't right for each other, starting with the way they drove each other crazy! He could think of a thousand more reasons why things would never work between them, but as the old saying went, *the heart wants what the heart wants.*

And his heart wanted Jacey Maddox. "*Mi princesa,*" he muttered huskily, tightening his arms around her.

She snuggled closer.

Don was pulling up to the curb as they exited the

building. He looked surprised to see Jacey in Luca's arms but didn't ask any questions. He was too well trained. "Where to, sir?"

"Home."

The car started moving, and his driver closed the window to the main body of the vehicle, giving them their privacy.

Jacey revived somewhat at the sound of Don's voice. The moment Luca set her on the black leather seat, she tried to put some distance between them. She smoothed the skirt of her wrinkled dress, a hopeless task. "I prefer to be dropped off at my place, thank you," she informed Don cooly.

"Not a chance," Luca growled and climbed in next to her, slamming the door shut behind him. "I'll give you three choices, *chica*. The hospital, your sister's place, or mine. No decent person would leave you alone tonight, especially not in the part of town where you reside."

Her face snapped to his. "You have no right," she hissed.

"As a matter of fact, I do. You're carrying my niece or nephew inside you," he shot back. "Hate me all you want, but we're family, and family looks after family." He couldn't stand the thought that she'd been living in a rough section of the city the whole time she'd been working for him, but he was mostly furious at himself for not knowing.

"Family? Seriously?" she mocked. Her anger

seemed to energize her. "That's the line you're going with? We both know you've been trying to get rid of me since the day I came to work for you."

"That was before I knew you were about to make me an uncle." *An uncle.* The title filled him with awe. A real, living part of Easton would live on through Jacey. It was a miracle, one he didn't deserve. It was both wondrous and humbling.

Some of the rage mottling Jacey's cheeks dissipated as she took in his expression. "I think I have the right to raise my child far from the reaches of both our hateful families," she returned icily.

"Yes, I suppose you do." He could understand why she felt that way. She'd been treated poorly by both their families. However, the thought of her leaving town twisted his heart into painful knots. "Do you really think that's best for the baby?"

"Yes," she whispered, dropping her gaze. "I don't know," she amended, with a crack in her voice. Her soulful blue eyes were locked on the quickly disappearing airline terminal through the tinted limousine windows. The moment it winked from sight, she started to weep. Deep, jagged, heart wrenching sounds of misery.

If Luca had ever thought he'd been in pain, and he had — deep, gaping-hole-in-your-heart-pain after the loss of his parents and youngest brother — this was far worse. Hearing Jacey cry was like having his heart ripped from his chest and flayed into tiny strips.

He listened until he couldn't stand it any longer. With a muttered exclamation, he hauled her onto his lap. Burying a hand in her hair, he pressed her face to his shoulder.

"I'm going to find a way to make this right, *carina*. I swear it." From now on, anyone in either of their families who tried to hurt Jacey would first have to go through him.

Thank God she didn't protest or try to push him away. He wasn't sure he had the will power to ever let her go again.

DON GAVE HIS BOSS A LONG, searching look when he opened the door. It softened to the consistency of melted butter at the sight of Jacey's limp form in his arms.

"Give MaryBeth a ring." Luca carefully eased himself from the car with Jacey in his arms. "Tell her I need a hospital bed for the weekend and a home visit as soon as possible, preferably tonight. I'm willing to pay whatever price she names."

He prayed MaryBeth would be able to deliver everything he asked for. Otherwise, he'd have no choice but to take Jacey back to the hospital.

Don nodded and whipped out his phone.

MaryBeth was a Family Medicine doctor Luca had dated a few years earlier. She'd wanted more, but that was impossible for him to give while running Genesis & Sons. They'd managed to remain friends after their mutual breakup. Last he heard she was dating a high school history teacher.

Luca crossed the portico and paused before the double front doors. His housekeeper, Merl, swept them open. She was a thin, middle-aged woman with salt and pepper hair pulled in a French twist. A single strand of saltwater pearls adorned her neck. Although he didn't require it, she insisted on wearing a black dress and white apron as the uniform of her office, a look she pulled off as regally as housekeepers did in the movies.

"Sir!" Merl hurried to his side. "How can I help?"

"Thank you for your concern, Merl." He was ever grateful for her assistance. "As you can see, my guest is ill." He hurried past Merl across the marble entry tiles and headed for the elevator. He was more than capable of carrying Jacey up the long, winding flight of stairs to the catwalk, but he hated to jostle her any more than necessary. "Don is calling the doctor. Bring me anything you can think of to make her comfortable. A thermometer, hot tea, extra blankets…" His voice trailed off. He had no idea what Jacey needed and could only pray MaryBeth would be able to pay them a visit tonight.

He hadn't put any thought into where Jacey would stay in his 17,000 square foot mansion. It boasted nine bedrooms including six furnished as spare rooms, but his feet naturally led him to one that was two doors down from his master suite. It was where Waverly and Edric stayed when they visited for any length of time.

Luca set Jacey in the middle of the oversized king bed, noting how fragile she looked against the navy silk duvet and creamy sheets. He raised one of her fine-boned wrists to check her pulse. It felt normal. He resisted the urge to lace his fingers through hers, knowing there would be no answering clasp.

He gently returned her arm to her side and perched on the edge of the bed to unbuckle her red sandals. He'd never understood why women liked to wear such torturous contraptions. He paused over a chip in the cherry nail polish in her otherwise perfect pedicure. He'd ask Merl to fix it before Jacey awoke.

He frowned at her rumpled black sheath dress. He didn't know how a woman was expected to breath in such a constricting outfit. The darts slashed brutally inward against her tiny waist, yet the fabric appeared loose. She was too thin, way too thin to be carrying his brother's baby. They were going to have to do something about her eating habits immediately.

Merl arrived with the blankets and busied

herself with the task of making their patient comfortable.

Don, his miracle-working right hand, ushered MaryBeth inside the bedroom within the hour.

A stunning woman with long, curling, coffee-colored hair, she greeted him with a warm smile and a familiar peck on the cheek. Then she turned to their patient. "So this is your inner sanctum." She glanced curiously around the large room.

"It's one of my guest rooms, actually." They'd only gone on a few dates. She'd never been inside his home.

"Ah. Well, it's a lovely room. Who's the sleeping beauty?"

"My sister-in-law, Jacey Maddox," he supplied curtly. "She's pregnant. I'd appreciate your discretion on the topic. The paparazzi hasn't yet gotten wind of her condition." They would, soon enough, but he'd rather it not be tonight.

"Discretion is my middle name," MaryBeth breezed, her expression going blank. She bent over Jacey. "Yours, I presume?" She shot an enigmatic look over her shoulder at Luca. He chose to classify it as enigmatic; it was easier than dissecting the envy and confusion he saw there.

"No." He was horrified at the assumption. Though it was none of MaryBeth's business, he gave her the bare minimum explanation. The truth was certainly better than the false conclusion she'd jumped to. "We just found out she's expecting my late brother's child."

"I see. Tell me what I need to know." At his scowl, MaryBeth hastily added, "Medically speaking."

"She hasn't been taking care of herself." His fault. He'd pushed her way too hard the past several weeks. "Going through a very tough time personally."

"I imagine she's grieving."

"Plus, working long hours, not eating enough, and not sleeping enough." Again, his fault. "I intend for that to change."

"Hmm." Looking intrigued, MaryBeth pressed her stethoscope to Jacey's chest through the thin sheet. She took Jacey's vitals and pinched her arm to check her hydration levels. Then she raised one of Jacey's eyelids and shone a small pencil light at her eye.

Jacey stirred and mumbled something.

Luca scowled and bent closer but was unable to make out what she was saying. "She collapsed earlier today during a board meeting. I took her to the E.R., and they put her on an I.V. They decided to keep her for observation a bit longer, but she left the facility against doctor's orders."

At MaryBeth's puzzled glance, he added, "It was *after* her sister and I left the hospital. The moment we realized she was missing, we went in search of her. I found her at the airport trying unsuccessfully to purchase a flight after misplacing her driver's license. Long story short, she agreed to let me keep an eye on her for the weekend." More or less. By default, Jacey had mostly chosen to stay with him over returning to the hospital. "She's been sleeping ever since."

MaryBeth stood, looking more puzzled than ever, and smoothed her white coat. "Please don't take offense at what I am about to say, Luca, but you mentioned Ms. Maddox was trying to leave town. Naturally, that prompts the question of her safety." She trained a blandly professional gaze on him. "Do you have any reason to suspect she or her baby are in any danger? Emotionally or physically?"

"Good heavens, no!" he exploded. What an awful position to find himself in! It was not every day a man had to explain his intentions toward his sister-in-law to his ex-girlfriend. Drawing a sharp breath, he ran a hand over his face, trying to tamp down on his irritation and mortification. "Without going into any unnecessary details, things have been difficult between our two families for years. It is my opinion Jacey was hoping for a fresh start elsewhere. That is all."

"Ah." The wrinkle in the center of MaryBeth's forehead smoothed. "Well, her vitals are normal. That's a good sign. My professional opinion is she's just run down and in need of rest. Not surprising, considering her condition and the fact she recently buried a husband. I imagine her new position at Genesis & Sons has been no walk in the park, either."

At Luca's raised brows, she shrugged. "Hey, I follow the local news, including the part about how you snapped her up ahead of the competition." She winked. "After dating you, myself, I know exactly what that means. Number one, she is very good at what she does. And number two, she's putting in some insanely long hours if she's keeping up with you." She wagged a warning finger in his direction. "You'll either lighten her work schedule, or the next doctor she sees will likely put her on bedrest."

"Already done." Luca clenched his jaw, mildly incensed at the underlying accusation in MaryBeth's tone. "None of us knew she was pregnant. Not even her."

MaryBeth threw up her hands, palms out. "No need to go into attack mode. I'm just doing my job. Which means the fact that Ms. Maddox is currently asleep in one of your guest beds, well, that's where my utmost professional discretion kicks in when I leave your home."

"Thank you." The doctor's curious expression was starting to grate on Luca's nerves, making him anxious to end her visit. "Did Don ask you about how to secure a hospital bed for her?"

"I can have one here by tomorrow." MaryBeth

made a face. "Are you sure it's necessary, though? She needs rest, but I expect she'll be back on her feet by the end of the weekend. Most pregnant women don't wish to be treated like invalids. Or so I've heard," she added wistfully, her hand straying unconsciously to her flat abdomen.

Luca studied Jacey bleakly. No, he certainly didn't wish to make her feel like an invalid. He just wanted her well again. And in his life in some capacity, not bolting out of town to avoid him or their complicated families.

When he didn't respond, MaryBeth shook her head, sending her dark waves dancing around her shoulders. "I'm glad you finally found the time," she murmured.

"What?" Luca blinked, trying to focus on what his ex-girlfriend was saying. He was having difficulty tearing his gaze away from the still figure in his guest bed.

"To look after somebody."

What was that supposed to mean? Luca bustled MaryBeth to the front door as swiftly as good manners would allow, nodded a brief farewell, and hurried back to the guest room where Jacey was still sleeping. *Come on, princesa. Open your eyes and assure me you're okay.*

He stayed with her for another hour, silently begging her to awake. She shivered once, and he hastily covered her with a second blanket. He checked her vitals several more times and finally left the room, satisfied she was sleeping as peacefully as MaryBeth claimed. He took a few minutes to snag a shower and change out of his suit. Then he returned to the guest room to drag an overstuffed leather armchair to Jacey's bedside.

He kept vigil until past midnight. He tried to catch up on his emails by scrolling through them on his cell phone, but his mind refused to focus on work. His gaze kept straying to his sleeping guest. He finally gave up and laid a hand over hers, so he would feel her movements when she awoke. Then he settled deeper in his chair and closed his eyes.

CHAPTER 17: COBRA'S LAIR

JACEY

Jacey was surprised to wake in a cocoon of silky sheets. She was also surprised to feel the warm, heavy hand covering hers. She yawned and stretched, allowing her gaze to follow the hand to the dark sprinkling of hair along the very masculine, very well-corded bronze arm connected to it. She jolted into full awareness the moment she ascertained the identity of the man sleeping in the chair next to her bed.

Luca!

The memory of her near escape at the airport flooded back. He'd flat out refused to drive her to her apartment, insisting she stay with someone who could look after her for the weekend. She hadn't expected him to volunteer himself for the task. She gazed at the dark, heavy furniture in the massive room that was the size of her entire apartment. Was this his master suite? Because that would mean she'd been sleeping in his bed.

Heat stole along her cheekbones as she sat up and squinted at him. With his long legs crossed in front of him and his expression relaxed in sleep, he looked like a very different man than the one who'd waylaid her at the airport. Gone was his suit and tie and overbearing demeanor. In the dim light pouring from the half-open door on the other side of the room, she could make out a dark t-shirt hugging the delicious contours of his chest. It tapered to a narrow waist encased in faded jeans.

Um...wow!

He was even more gorgeous out of a suit than in one. She swallowed hard and forced her gaze back to his face. An evening shadow turned his firm jaw rugged, and the hank of hair lying across his forehead made her think of Easton's ever-tousled appearance. She wanted to reach over and smooth it back from his face.

But it wasn't her place. *Only look, don't touch. He's not Easton, and he's certainly not yours.*

For the first time, it struck Jacey how much the two brothers resembled each other. Not Luca's usual suited version but rather this less slicked up version. In jeans and a t-shirt, he looked so much like the careless, laughing Easton she remembered that it made her heart ache. They shared the same bronze skin tone and basic familial facial structure, but that's where their similarities ended. In every other area, Luca was bigger, broader, and harder.

She didn't realize she was squeezing his hand until his eyelids snapped open.

He sat up in the armchair, rubbing his eyes. "How do you feel? Are you in any pain?"

"Do you interrogate all your patients the moment they wake up, doc?" She tossed her hair over her shoulder.

"Only on Saturdays," he shot back.

She scowled at him. "I demand a shower and a toothbrush first. That's my price for talking."

"I'd like that, Jacey. Very much." The humble timbre in Luca's voice caught her off guard. She'd never seen the *please* and *thank you* side of him before.

"Don't get your hopes up, Uncle Luca. I can't promise to tell you what you want to hear, and I absolutely will not promise to continue living in this city."

Unless she was mistaken, fear leaped across his features as she spoke. His grip on her hand tightened, but he loosened it when he saw her wince.

"I'm sorry, *princesa*. For everything."

Another apology? She made a face at him, not knowing what to say.

"You look rested. How do you feel?" He sounded genuinely anxious.

Vulnerable and exposed with the way you're

looking at me, not that I'm going to admit that to you. Wait a blessed minute! Speaking of exposed... She peeked beneath the sheets and blushed with all the blood she had left in her. She was wearing a thick, white bathrobe that didn't belong to her! Yanking the sheet back around her, she ground out through clenched teeth, "Where is my dress?"

"My housekeeper is laundering it," he assured, a slightly elevated color staining his own cheekbones. "She insisted on changing you and making you more comfortable."

The glance they exchanged was charged with tension. That was when she noticed how weary he looked. There were lines creasing the edges of his eyes and shadows beneath them.

His weariness didn't keep him from jumping to his feet when she slid her feet over the side of the bed. He reached for her hands. "Here. Let me."

She swallowed and wrapped the borrowed robe more tightly around her before allowing him to assist her down from the bed.

His fingers wrapped around hers, warm, firm ,and steady, making her feel delicate and feminine... and cherished. All she needed to do was take one more step forward and she would be able to lean into his strength, to rest her head on one of his broad shoulders.

She squeezed her eyes tightly shut for a moment to block out such a crazy thought.

"Are you alright, *carina*?" he asked quickly.

Her eyelids snapped open. "I'm fine." *Just pregnant and hormonal and way too attracted to you for my own good.*

"Well, then. Your shower awaits, *princesa*." He gave her a mock, courtly bow and motioned her toward a door on the opposite end of the suite. Whether purposefully or not, he continued to stand directly in her path.

They stared at each other for an emotion-charged moment. "Do you need something else?" he asked huskily.

It had to be the hormones at work, because she wanted his arms around her so badly she could hardly think straight. She wanted his lips on hers again. She wanted... *Stop!* What she wanted was completely foolish. He'd proven that already, kissing her one afternoon, then kissing a different woman the next day. His only lasting interest in her surrounded the unborn child in her belly and nothing more. She'd be wise to remember it.

"I'm fine," she repeated firmly. "If you'll excuse me." *And move out of my way, please, before I do something to embarrass myself. Like throw myself in your arms...*

He lingered in front of her a few heartbeats longer. "Would you like me to call Merl to assist you?"

A servant to assist me? Seriously! "I'm fine, Luca.

Being pregnant doesn't make me an invalid." Mouth tightening with indignation, she stomped around him and shut the bathroom door a little harder than she intended.

She immediately felt guilty for acting so childish. There was no point in taking her anger out on Luca when the worst part of it was directed at herself. The truth was, she was longing to be held, coddled, and spoiled by someone right now. Most unfortunately, she wasn't Luca's to spoil.

A moan of defeat escaped her, and she muffled it by raising the lapel of her robe and pressing it to her face. Heaven help her, but she appreciated his concern far more than she had the right to and that was going to be a problem. She was going to have to figure out a way — fast — to hide her feelings from him, because he had years of experience exploiting the weaknesses of others. He was gorgeous and brilliant and apparently irresistible to her hormone-befuddled mind. He was also clever and conniving, a master manipulator. She couldn't allow herself the luxury of letting down her guard, especially while spending the weekend in his home. His turf. The beast's own lair.

A second moan escaped her for an entirely different reason as she slipped out of her borrowed robe. She stepped around the single clear, glass wall barrier into his marvelous guest shower. Rain shower heads were low-lit with faint blue lights. The water cascaded over her and fell on wide, slate tiles. It trickled along the floor and disappeared into a rocky basin separating the shower area from the sunken tub.

The *piece de resistance*, however, was the rear wall of the shower. It enclosed an enormous saltwater fish tank. Tiny turtles, fish of varying hues and sizes, and a waterfall of green vines turned the room into a marine-lovers paradise. It was exotic and breathtaking, just like its owner.

She tried not to think of him showering here. Standing right where she was standing. All six feet two inches of his broad and beautiful frame. With his intense gold eyes and hard mouth. The one she longed to feel on hers again.

Stop, Jacey. Just stop. On a shuddering sigh, she turned down the water temperature a few degrees.

Not only were heated towels waiting for her, but a duffle containing some of her own clothes rested next to it. *How in the world?* She cringed at the thought of Luca visiting her itty bitty apartment and finding out how financially strapped she was. How desperate. Maybe Alora had delivered her clothing to Luca's mansion. Jacey would call her at first opportunity to verify it.

She tugged on a white tank top, an off-the-shoulder pale pink sweatshirt, and a comfy pair of jean jeggings. What had Alora been thinking to pack something so hip-hugging and comfy? She dug in the duffle a second time, hoping for something more along the lines of business casual, but there was nothing else in the bag. *No way! That was it?*

Jacey wiggled her toes. At least her pedicure was still fresh. She opened and closed a few drawers in the vast vanity and found a hair dryer. Despite her unsettled state, she couldn't help reveling in the warmth of the pressed hot air and wafting scent of the shampoo she'd helped herself to from the basket of bottles on the sink. It was something with vanilla in it. She'd always considered it a comforting and soothing scent.

She turned off the dryer once her hair stopped dripping and finger combed it into some semblance of order. She preferred not to dry out her hair with too much heat. Staring at herself in the mirror, she placed a hand on her still-flat belly, reminding herself there was a little human growing inside her.

It made her eyes fill. "This wasn't supposed to happen without you here, Easton," she whispered. They were supposed to have gone to pastoral counseling together, worked out their differences, and gotten their marriage back on track. Instead, he was gone. For good. He would never get to meet their child.

A sob worked its way up her throat. "Without you here," she repeated softly, as the lyrics to a new song began to flow through her head. Gritty and wrenching, they grabbed ahold of her insides, demanding to be written down. It was something she'd not bothered sharing with anyone. Not even Easton. She was more than a singer. She wrote music, too, both the lyrics and the score, though she hadn't been inspired to write a single word or note for months.

Jacey dashed from the bathroom and nearly collided with Luca.

"What's wrong?" he demanded, gently clasping her upper arms to steady her.

"I need a pen and paper."

He strode across the room and yanked open the drawer to the closest nightstand. "Here." He handed her a fancy pen and a good quality pad of paper monogrammed with a scroll-like C.

Half weeping, half singing, Jacey perched on the edge of the guest bed and scribbled out the chorus.

> Without you, all I have is unfilled
> promises.
> Without you, all I have is half-lived
> dreams.
> Without you, I spend all my time
> remembering.
> Holding on to every moment I had
> with you.

The verses would come to her later. The magic was in the chorus right now. The "without you" part encompassed so much. Her long-lost youthful invincibility. Her too-hasty marriage that had quickly spiraled south. Her languishing dreams. Her fledgling musical career she'd abandoned after Easton's fatal wreck. And Easton, himself, with his insatiable taste for life and adventure that had been utterly extinguished without warning. Anyone who heard the song would probably assume it was a grieving widow's cry — no more and no less, and that was okay with Jacey. She was the only one who needed to know the song was about much more. She would sing it to their baby when he was born; and when he was older, she would tell him all about the father he never met.

Funny how she already thought of their unborn child as a son.

Jacey clasped the notepad to her chest and closed her eyes, letting her voice close huskily and full-bodied around the final line. "Holding on to every moment I had with you."

The rasp of jeans against the bedsheets made her eyelids fly open. Luca was standing close. So close. Her lids drooped from the dizzying sensation his nearness brought.

"You have a lovely voice." He cupped her face with both hands. "It's like magic."

So was his touch. The notepad and pen slipped from her fingers, skittered across one of her knees, and landed on the floor. Jacey had known, way down deep, the moment she'd woken up in Luca's home that this time would come. She just hadn't expected to feel so powerless to resist him when it did. As naturally as a flower opening to the sun, she tipped her face up to his.

"Jacey." His voice was a reverent whisper as he drew her to her bare feet. One of his knees bumped hers as he leaned forward to capture her mouth.

Instant heat fused their lips. The melancholy left her. There was no more looking back. No more regrets. Only Luca.

With a soft sound of capitulation, she kissed him back. His warm fingers cupped her chin, searing her all the way to her soul.

I can't believe this is happening. Again. It's still too soon, but...

She ignored the warnings going off in her dazed mind and entwined her arms around Luca's middle, soaking in his scent and nearness and strength. It wasn't a casual kiss, either. Or one from a person simply offering comfort. It was more. They were two hurting souls who had found something vital in each other to hold on to. Something real, potent, magical, and healing.

Something that inspired cautious hope and crazy little explosions of joy.

The last twenty-four hours of bottled-up frustration, hurt, and anger in Jacey evaporated. So what if the timing of things between her and Luca was completely off? Or worse...what if the two of them were completely wrong for each other? Her traitorous hands traveled up the smooth fabric of his t-shirt, over broad shoulders that could handle anything a mega corporation could throw his way, and circled his neck, tugging him closer. She needed his strength right now, and she craved the man beneath the strength.

He was the first one to break off the kiss. "We better stop."

"Luca," she breathed, touching his cheek. Who would have dreamed in the past few miserable weeks that he was capable of such passion, such tenderness?

"I know, *princesa*," he assured huskily. "I feel it, too. I just want the timing to be right when..." He shook his head and ran a hand through his dark hair.

Her face fell as thoughts of Easton came inevitably crashing back. "You're right. We can't. This isn't a good idea," she mumbled. As the brother of her dead husband, Luca wasn't hers to kiss like this. He was an angry, grieving man whom she'd taunted and teased every bit as mercilessly as he had driven and punished her during the short time they'd worked together. Both of them were a hopeless tangle of conflicting emotions, too often held in check in each other's presence.

Which was the only logical explanation as to why they kept erupting on each other. What was happening between them had no foundation and didn't equivocate any lasting emotion. Nothing even close to love. Best to put a stop to whatever it was before either of them did something they would regret.

"Believe me, it feels right even though I know the timing is off." He tipped her face up to his with a single finger.

She sucked in a breath. He didn't play fair. He never played fair. One of them had to start playing fair.

"Don't," she said quietly.

He immediately dropped his hand.

"What is it, *princesa*?" The fear in his voice blazed through her, warming her to her toes. It had been way too long since anyone had shown so much concern for her.

When she didn't answer, his expression grew stricken. "Talk to me, *carina*. Did I do something wrong?" The genuine anguish in his voice made her eyes widen.

"No, you didn't, and I'm fine. Really." She smoothed her hands down her sweatshirt.

His expression grew shuttered. "Then what's wrong? I can tell something's wrong."

She gave a shaky, rueful laugh. "Me. I'm what's wrong. Going crazy all over you like that. It's the hormones, you know." A raging mass of hormones that shifted into insane overdrive every time he was near her.

His expression grew soft again. "Is it, now?" He leaned closer to touch his lips ever so softly to hers.

She fought a moan, beating it down to what turned into a much smaller, more helpless sound. *Good grief!* How could she ever hope to resist this man? "Yes."

He touched his lips to hers again and spoke against the edge of her mouth. "I think it's something more. Why fight it, Jacey? I'm tired of fighting it. Maybe we could call a truce?"

You're killing me. You're absolutely killing me. "This isn't about us, and you know it. Not really." She scrambled for the right words. "We're both grieving."

"Call it what you want, *mi princesa*." He treated her to a tender smile. "Being with you makes me happy."

"Happy?" She shot him an incredulous look. "All we've done is rip at each other's throats since the day you hired me."

"Because neither of us was looking for this." He made a back-and-forth motion between them. "We both fought it, but it happened anyway."

Her lips formed a silent O of disbelief. She made Luca Calcagni happy? The wildly successful billionaire CEO of Genesis & Sons? The man who'd spent nearly the entire time they'd known each other acting like he despised her? Except for the few times they'd kissed. Like today.

She wanted to believe him, but nothing was ever simple with him. Her gaze narrowed, as her suspicions unfurled. Luca always had an agenda.

It was entirely possible the only reason he was being so sweet and romantic right now was because he wanted her to stay in town. Because he intended to lay the claim of the Calcagni dynasty on her unborn child, his brother's baby. This was very likely just another one of his attempts to control her. She knew this and yet...

Her heart gave a spasm beneath her ribcage as his warm fingers tucked a loose strand of hair behind her ear. How was she supposed to resist such an expert manipulator when she was already half in love with the man?

She couldn't, that's what. He'd managed to uncover all her weakest points, her furthest limits. *Darn him!* She absolutely couldn't resist this side of him, which was the real reason she needed to leave town — as soon as possible!

CHAPTER 18: PROPOSITION
JACEY

As if sensing her inner turmoil, Luca dropped his arms and stepped back. "You really should get back to bed."

She scowled at him. "I can't lie around all weekend," she protested.

His brown-gold eyes sparkled with amusement. "Why not? You need rest, *princesa*. Lots of it. Doctor MaryBeth's orders."

"Doctor who?" she asked suspiciously.

"A friend of mine. She paid a house call and pronounced you in perfect health. Just run down."

Thanks to all your slave driving. Her scowl deepened.

"Blame me all you want, *mi querida*," he muttered. "I deserve it, but that won't change the fact that you need your rest."

Jacey laid awake long after he left the room,

squeezing her eyes shut and trying to imagine what it would be like if Luca truly loved her. If he wanted her to stay in town, not because she carried the next member of his family dynasty in her womb, but because he truly wanted her in his life.

She had no doubt he would care for her and the baby if she remained in town. He possessed a solid sense of duty, especially to his family, but it would never be enough. She would never be able to stand on the sidelines and watch him date other women, like the one he'd brought to his office the other day. If she stayed, she would always long for more from him. She would always want *him*.

Tears stung the backs of Jacey's eyelids. She squeezed them tighter, trying to hold them back, but one slid hotly down her cheek, making her angry at herself for her show of weakness. *Stupid hormones!* She hated herself even more for falling for a man who would never love her in return. Foolishly setting her sights on a man like Luca Calcagni was yet another failure to add to her growing list of failures. And leaving him was going to be the hardest thing she'd ever done.

Forget sleep. With Luca finally out of the room, it was her chance to make her getaway. She hurried to the restroom to freshen up one last time, then returned to the guest room to help herself to a few items from the morning bar near the door. Bottled water, orange juice, granola bars, and a few pieces of fresh fruit. Hopefully, it would tide her over until she reached her destination, wherever that might be. She would take the bus this time and pay cash for her ticket since her driver's license was still unaccounted for.

"What are you doing?" Luca's voice made her jolt.

Jacey paused in the middle of zipping her duffle, irritated to be caught in the act of leaving. She'd tried to be so quiet. Looked like she should have shut and locked the door, as well. *I'm leaving. What does it look like?* She peeked at him from beneath her lashes to gauge his expression.

He was standing in the doorway, fists clenched at his sides.

Her mouth turned dry at the glare riding his handsome features, making it nearly impossible to swallow. He looked so distraught, she wanted to launch herself back in his arms, to assure him everything was okay, to feel his mouth on hers again. But she knew better. Her baby was the only reason he was hounding her to stay in town. She needed to remain strong and stick to her original plan.

"I'm going home." The lie slipped out easily. "Thank you for everything, but I've burdened you long enough."

"Before breakfast?" His mouth tightened into one of his infuriating judge-and-jury expressions.

"Do you really think that's wise, considering your condition?"

"I'm not an invalid."

"So you keep telling me, yet you've collapsed twice in the past forty-eight hours. You really need to start taking better care of yourself."

It irritated her how Luca was so right all the time. Couldn't he be human for once and be dead wrong about anything? She allowed her duffle to sink to the floor. "Fine. I'll stay for breakfast. What are we having?"

His brows rose. "Anything you like. My chef is very skilled."

A chef. Jacey closed her eyes for a moment, absorbing the luxury of Luca's offer. *Anything I want?* Without opening her eyes, she spoke softly. "Tarragon egg salad on slivered cucumbers with a slice of pumpernickel bread on the side. Toasted."

He repeated her order. "Tarragon egg salad on slivered cucumbers with a few slices of pumpernickel bread on the side. Toasted and dry."

"How many servings, *monsieur*?"

The female voice made Jacey's eyelids fly open. Luca hadn't repeated her order to remember it. His thumb was pressing a button on the wall. He was speaking into an intercom system.

"Breakfast for two. Oh, and bring up a carafe of cucumber water and a side of watermelon balls. Thank you, Colette."

"My pleasure, *monsieur*."

Jacey shot Luca a wistful look. "I miss this. All of it." The words flew from her mouth before she gave them permission to leave. She'd enjoyed a childhood pampered and spoiled by an entire staff of servants, many of whom she adored as much as her family. It had been tougher than she imagined to give it all up and fend for herself in the regular world.

Luca's answering nod held none of the mockery she expected. "Then maybe you will consider the proposition I'm about to make."

A whispery sigh escaped Jacey as she wrapped her arms around her body. She already knew what he planned to say. He was going to try to convince her to remain in town, which would never work for them. For every reason she could think of, it was best if she left. She would pretend to listen to what he had to say, then follow her own path like she always did.

Luca beckoned for her to follow him into the adjoining solarium where the rising sun was no more than a distant glow on the horizon. Towering tropical plants graced the corners of the room and curled against the glass ceiling. Creamy leather lounges faced each other in the center of the room with a glass-topped coffee table between them. It was a cozy scene despite her coming confrontation with Luca.

He motioned for her to be seated first and eased

himself down beside her, tossing an arm across the back of the sofa and toying with a strand of her hair.

It was an unfair move, swooping in on her like this with all six plus feet of his beautiful frame stretched out next to hers. If Jacey allowed herself to look too long into his golden, soul-searching gaze, she might swoon or give in to whatever he was about to propose. So she looked away, instead.

She caught her breath when his thumb traced a lazy pattern on her shoulder blade. "You know I don't want you to leave, Jacey."

She flinched and dragged her gaze back to his. Of course, he went for her most vulnerable spot first. The man absolutely didn't know the first thing about fighting fair. "No, Luca. You only want my baby, your nephew. That's the real reason you want me to remain in town."

"Not true. I want both of you."

She hugged her middle tighter. "Why?"

He leaned closer to push back the curtain of hair she'd let fall forward to cover her face. "Your baby? That's easy. He's the last living link I have to my brother, and family means everything to me. You?" he sighed. "I'm afraid I don't have any clear answers concerning my feelings for you. All I know is I want you to stay."

Well, wanting her to stay wasn't going to put food in her baby's mouth, neither was working a job that barely brought in twice minimum wage. Jacey leaned away from Luca's mesmerizing touch and rose to her feet. "Forgive me for passing on such a compelling list of reasons to remain in town, but I have a baby to raise. I'll admit I didn't plan this and I literally have no idea how to be a mother, but I'm sure about one thing. I'm raising my child as far away as possible from all the feuding, corporate missions, professional jealousies, and private agendas of both the Maddoxes and Calcagnis." There! At least one of them knew what they wanted and wasn't afraid to say it aloud.

Luca stood and reached for her hands. "Living on soup and crackers on the cheap side of town might have been okay for a very tough, very determined widow. But it won't be enough for your baby. Think about it, Jacey. What kind of home can you give your child? What kind of insurance and benefits? What kind of life?"

Mortification flooded her from her hair roots to her toes. "Go ahead," she choked. "Mock me all you want." Years of enduring her family's disapproval had helped her grow some very thick skin.

"Why would I mock you?" He looked shocked.

"I made my bed, and now I get to sleep in it," she retorted bitterly. "Believe me, I've heard it thousands of times."

"Yes, you did make your bed, and you've done a really good job of sleeping in it. Ask me to repeat this in public, and I'll probably deny ever saying it, but there's a part of me that admires you."

The sting of tears was back, but Jacey was too surprised at Luca's words to hide them this time. "Right. I've made an absolute disaster of my life. What could you possibly admire about that?"

"Not true." He glared at her. "For one thing, you made my brother happy."

Her face fell. Actually, she hadn't. It was a regret she would take to her grave.

Not knowing her thoughts, Luca plowed onward. "As your boss, I've seen your capabilities first hand. And don't forget I heard you sing."

"What does that have to do with anything?" She flushed at the memory of blubbering over his monogrammed notepad while she scribbled down the words pouring from her heart. Despite the unwelcome burst of emotion it had elicited in her, it had been a healing and comforting exercise. One more step towards achieving closure from her tragic marriage.

"You have a special gift, one that you sacrificed all the benefits of being born a Maddox to pursue. As much pride as it costs me to admit this, I was wrong about you, Jacey. Wrong in my assumption you were just like my wayward brother, may he rest in peace." His voice cracked.

The emotion in his eyes ripped at her heart.

"Luca, please. We don't need to go there." The pain was still too fresh, her regrets still too raw.

"I'm sorry, *carina*, but I think it's time to be honest with each other about him. Easton was a thrill seeker and a rolling stone. I imagine no one knows this better than the woman who married him. Yes, I loved him, but I wasn't blind to the fact he was unable to accept any meaningful adult responsibilities. My grandparents and brothers weren't oblivious to the fact, either. He was like..." Eyes red-rimmed, Luca seemed to be struggling for the right words. "Like Peter Pan. The boy who never grew up."

Luca's description was agonizingly accurate. It was painful to talk about Easton, but he'd summed up their failed marriage in one simple sentence. Jacey had been married to a boy who'd never grown up. She'd never forget all the lonely nights she'd spent without her husband. She'd tried to convince herself it was because he worked days and she mostly worked nights, but it was more than that. In the end, Easton hadn't been committed to anyone or anything. Not her. Not her vain attempts to start attending church on Sundays as a married couple. Not even racing. Heavens, he'd been debating joining a skydiving team if he failed to win the race that had ultimately claimed his life. Jacey and her trust fund had simply been the enablers of his flighty temperament.

"You agreed to stay for breakfast," Luca

reminded mildly, squeezing her hands and pulling her back to the present. "Sit with me a few minutes, Jacey. If you don't like the proposition I have to make, then you're free to go after breakfast. I give you my word. No tricks. I'll drive you back to the airport, myself, if that's what you want."

Again, she wanted to believe him, but her heart was wary as she sat back down on the couch.

"Free to go where?" she asked bitterly. "I already know how this is going to play out. The Calcagnis will sue me for rights to my child. Whether you'll try to take full guardianship, settle for visitation rights, or pull some other legal stunt I haven't yet considered remains to be seen. Regardless, I fully expect your team of expert attorneys to dog my heels, starting today, in the attempt to bend me and my unborn child to your will."

Throughout her tirade, a myriad of expressions wafted across Luca's features, from surprise to anger to mortification. He sucked in a slow, deep breath when she was through.

"Hiring lawyers would be a pointless move, don't you think, if we're married, *carina*?" he asked softly.

Thankfully, Jacey was already in the act of sitting, because her knees gave out. She collapsed atop the sofa cushions with a short bounce. "What did you say?"

"Marry me, Jacey. It's the best solution." Luca sat down beside her, his expression pleading.

She studied his features, distressed at his cavalier approach to such a serious topic. "Marriage isn't supposed to be a solution. It's supposed to be —" *A holy union between two people who are in love.*

"Eighteen years," he pressed. "That's how long I'm asking you to stay married to me."

What? Incredulous, Jacey scanned his features, but he appeared deathly serious. He was offering her eighteen years of marriage in the same cold and calculating way he negotiated his business contracts. It was un-romantic and ill-advised of her to even consider something so preposterous, though the practical side of her knew it would mean no child custody or visitation battles. Her son would be an adult by then, never to be fought over in court.

"If you choose to leave at that point, you won't go empty handed, either. I'll draw up a prenuptial contract to guarantee you a generous settlement. I take care of what is mine. You know that as well as anyone, Jacey."

His. She wanted to dwell for a moment on the thought of being his, but he'd spoiled the mood by placing a price tag on it. She gulped air, instead. "You want me to live here." She spread her hands to take in the room. "In this house with you for the next eighteen years?" Her voice escalated to a ridiculously high pitch. *In exchange for a generous settlement because you think you can buy me.* Her insides crumbled like dry, brittle soup crackers.

"I already admitted I want you in my life." He chuckled, a beautiful baritone sound that resonated across each and every raw nerve ending inside her.

Jacey could only stare, incredulous, drowning in his gorgeous eyes, trying not to tremble beneath the delicious pressure of his fingers clasping hers.

"I'll help you raise your child. Treat him as my own. He'll have a safe home, a good education, the best opportunities, Jacey. As my wife, you'll also have everything you need. All the things you previously gave up." His voice turned teasing, and he treated her to a wink. "To include the funds you'll require to continue growing your impressive shoe collection."

A strangled sound escaped her. This was no joking matter. What he was offering her was everything she'd dreamed of, minus one important detail — his heart.

"I can secure you a recording audition with a major studio, as well." His tone turned cagey. "I know an agent down in Nashville who's always scouting for new talent. He's a bit of a carpet-bagger and a little annoying at times, but he knows the industry."

Jacey felt the threads of resistance snapping. "Luca!" She found her voice at last. "I don't understand. Why would you do so much for me when you could fight me in court for the same outcome?"

"Because fighting you in court will *not* produce the same outcome." He shot her a wistful half-smile.

"I want you in my life, *cara*. In my home. And when you're ready, I hope for more than that."

She was feeling lightheaded again. "So you want a marriage of convenience with *all* the conveniences?"

"I said when you're ready, but yes."

She was pretty sure every inch of her turned pink.

Luca moved closer, draping an arm behind her on the sofa, once more. "It's the best solution, and you know it. If you're worried about whether my attraction for you is real, let's just say not many women can grace a centerfold the way you did last year."

Jacey groaned and covered her face with one hand. "We needed the money. Easton's racing expenses were draining us."

"I know that now, and I am sorry for it. More sorry than words can express. It was a decision we made as a family. We hoped freezing his assets would return him to his senses and bring him home to us. We didn't understand how financially invested you were in the marriage and how our decision was affecting you, as well."

It had bankrupted her, that's what, but there was no way Luca could have known.

"We certainly never intended to hurt you in the process. Not in a million years."

Luca's apology wasn't given lightly. It meant

something. It settled over Jacey like a balm on a thousand open wounds.

"So you see?" He glanced away from her. "You aren't the only one who feels the need to atone. I've been drowning in guilt ever since you collapsed in the board room. Not only did I bungle things with Easton, but I've been bungling things with you ever since you came back to town. I've never been much of a religious man, but I begged the good Lord last night for another chance to make things right with you. Please believe me when I say I truly want to help you and your baby."

Jacey shook her head. What Luca proposed was tempting but preposterous. "You don't have to marry me to help us. Marrying me might actually make things worse. Both our families would oppose the union. Adamantly."

He offered her a fiercely grim smile that made her heart leap. "Let them." He bent over her to brush his lips against hers. "Just be mine, Jacey."

His. Her tenuous control over her emotions melted at the word. She knew Luca was capable of championing her every bit as much as he had opposed her the past several weeks. She'd watched him in action often enough to understand once he made up his mind about something, he was a force to be reckoned with. It was tempting, so deliciously tempting, to work with him instead of against him.

"Say something," he whispered against her mouth.

"I don't know what to say," she whispered back.

"How about yes?"

He brushed his lips against hers again. She suppressed a sigh at the tender caress. Maybe she wasn't thinking straight. She'd never been able to think straight around Luca, but for the life of her, she couldn't fathom how running away from her hometown a second time, this time with a baby inside her, would be any easier than accepting his insanely generous offer. The biggest risk she could see in his whole proposition was losing her heart to him, and the horse was already well out of the barn on that issue.

"Okay, Luca," she sighed. "You win. For the next eighteen years, I'm yours."

With a sound of exultation, he drew her into his arms and buried his face in her hair. They sat wrapped together for several minutes, just breathing each other in.

A woman cleared her throat delicately. Jacey raised her flaming face in the direction of the sound. It was Merl, standing in the arched doorway, bearing a tray of food.

"Breakfast is served," the middle-aged woman announced somberly, averting her eyes.

"Come in, Merl." Luca's jovial offer made his

housekeeper blink in surprise. "You can be the first to congratulate us. Jacey has just agreed to marry me."

For a moment, Jacey thought Merl was going to drop her tray. "Oh my, sir!" she said faintly. "That is happy news, for sure!"

CHAPTER 19: WEDDING PLANS
JACEY

Merl was so flustered she spilled the hot tea she was pouring Jacey. Gasping out an apology, she mopped it up with a white linen napkin.

"I'll take care of it." Luca's hand closed over Merl's. "Thank you for all your extra help this weekend. Why don't you take the rest of the day off?"

"I couldn't possibly, sir." His housekeeper stood and smoothed her hands down her perfectly ironed apron. "There's this week's meals to plan yet and—"

"I insist," he said firmly. "Go rest or go on one of your famous nature walks, whatever you like. Everything else can wait until tomorrow."

"But, sir!"

They engaged in a dual of gazes until Merl turned away with a sigh of defeat. "I suppose I could start working on your wedding quilt." Shaking her head, she left the room.

"Wow! An employee who actually enjoys being employed by you. Did you have her hypnotized or what?" Jacey wanted to bite her tongue as soon as the words left her mouth.

But Luca didn't seem to take offense. He gave a low, rumbling chuckle that made her knees go weak and turned to cup her face with both hands. "It's because I'm irresistible." He brushed a thumb across her lower lip. "The same reason you agreed to marry me."

Jacey shivered, resting her hands on his shoulders and wondering if she'd ever be able to resist the man.

"Cold?" he asked, running his warm hands up and down her arms.

"More famished than cold," she countered, making a fist and tapping him on the chest. "I'm going to wither away if you don't hurry up and feed me."

For an answer, he reached for the food tray and set it on his lap. They faced each other, taking each other's measure.

"Really? I was sort of kidding about the feeding part," she confessed dryly.

"Really." He mimicked her tone, swooped up one of the slivered cucumbers, and stuffed a bite heaped with Tarragon egg salad in her mouth.

The melody of flavors burst over her hungry tastebuds like sunshine. She moaned and briefly closed her eyes while she chewed. It had been a long time since she tasted anything so well prepared. She'd been eating way too much fast and frozen food lately.

"You like?"

Her eyelids fluttered open in time to watch him lick a drop of the egg salad off his thumb.

"It's divine," she admitted. "More, please."

He fed her another bite, watching her from beneath heavy lids.

The thought struck her that Easton had never been so focused on her. The few times they'd snatched a meal together, he'd immediately launched into talk of cars or races or something else related to his career and personal ambitions. Not Luca, though. Luca was absorbed in the moment. In her. Studying her with pure male interest.

There was an uncharacteristically gentle set to his normally curled lips, and he didn't seem to feel the need to fill every moment with conversation, either. He fed her in leisurely silence, punctuating the bites he offered her with nipping little kisses on the corners of her mouth and on her fingertips.

"Thirsty?" He reached for the gold-rimmed teacup Merl had filled minutes earlier.

"Yes." To Jacey's delight, it was swimming with autumn spices and cooled down just enough to sip on. Luca played with the seam of her jeans while she drank, tugging idly at a loose thread.

Jacey took a larger gulp than she intended of her tea and coughed.

Eyes tinted with knowing humor, Luca took the mug from her and returned it to the breakfast tray.

"You okay there, *cara*?" His arms came around her.

Maybe. She hoped. His fingers traced a lazy little circle on her lower back. *No, not even close.*

"How would you like to get married outside?" she asked desperately, needing a little more time to adjust to the change in their status. *I'm actually engaged to Luca Calcagni!* It was still sinking in.

"It's November," he reminded mildly, hitching her closer. "It's starting to get pretty chilly out there."

"I don't mind," she assured breathlessly. She wanted everything about her second wedding to be different from her drive-by first one at a small chapel in Vegas. She'd not had flowers or a wedding dress the first time. Or a cake.

"If that's what you truly want, consider it done." Luca searched her face. "We should probably get married before the snowy season sets in. How soon can you be ready?"

Jacey's laugh bubbled up like sparkling cider and spilled into the solarium. "I'm between jobs, remember? My schedule is wide open."

He treated her to one of his beautiful, rare smiles. "Then there's no reason to wait. We'll get married right away. I'll show you Mother's wedding ring after breakfast. If you like it, it's yours. If you don't like it, we'll go ring shopping."

Luca wanted her to wear his mother's ring? Jacey twined her arms around his neck and rested her head against his shoulder. She was too moved for words. It made their eighteen-year wedding seem more like a real one.

"*Mi princesa,*" he muttered, pressing a kiss to her hair.

◊

LUCA HELD Jacey to their agreement to marry quickly, giving her just enough time to purchase a dress, have it altered, and order a small wedding cake.

Two weeks later, they stood beneath a tall, white hexagonal tent in the rear courtyard of his estate. Though Luca had agreed to her wishes for an outdoor wedding, he'd insisted on the tent and an array of outdoor space heaters. The officiating minister awaited them beneath an arched rose trellis, handwoven with hundreds of hothouse blooms that would have otherwise been out of season. Roses of white, gold, and ruby hues.

It seemed wrong to wear white so soon after Easton's funeral, and there was not enough time to order and be fitted for a proper wedding dress. So Jacey wore a multi-hued silk fabric that was part pink and part gold depending on how the light caught it. It was a stunning gown of lace and silk from a local evening wear shop. When the owners had learned about her rapid-fire wedding, they were happy to escalate the needed adjustments.

Jacey lifted the skirt of her gown a few inches to make sure her shoes weren't snagged on the hem and let it settle again. It was a strapless gown that showed off her slender form to perfection. She knew Luca considered her to be too thin, so she'd chosen a high-waisted gown that de-emphasized her recent loss of weight.

Luca wore a charcoal tuxedo with a dark wine cummerbund and matching tie over a snowy white shirt. He bent to speak in her ear. "You look stunning, *mi princesa*." His minty breath stirred the tendrils of hair the light breeze had set to dancing against her cheek.

She didn't require compliments. The look in his eyes always made her feel beautiful, but it was nice to receive one from him. "You look pretty incredible, yourself."

"Thank you." He raised her hand to his lips and kissed it lingeringly before tucking it over his arm. "Ready?"

Was she ready to become Luca Calcagni's wife? It was a heady question. Jacey nodded, lost in the surreality of the moment. She pressed her bouquet of roses and star-gazer lilies to her belly. *This is for you, little one.* She prayed she was doing the right thing.

The wedding tent was positioned over the central garden pathway leading from Luca's terrace. Edric, Waverly, Rhys, and Knox lined one side of the path. Alora and Greyson stood on the other. Her remaining two siblings, Bailey and Kellan, weren't present. Neither were her parents or her grandparents.

Jacey's thoughts turned dark at how thoroughly her parents and grandparents had cut her out of their lives. As if divining the direction her mind had wandered, Luca placed his free hand over the one she had resting on his arm and squeezed.

The diamond choker, which he'd claimed had been worn by every Calcagni bride (other than Easton's), warmed her neck. Her breathing suddenly constricted beneath it.

Her fingers tightened on his arm. "It's not too late to back out, Luca," she declared quietly but firmly. "We haven't said our vows yet."

He glanced down at her, his expression going blank. "Have you changed your mind, *carina?*"

"Me? No. There's just something about this whole thing that doesn't seem fair to you."

He flicked a finger beneath her chin, scowling and tipping her face up to search her features. "What's not fair about it?"

Out of habit, she nearly bit her lower lip but

stopped just in time. Pink lipstick. White teeth. She wanted to keep them that way. "For one thing, I'm widowed and pregnant, while this is your first trip to the altar."

His scowl deepened. "So? Back in ancient times, it was common practice for a surviving brother to marry his brother's widow. Taking care of one's own is a longstanding and very honorable tradition."

A beautiful thought, yet it scared Jacey to think that Luca was sacrificing himself on the altar of duty. Ancient tradition or not, a modern man like himself was in no way obligated to fix everything his brother had messed up. *Like her.* Jacey started to step away from Luca, but his hand settled on her shoulders, holding her in place.

"If you're only marrying me out of your enormous sense of family duty, Luca, please don't. Someday you'll regret it. I know all about regrets."

He silenced her with a kiss on the edge of her mouth. Tender and sweet. One that didn't muss her lipstick. "Believe me, *mi querida*. I am marrying you because I want you, and I will prove it to you. Soon."

She was grateful he'd insisted she didn't wear stilettos, because his words unbalanced her.

The stringed quartet he'd hired played the opening stanzas of the wedding march.

Luca placed his hand over her gloved hand on his arm. "It's time, *cara*." He guided her between their assembled family members. A cameraman followed them to snap pictures, bulbs flashing wildly.

The minister smiled benignly when they took their place beneath the trellis and waited for the music to end. "Dearly beloved..." He launched straight into the simple ceremony they'd planned.

Luca slid an enormous square diamond on Jacey's ring finger. It was at least five carats and probably worth more than any single item of jewelry she'd ever worn, with possibly the exception of the choker around her neck. It was surrounded by a cluster of smaller, round white diamonds and set in a white gold band. The gems winked and flashed like fire.

The heirloom beauty of them was so breathtaking that it made Jacey's hand tremble.

Luca bent to speak softly in her ear. "It matches your eyes, *mi angel*." He drew a white gold band from his pocket for her to slide on his hand.

He didn't wait for the minister's permission. He sealed their vows with a gentle, possessive kiss.

When they turned to face their families again, they were married. A sense of finality swelled in Jacey's chest. And enormity. And lightheadedness. She wished someone would assure her she hadn't made yet another monumental mistake.

Luca's grip tightened on her arm as their families closed in on them. Waverly and Edric reached them first.

"Congratulations." Waverly kissed Jacey's cheek. "For your marriage and for conceiving my first great-grandchild." With a firm nod and glistening eyes, she took a step back to stand by her beaming husband's side.

They knew about the baby.

Rhys leaned in for the next kiss, brushing his lips against her cheek and stepping back to survey her gravely.

"Thank you, Rhys," she whispered. "For everything."

He nodded, still searching her face. Knox stepped up to her next and shook her hand. He didn't say anything, but he regarded her with a gentler expression than the hard look she was accustomed to receiving from him.

Jacey was confused. It was as if Easton's baby had changed the way all the Calcagnis viewed her in an instant. Did her unborn child really mean that much to them? It was both humbling and unsettling to know her womb was carrying something so treasured by their entire clan.

The legal paperwork Luca had drawn up required her to take on his surname. He'd moved Maddox to her middle name. No hyphen. It looked right somehow. He wasn't asking her to give up her identity entirely, but he was claiming her as a Calcagni. As his.

A few weeks ago, Jacey would have balked

against such a change but no longer. Not after her family had so thoroughly betrayed her. She signed the marriage license and prenuptial agreement without questioning them and became Jacey Maddox Calcagni.

Mrs. Jacey Calcagni. Mrs. Jacey Maddox Calcagni. She rolled every variation of it over in her mind. Her new name was going to take some getting used to.

Then again, change was in the air. The most important change, however, was taking place inside her body. Why shouldn't her name reflect the wonder and miracle of all that was happening to her? Plus it meant she, Luca, and her son would bear the same surname. Things would be easier that way for all of them.

When Jacey laid down the pen after signing the last signature field, Alora was there to envelope her in a hug while Greyson patted her awkwardly on the shoulder.

"You better keep calling," her sister threatened with a fierce hitch to her voice. "Even if you don't need any more favors from me, now that you've married a sinfully rich man."

"I will," Jacey promised, grateful her sister had chosen to attend the simple wedding ceremony. "Ah...how are the others?"

"They're doing well. Bailey wanted to come

today, but she and Mother are really tight. Awkward, you know?"

It meant their mother, Nora, had outright refused to come.

"As for Kellan?" Alora fluttered her hands. "You know him. Always traveling. This time he's on business in Rome. He sends his regrets and says to expect a big, expensive wedding gift from him when he returns. Dad is furious, of course. Not going to lie. He can't believe you're hitching yourself to another Calcagni, and our grandparents refuse to acknowledge the union at all."

Jacey wasn't surprised. She just wished she could finally reach the place where she didn't care. "Do they know about the baby?"

Alora drew back, shaking her head. "Not yet. Greyson and I decided it was your news to share whenever you're ready." She spared a glance at Luca, who was engaged in a stilted conversation with the unsmiling Greyson and lowered her voice. "Not that you asked for my opinion, but I think you made a better choice this time around. Luca Calcagni is exactly the kind of man you need."

"A fire-breathing dragon to keep your wayward younger sibling in check, eh?"

Alora belted out a laugh that made all heads turn their way. "True, but that's not what I meant. This one's all grown up, love. Now go be happy with him."

GO BE HAPPY WITH HIM. Alora's words swam through Jacey's chaotic thoughts as she removed her wedding dress and hung it in her vast new walk-in closet. Her designer shoe collection was already on display, accentuated by clever recessed lighting. Luca had wasted no time moving her things from her tiny apartment and terminating her rental agreement.

He'd made it clear from the beginning he wanted her to share his master suite, though he'd promised she could use the guest room next door until she was ready for...other things.

She shivered and tugged on a white silk robe, another one of his many gifts. *This is it.* She drew a deep and bracing breath. Time to face the complicated and unpredictable man she'd married.

He was waiting for her at the side bar of his suite in a navy silk robe. At the sight of her, he stilled for a moment to drink in her approach. She loved the way he did that, the way he made her feel like she was the most important thing in his world.

He held out a glass of sparkling white grape juice.

She accepted it and cupped the glass with both hands. She faced him, acutely aware of every move he made, every breath he took. She was a mass of thrumming, ultra-sensitive nerve endings.

Luca took her glass when she finished sipping and set it down. "Mrs. Calcagni, you make a lovely bride."

"Thank you." She was unsure of what to say next. Compliments had always made her uncomfortable.

He swooped in on her, backing her against the paneling. He laced their fingers together and pressed her hands to the wall on either side of her head. "I can't believe you're finally mine. Ever since I first laid eyes on you nine years ago, I've wanted you to be mine." His amber gaze glinted with tender exultation.

Nine years, huh? All the way back to that silly, teenage stunt I pulled in full view of you on the beach.

"Could have fooled me." Was that thin, breathless voice really hers? "You were pretty crabby during our first encounter and even more venomous during my job interview." All those verbal slaps they'd exchanged and the way he'd tossed her resume in the wastebasket seemed like eons ago.

"Only because I was trying to keep it professional when what I really wanted to do was this." He claimed her mouth at last.

CHAPTER 20: WEDDING NIGHT

LUCA

They stood together in Luca's enormous floor-to-ceiling bay window and watched the night fall over the waters of the Cook Inlet that connected their hometown to the Alaskan Gulf. It was a lovely night with a full moon and a star-spattered sky.

His arms were loosely draped around Jacey, and her head rested on his shoulder. She couldn't remember ever feeling so many emotions at once: breathlessness, nervousness, hopefulness. It was a relief not to be huddled and shivering in her cold apartment tonight. She knew, without a doubt, she was safe in Luca's home, in the physical sense at least, but she wasn't near as certain about the safety of her heart. She was wildly anxious to learn what he expected of her now that they were married. He'd made it clear he wanted a marriage with all the conveniences, but how soon would he demand those perks?

He turned his head to brush his lips against her temple. "We should date," he said softly.

Date? He wanted to date her? Jacey's breath clogged in her throat as she tipped her face up to his. She scrutinized his expression. He looked serious and a little worried.

"What are you trying to say?" she whispered.

"I am grateful you accepted my proposition to marry quickly. More grateful than you can imagine." He hugged her tenderly. "But we skipped some important steps along the way, and I fear I'm not the first Calcagni who skipped those steps with you."

Jacey froze. *He knew?* How was that possible? She'd told no one how difficult her marriage to Easton had been. How lonely. How heartbreaking. She blinked as the start of tears burned behind her eyelids.

"I'm sorry. I didn't mean to make you sad." Luca shook his head in regret and glanced away. "Guess this isn't the most romantic conversation to be having on our wedding night."

She gulped and swallowed. "It's okay." Her voice trembled. "And you're right. I haven't done much dating." There. Her ugly secret was out. Or a good part of it, at least.

His jaw clenched at her affirmation, and it was his turn to look sad.

"Where will we go?" she asked quickly, trying to distract him from his unpleasant thoughts.

He offered her a half-smile that didn't quite erase the grief in his eyes, but any smile from him always did crazy things to her heart. Their gazes clashed and held for several breathless moments. She half-expected him to kiss her again, but all he did was touch her cheek.

"I was hoping you would take a dinner cruise with me tomorrow evening."

Her smile turned tremulous. "I would love to." Excitement raced through her at the thought of dressing up and going out to dinner with Luca. It meant he wanted to be with her. It also meant he didn't mind being seen with her in public.

Or was it simply part of his carefully crafted public image? Play the hero by marrying his brother's widow, then make sure the paparazzi gets plenty of publicity shots of it?

Uncertainty twisted Jacey's insides. She slid from his arms, suddenly wishing to be alone. "I think I'll turn in for the night."

"Good idea." He watched her with curious longing as she walked to the door of his master suite. His lips parted to say something.

She stopped him by holding up a finger. "Don't even think about it. If you say another word about me needing more rest, I will probably throw something at you."

He grinned and bent to snag a water bottle from the drink fridge at a side bar. "Temper, temper, Mrs. Calcagni. I was merely going to ask if you wanted to go shopping tomorrow morning."

"Shopping?" She blushed at his use of her married name, unable to process the rest of what he said.

"You'll be needing things soon, *cara*. So will the baby." He strode her way, uncapped the bottle, and pressed it into her hand.

She wrinkled her nose at the reminder she was about to lose her figure but took a sip of the water. She hadn't realized how thirsty she was. Luca was turning out to be a very attentive husband and father-to-be. It was a novel experience to have someone looking after her after so many years of fending for herself.

"Thank you. For the water."

"My pleasure."

The way he said the word *pleasure* made Jacey's toes curl against the hardwood floor.

"Want to call it another date?" He winked at her.

"You mean going shopping?"

"Yes."

More doubts assailed her. For one thing, there was the dire matter about how little money she possessed. Her few thousand dollars in her checking account wasn't going to go far when it came to stocking up on baby supplies. "I guess I haven't put much thought into the nursery." There wouldn't have been room for a nursery in her old apartment. She probably couldn't have fit much more than a bassinet there.

"We don't have to purchase everything in one day, but we can at least get started. I have Don working on getting you a credit card issued."

Jacey's blood chilled a few degrees. She'd known the topic of money would arise, but she hadn't expected it to happen on their wedding night. "I didn't marry you so I could go on shopping sprees." Defensiveness crept into her voice.

"What?" Luca looked startled. "I wasn't suggesting you did." At her stubborn silence, he exploded. "Oh, come on! You had to have known becoming my wife would come with a few financial benefits."

She took another sip of water and had to choke it down. Maybe it was just the hormones at work again, but the idea of blindly swiping a credit card and having her new husband pick up the tab made her uncomfortable. After a few straight years of scrimping and watching every penny, it didn't feel right, somehow. She wasn't a spoiled young debutante any longer. She now understood that money didn't grow on trees and how hard it was to come by.

"I don't think we need to go shopping tomorrow," she muttered. "My clothes fit fine, and the baby is a long way off."

"Fine." Luca's mouth twisted in defiance. "But you're still getting a credit card."

"If you insist." Her chin came up. He couldn't force her to use it. "Goodnight, Luca."

"Goodnight, Jacey."

She felt his frustrated gaze on her as she exited the room. What an awkward way to part on their wedding night! She should have seen this coming.

CHAPTER 21: BATTLE OF WILLS
JACEY

Luca flatly refused to return Jacey's job to her at Genesis & Sons. It was a sore point between them that had her practically climbing the walls of his mansion. There was only so much time a person could spend in his private gym, elaborate game room, and home theater. She longed for a real project to sink her teeth into again.

"I can't believe you!" she seethed, meeting him at the door to his seven-car garage when he returned home from work one evening. "I agreed to marry you, and you still won't un-fire me from Genesis & Sons?"

He chuckled and cuddled her close. "It's only been two weeks, *princesa*." He swooped in for a lingering kiss. "You need your rest. The doctor said so."

"There's that R word again. It feels like jail,

Luca," she groused, fisting her hands in his shirt and tugging him down for another kiss.

He eagerly indulged her. "Whatever it is, it's working." His voice turned gravelly. "You look well again, *carina.*" He laughingly laced his fingers through hers to imprison her hands. "I couldn't be happier about how much better you're feeling."

She was also eating better and growing stronger, thanks to his five-star chef, Collette.

"I mean it. I can't sit around forever," she protested. "You can't expect me to, either. I proved I have a lot to offer while working as your assistant. We made a great team, whether you ever choose to admit it or not."

He rested his forehead against hers. "I think marrying you proves how I feel on the topic of our compatibility."

"I'm a girl. I would prefer to hear the words."

He grinned. "We make an incredible team, Mrs. Calcagni."

Make not made? As in the present tense? It was one of the nicest things Luca had ever said to her. Jacey was still getting used to her new name, but she loved the way it sounded in her husband's caressing Hispanic accent. "Well, your partner in crime is way past ready to take on a new challenge. Seriously, Luca! I've slept at least a hundred years, and I've gained three pounds."

"Three whole pounds, eh?" He tipped his head

back to study her. Worry flashed briefly across his handsome features.

She made a face at him. "Before you start your whole growly bear routine, I'm following every line item of what my dietician says I should be doing. That does not include stuffing my face and turning into an elephant."

He raised his brows. "I don't growl. I'm too civilized."

"Maybe not, but you sure can strike like a cobra."

He looked more amused than offended. "I'm a CEO, *cara*. Not a girl scout."

No. He was definitely *not* a girl scout. She muffled a laugh at the picture her brain conjured at his words. "Back to the topic of my career, Mr. Calcagni. I believe you made some specific promises on the subject when I agreed to marry you."

"I did and I fully intend to keep those promises. Soon. Just not tonight." His jaw took on a stubborn clench.

She poked a finger at his chest. "There's no use continuing to fight me on this. I *will* wear you down."

"As much as I enjoy seeing you in full battle mode, that won't be necessary," he assured, eyes glinting with wicked humor. "If you'll just give me a few more days, I think I might have the perfect solution for what comes next for you."

No amount of wheedling on her part would make him explain himself further.

◊

IT TOOK two more weeks for Luca's promise to come to fruition and it came in the form of a singing audition.

"Please tell me I'm not dreaming." Jacey gripped her phone so hard while staring at the email invitation that it was a miracle it didn't shatter in her hand. She'd been practicing for days in the makeshift studio Luca had put together for her, a soundproof room on the lower level of his three-story mansion. She'd finished writing *Without You*, score and all. It was the song she planned to audition with when the time came; she just hadn't imagined the opportunity would come this quickly.

"Nashville bound," she sang, turning the words into their own little jingle as she packed an overnight bag the evening before her trip.

Luca lingered around the house the next morning.

"It's Monday," she reminded. "Aren't you heading to the office?" Normally, he would have departed an hour earlier.

He leaned across her suitcase to brush his lips over hers. "No, *cara*. I was able to rearrange my schedule the next few days. I'm going with you."

"That's nice." She grew still, unsure if it was. It was one thing to put herself out there during an audition. It was another thing entirely to have Luca present while she put herself out there. All her hopes and dreams would be at stake. What if she failed?

She dawdled in the bathroom over her makeup, growing more irritated by the second at his last minute change of plans. Why hadn't they discussed it in advance? Didn't he trust her? Or was he afraid she would try to disappear again?

He knocked on the door. "Are you about ready in there? We're scheduled to take off in less than an hour."

Less than a— Jacey threw the door open, aghast. "You told me to be ready by eight. What were you thinking? There's no way we're going to get to the airport in that amount of time, get ourselves checked in, get through security—"

"It's a good thing I have a pilot's license, then."

Are you kidding me?

His gaze heated as he took in her stunned expression, but he merely treated her to one of his mocking smiles. He lounged against the doorway, arms crossed and looking way too good in his cream cashmere sweater and black slacks.

She waffled between wanting to slap him for giving her a near heart attack and wanting to run to him and drag his head down for a kiss of gratitude. "I would have been fine flying commercial." *Alone.*

"You're pregnant."

"Last time I checked, that's not a crippling disease." She snapped her makeup kit closed, eyeing herself in the mirror and trying to be satisfied with what she saw. She'd gone for the dramatic look. A red sequined showgirl top, black leather pants, and a temporary eyelid tattoo that extended over her left check with black scrollwork. It might need a little touching up after their arrival, but she wanted to be ready for anything the moment she stepped off the plane. They were scheduled for a late meeting over snacks and beverages with Luca's contact in the recording industry.

"You lost two pounds last week," he pointed out in a voice strained with concern. "According to the doctor, you should be gaining about a pound per week. Not losing."

He caught her as she tried to sweep past him through the doorway. His long fingers enclosed her waist and did crazy things to her heart. "Auditions can be stressful. I figured someone needed to come along and make sure you eat and drink properly. Heaven knows, you can't be trusted in that area."

Whatever! Jacey wrenched free of his grasp and stomped to the bed to stuff her makeup kit into her carry-on bag. "I'm trying my best. You know I am." She couldn't help it if she was too sick most mornings to keep much of anything down. She tried to make up for it by eating more in the afternoons, but Luca was entirely too right. She was still underweight, and it worried her as much as it was worrying him.

"Yes, well, it's a husband's job to worry about his wife, so get used to it." He lifted her bag the moment she zipped it shut. "Allow me, *princesa*." He glanced down at her silver platform heels. "Do you really have to wear those things?"

She whirled to place a finger over his lips. "Not another word about my delicate condition. I'm healthy and fit, and my image is just as important as my voice if I'm going to nail this audition. Which I am."

He kissed her finger and lowered it to her side.

She couldn't read his expression, and that bothered her. She would have appreciated a little more well wishing. Or even another round of bickering. Anything but his insufferable silent hovering. She needed to focus on her art, not on every minute she spent resting or on every bite she put in her mouth. Or chose not to put in her mouth…

CHAPTER 22: JACEY'S WORLD
LUCA

All big boys possessed a few big toys, and Luca saw no reason to be an exception to that fundamental truth. He adored his private Boeing 747 with its custom interior and had been personally involved in every step of its design. As a result, it suited his needs to perfection, both personally and business-wise.

The interior was divided into four parts. The front section was the captain's quarters, of course. Directly behind it was a full master suite with a luxury bathroom, complete with a jacuzzi tub and sauna. The middle cabin held a skylight seating area on the top level and a plush movie theater on the bottom. The rear cabin was strictly for business. It held a conference room, a lounge area with a wet bar, and an office nook in the tail.

He proudly gave Jacey the tour, hoping to impress her.

"Where's the music room?" Her tone was teasing.

"Where would you like it to be?" he countered and was rewarded with the surprised widening of her eyes.

She shook her long, gorgeous, white-blonde hair back. "I've always enjoyed a room with a view."

His new bride was stunning — all the time — but she positively took his breath away every time she smiled. "The skylight room it is. I'll have the specs drawn up for you to review them."

"Luca! I was kidding."

"I wasn't. You can thank me with a private concert." He hooked an arm around her waist and tugged her closer. "I'll never tire of hearing you sing, *cara.*"

She laughed, and it was all the thanks he needed. He would never tire of hearing her laugh. Not in eighteen years, fifty, or a hundred.

His chef, Colette, and Don joined them before take-off. The petite, sassy-eyed French chef was making her usual attempts to flirt with his stoic co-pilot and otherwise engage him in conversation. Don maintained his usual brevity, answering her in monosyllables, though Luca sensed an odd restlessness in him today.

Don had received a phone call earlier when they

were prepping the plane for departure and had excused himself for more than ten minutes to take it. He'd returned from it, quieter and more tight-lipped than usual. Luca had always suspected there was more to the man's past than his stint in the special forces, but he respected Don's privacy and didn't ask questions. He hoped and prayed there was nothing in his past coming back to haunt him now. The man was irreplaceable.

Jacey stared at Colette and Don with disapproval. "It's only a ten or eleven-hour flight," she hissed in undertones to him. "There's no need to take over half the household."

He winked at her. "I didn't want you getting lonely while Don and I are in the cockpit."

She glared at him, lips parted, apparently at a loss for words. He treasured the moment; his wife was rarely at a loss for words.

"You'll be thanking me after you sample the breakfast Colette has planned for us," he continued smoothly.

If looks could kill, he'd be suffering a mortal wound. Instead of destroying the siren red paint on her lips, he settled for pressing a kiss to her forehead.

"You're impossible," she sighed, but he could feel her resistance melting beneath his touch. It filled him with a crazy amount of joy to know he remained one of her biggest weaknesses. It gave him hope that at least some small part of her was falling for him the way he was falling for her.

"On the contrary, I aim to please, *mi princesa*." He brushed his lips against her temple, adoring her warmth and flowery scent.

◊

DON DIDN'T REQUIRE a lot of conversation, so Luca had hours to simmer in his growing concerns for Jacey and the baby. If she dropped many more pounds, the doctor was threatening to either admit her to the hospital or put her on full bed rest. It was a threat she clearly didn't take seriously enough. Knowing it would crush her spirit to be so thoroughly confined, Luca had to find a way to get her to eat more, and soon. Bringing Colette to the audition was the first step in his plan to do exactly that.

It also bothered him that Jacey was still pacing around his mansion like a caged animal. He'd expected her to be more settled in by now. To buy more clothes or redecorate a room, to do something to carve out her own space there and leave her mark on his world. Instead, she continued to act like a guest. It made no sense. It wasn't as if his luxurious lifestyle was completely foreign to her; she'd been raised wealthy.

Other than his first attempt to take her shopping, however, she hadn't said one word about setting up a nursery or purchasing baby supplies. He'd tried to bring up the topic a few more times, but she'd brushed him off, saying there was plenty of time and he'd already done enough for her. Which made little sense. He knew for a fact she hadn't swiped the credit card he'd given her — not even once — and his generous monthly stipends were piling up in her checking account, untouched.

Accustomed to handling things, Luca hated the feeling of helplessness he always felt when attempting to care for his new wife. As the hours of the flight wore on, he found himself silently praying for divine guidance on how to be a better husband. He desperately needed to master that role before becoming a father.

Though his prayers brought no earth shattering revelations, they did bring him a bit of peace. He landed his plane at the Nashville airport and escorted his wife across the runway to their rented limousine. Despite the nearly eleven-hour flight, she looked more agitated than tired.

They had half a dozen voicemails waiting for them from Luca's contact. Apparently, the owners of the studio wanted to meet Jacey at the office instead of the restaurant. Which most likely meant they wanted to hear a sample of her music tonight.

Luca was furious at their lack of sensitivity. They'd traveled all day, and his wife was pregnant, for crying out loud! Not that the men they would be meeting knew about her condition. Jacey had insisted on keeping it a secret, fearful it would interfere with their decision on whether to offer her a contract.

"It's okay," she assured him softly. "I can do this."

No. It wasn't okay, but there wasn't much he could do about it at this point. He continued to fume during their brief ride to the music studio. Jacey was silent also, her gaze distant and distracted.

She clutched his shoulders when they stepped from the car, her blue gaze clouding with some unspeakable emotion. "Whatever happens in there, Luca, I just want to say thank you for this opportunity. It means everything to me."

It took a second for him to absorb the quick stab of pain her words brought him. He wished *he* meant everything to her. He touched her cheek, trying to swallow his longing and come up with the right words. "I've seen you in action, *princesa*. You're going to slay them in there. I can feel it."

"Thank you." She squeezed her eyes shut for a second.

"Do you prefer for me to listen in or wait outside?"

She opened her eyes, and it was like a different woman was standing before him, one who took his breath away all over again. "By all means, come in, Mr. Calcagni. Bring your whole entourage, if you wish." She waved a hand in Don and Colette's direction. "We musicians thrive on an audience."

Her answer both pleased and charmed him. He was utterly mesmerized by her glow of excitement, her almost palpable anticipation. He'd never seen this side of her before.

The pre-show version of Jacey in no way prepared him to watch her in full performance mode. Like an actress switching costumes, she took on an entirely different persona in the presence of her prospective agent and the man's recording crew. Animated and flirtatious in a larger-than-life way, she took control of the room and its occupants. She was no stranger to the recording equipment, either, donning her headset with ease and making a few practiced hand signals to the band.

"This is J.C. Crew, with an original, never-before-recorded single called *Without You*. The lyrics are very close to my heart. I hope you enjoy listening to it a fraction as much as I enjoyed writing it."

J.C. Crew?

Luca glanced down at the sheet music Jacey had handed him before stepping behind the glass. Sure enough, it was titled *Without You* by J.C. Crew. His wife was J.C. Crew? No wonder his agent friend had been so quick to agree to the audition. She was a rising singer and songwriter on her own merit, who had the world of social media buzzing with speculation. Actually, they'd been in a downright tizzy lately, debating to no end the reasons behind her extended absence from the stage.

Meaning she'd purposefully and willingly sacrificed one of her biggest dreams to come to work for Genesis & Sons. And him. *Incredible!*

Luca couldn't have been more stunned. Any last doubts about the character of the woman he'd married vanished. She was no longer the maddening teenager he'd once known, hellbent on having her own way no matter the consequences. All her efforts to atone for past wrongs and to make things right with his family had been genuine. And they had come at a great personal cost.

He raised his head from the sheet music, gazing at his bride with new eyes. She was a uniquely talented and capable woman with an impeccable sense of work ethic and unshakable integrity. Lord, forgive him, but he hadn't given her near enough credit until this very moment. He suddenly had no doubt she would land the recording contract.

She signaled the band again, and they played the opening sequence. She nodded and smiled encouragingly at them, swaying to the music and cradling the microphone in both hands as she lifted it to her lips.

It was the same song she'd sung to him the morning after he'd circumvented her attempted flight out of town, except this was the full, uncut version.

He stood riveted as her husky, one-of-a-kind alto

swept through him, rich and mesmerizing. It filled the room, surrounding him and sweeping him beneath her web of magic.

During the bridge sequence, she sashayed her way to the keyboard, still singing. With a flourish of her wrist, the man who'd been playing for her stood and yielded his stool. Luca watched open-mouthed as his wife ran her fingers over the keys in an elaborate instrumental solo before plunging into the chorus. It was a seamless transition. Not a beat was missed.

As it turned out, Jacey played as beautifully as she sang — not only with extraordinary skill and style, but also with a soulful quality that left her listeners emotionally moved.

Her prospective agent stopped writing and simply watched her, mouth every bit as agape as Luca's. The DJ and sound crew nodded gleefully, rocking their heads to the beat. Like the agent, they also seemed unable to tear their gazes from the woman behind the glass.

Jacey sang directly to them, not looking over their heads and beyond her audience as so many performers did. There was no stage fright in her stance. If anything, she seemed to draw energy from their animated response to her music. She sang of love and loss, freedom and captivity, mistakes and redemption.

At some point between the opening and closing

notes of the song, Luca finished falling profoundly and irrevocably in love with his wife.

◊

ONE OF THE most prominent booking agents in the industry, Chance Biggers knew his stuff. At the end of Jacey's audition, he held out his arms. A wide grin stretched his angular features. He tilted his head sideways, tossing his longish wavy auburn hair back from his face. "Make me your agent, J.C. Tonight. Right now, please."

She was ecstatic and required no further urging to sign her first recording contract. Luca was dazzled at the way she handled her victory. Joyous yet professional. She was so animated, so alive, so lovely, so his. He could hardly breathe properly as he watched her take the next steps to launch her musical career.

He tried not to think of the words she'd sung, but it was impossible. They were emblazoned across his soul.

> Without you, all I have is unfilled
>   promises.
> Without you, all I have is half-lived
>   dreams.
> Without you, I spend all my time
>   remembering.

> Holding on to every moment I had
> with you.

Discovering he was in love with his wife came with one serious complication, one Luca should have seen coming. Despite the many frustrations Jacey had undoubtedly grappled with in her marriage to his immature youngest brother, she was clearly still in love with him. How on God's green earth was Luca supposed to compete with a dead man?

He and Jacey rode a complimentary shuttle from the music studio to their hotel in near silence. She wore a dazed look on her face, while he nursed an aching heart. She reached for his hand on their short walk across the portico to the front entrance.

"Luca, this is it. Everything I ever dreamed of, and it's all because of you. I can't thank you enough for arranging my audition."

Congratulations to me! His thoughts churned bitterly. *I fell in love with you and lost you in the same evening.*

"Hey." She laid her other hand on his arm, stepping closer. "You haven't strung three whole words together since I signed the contract. Please tell me you understand this is the most amazing thing that has ever happened to me."

Ouch! Where did their marriage fit in that picture? Where did *he*? And their unborn son? Her words put him in an even more rotten mood.

"Congratulations, *princesa*." He wished he didn't sound so clipped, so ironic.

She caught her breath at his tone but didn't have time to respond before they reached the check-in desk.

Don was waiting for them with their suitcases in hand, and Colette was beaming at his side. "Welcome back, sir and ma'am. Well. Mrs. Calcagni?" He arched a brow at them. "How did the audition go?"

"I landed the contract!" Jacey sang out and launched herself at him, drawing him into a short dance. He hugged her back and swung her around once before setting her down. It was an uncharacteristic show of emotion for him.

Apparently, they'd become friends in the past month, a fact that did nothing to improve Luca's mood.

He hurriedly checked them into their block of rooms and bustled their small party to the elevators. For some reason, he was unable to bear the thought of how many people adored his lovely wife, or of how many ways he was losing her — to his brother's memory, to her ambitions, to her career, and to her rapidly growing line of fans.

Once inside their private suite of rooms, Jacey firmly shut the door behind them. "Okay, Luca. Out with it. What's wrong? I thought you, of all people, would be happy for me."

He should have known she wouldn't let it go. "I

am happy for you, *mi querida*." He drew a finger down her cheek. "And I'm not the least bit surprised by your success today. I knew you had talent the first time I heard you sing. The rest of it was just details."

"Details?" She fisted her hands in his shirt. He loved it when she got all possessive like that. It made his heart leap with hope.

"Are you kidding me?" she squealed. "This is everything I ever wanted. One of the biggest reasons I eloped and left town with Easton. This is," she shook her head, anxiously searching her husband's face, "rainbows and unicorns and pixie dust. All the things my family said I couldn't have and would never achieve. Don't you see? We proved them wrong, sweetheart. You and me. You're the first person who ever put yourself out there for me. You're the one who helped make this happen."

She had him at *sweetheart*. Fortunately, she no longer needed perfect makeup. Luca hauled his bride closer and slanted his mouth over hers. Drinking in her excitement and euphoria, he tried to be happy for her. Tried not to wonder if she wished she was sharing her victory kisses with the father of her unborn son instead of his oldest brother.

She pulled away breathlessly. "Be right back. I know I'm not showing much yet, but my bladder says there's less room in there than there was a few weeks ago."

Luca grinned. It was the most unromantic thing

that had ever tumbled from his lovely wife's lips, but even that was attractive coming from her. *It's about time.* She was finally talking about the baby, which thrilled him beyond belief. He pulled out his phone and recorded a hasty message to Don.

Tell Colette to take a couple extra hours of personal time in the morning. You, too. We're pushing back our departure by two hours. Jacey needs her rest.

And he desperately needed some quality time with his wife this evening.

By the time she returned from the bathroom, he had two sparkling waters poured and the curtains thrown back to reveal a starry night.

He handed her one of the fluted glasses. "Cheers, *cara*."

She clinked her glass against his. "Cheers, Luca."

They smiled at each other over the rims of their glasses and drank to tonight's success.

In no hurry for them to scatter to their separate rooms, he nodded at the gold sofa with its mountain of decorative throw pillows. "Sit with me?"

"Gladly." She yawned and slapped a hand over her mouth. "Well, that came out of nowhere." She hastily sat and took another sip of her sparkling water, but he could tell she was finally succumbing to the exhaustion she hadn't felt until now.

"Hardly. It's been a long day for both of us." He could almost visibly watch the waves of adrenaline-laced euphoria she'd been riding start to fade. Taking a knee before her, he slid off her platform heels and was rewarded with her soft sound of pleasure. To his concern, her feet looked a little swollen. That was something he could help out with.

Rising to take a seat beside her, he lifted her feet and propped them across his knees. He lifted the first one and slowly kneaded his thumbs across the underside of her arch.

She tipped her head back against the cushions and sighed. "Keep that up and I might never leave this sofa."

Having her all to himself like this made Luca's day a hundred times better. Her feet were as lovely as the rest of her — all porcelain perfect, slender, and delicate. Her nails boasted a fresh, glossy pedicure in her favorite siren red. He bent to kiss the tips of her toes.

When he raised his head and ensnared her gaze, she was watching him with flushed cheeks, lips parted. "Luca," she whispered, setting down her glass on the end table. They reached for each other.

But before Luca could gather her in his arms, her cell phone trilled. It was Chance Biggers. With a startled look, Jacey connected the line. "Hi, there, Chance! Just so you know, I've got you on speaker phone. Luca is with me —"

"Guess what, J.C.?" Her agent raised his voice to drown out the rest of her sentence. "I know it's getting late, but I've already secured the release of your first single with an advance that will make you smile all night long. The acquiring company wants to film a music video right away plus — get this — they're making noise about sending you on your first concert tour next spring. I expect to hear back from them soon with the deets. Wouldn't be surprised if they call again in the morning."

Jacey gripped the phone, grinning like a loon across the couch at Luca. "That's fantastic!" Her smile dimmed a little at his cautious expression. He knew he was being a stick in the mud and fought to muster up a smile for her.

"I know, right?" Chance chortled.

Something about the fast-talking little bugger rubbed Luca the wrong way. He leaned closer to the mouthpiece. "Luca Calcagni here. Glad to hear about the release of my wife's first single, but she's approaching the end of her first trimester. I'm not so sure a concert tour is the best idea for a woman in her condition."

Jacey's fingernails bit into his arm. "What are you doing?" she whisper-screamed in alarm.

"She's pregnant?" the man shouted. "Okay. Ah, sorry. I mean congratulations, of course. Holy moly, I didn't mean for it to sound like that. I'll certainly keep it in mind while scheduling her debut tour. It probably won't happen before next summer, anyway. These things take time to plan and promote. I'm just so excited about her I'm jumping the gun here." He gave a long-suffering sigh. "About that music video, though, we'll have to get real creative with the lighting and poses to hide her pregnancy. Unless, hmm. Let me think about it, okay? I'll get back with you."

When Chance abruptly ended the call, Jacey rounded on her husband, tight-lipped and stony-eyed. "Next time I give you the courtesy of putting you on speaker phone, your role is to listen. Although I appreciate the sentiment behind your concerns, this is my career. I'll handle it from here."

A strained silence settled between them, but Luca wasn't near finished interfering with her fledgling career. Not even close. They debated it long and hard the next several days. In the end, she agreed to shoot her first music video on his estate for health purposes. Chance balked loudly at first, grumbling over the added expense of traveling to Anchorage, but he was ultimately satisfied with the results.

The man could hardly stay in his seat during the pre-showing of the recording in Luca's home theater. "We're going platinum, baby," he announced gleefully. "Mark my words. *Without You* is going to rock the charts." He leaned across the armrest to kiss Jacey's cheek.

Luca shot him a warning look, and the man settled back in his seat, a speculative expression riding his narrow features.

But Chance was point on. *Without You* left the

gates at a full sprint and stayed number one on the pop charts for weeks.

The royalties poured into Jacey's accounts like a flood, and Luca's hopes of making her fall in love with him plummeted. The biggest things their marriage had offered her and her unborn son — a home and financial security — she no longer needed. She could provide everything for herself now.

His fear of losing her before he had a chance to win her heart increased exponentially.

CHAPTER 23: RACE

JACEY

Jacey was thrilled with the long-awaited launch of her music career and the new income stream it afforded. After five long years of stressing about money, singing for small crowds on the club circuit, and all but giving up hope of ever receiving her big break, she'd finally done it — finally become her own person, no longer beholden to anyone.

It was amazing how coming home and facing her past, including her personal mistakes and her family's deep-seated issues, had ultimately propelled her to success.

Her morning sickness disappeared, and her second and third trimesters flew past. She even started gaining weight, not enough to make the doctor stop harping at her, but at least she was moving in the right direction. The only thing dimming her happiness was the wall of tension that had risen between her and Luca following the launch of her musical career.

"So," Jacey instinctively knew her latest announcement wasn't going to make him any happier, "Chance Biggers just landed me an opening gig on the Lady Rock World Tour."

"World tour?" Luca's features tightened with disapproval. "Exactly how long are we talking about?"

She laughed. "Two years for the entire Lady Rock Tour, but I'm only booked for the Central U.S. leg of it. August through September. Chance says I'll need to spend most of July practicing with her band in Nashville to prepare for it, though."

"That's right after your due date," Luca protested, looking shocked. "It's too soon. You'll need time to rest and recover."

They were sitting on a swing in the backyard gazebo in the early morning hours. A space heater was blasting until the warmer mid-day June temperatures could catch up with them.

"It's cutting it close," she agreed, no more thrilled than he was about the timing. Her delivery date was only two weeks away, and Chance was banking on her being in Nashville in six weeks.

Jacey's hand rested on her blooming belly. The ultrasounds had finally verified it was a boy. "But I have to do it, Luca. It's my big break. An opportunity like this might never happen again." The last Lady

Rock World Tour had drawn record crowds at every stop, and her upcoming tour was already sold out.

Luca picked up her hand, studying it seriously. "You know I can't take two months away from Genesis & Sons to go on tour with you."

"I'm not asking you to." He looked so yummy in his pistachio pullover and khaki slacks, it made her fantasize about licking an ice cream cone; but she was too tired to go check on their ice cream supply in the kitchen. Unable to find a comfortable position the night before, she hadn't slept well.

"What are your plans for Race?" he asked. It was the shortened version of the name she'd picked out for her son — Easton Race Calcagni. "The road is hardly a place for a newborn."

"I'm torn," she admitted. "It's probably going to kill me to leave him behind, but I agree with you two hundred percent. The road is no place for a baby. I know this is a lot to ask, but I was hoping to leave Race with you. And his nanny, of course."

They'd been interviewing prospective nannies for days and had finally made a job offer to a young woman from the Netherlands. She'd informally accepted their offer, but they were still waiting for the agency to process all the necessary paperwork to make it official.

Luca looked moderately relieved, although the lines around his mouth didn't disappear entirely. "You know I will."

Jacey strained to hear more, longing for him to confess he would miss her for the two months she would be away, but he fell silent.

Her breath left her, leaving her chest deflated. His biggest concerns had always been, and ever would be, reserved for his new son. Race. The baby who would usher in the next generation of Calcagnis. Race was the main reason Luca had proposed to her in the first place. She savagely bit her lower lip. She was a fool to keep hoping for more.

Having her as his wife was nothing more than a side perk, a convenience for a busy, wealthy man who worked long hours and had little time to date and socialize after hours.

"Your lip is bleeding!" Luca stood and yanked off his t-shirt to press against her mouth. "Here. Hold this, while I run inside for some ointment and an ice pack."

Good heavens! Jacey hadn't intended to bite down that hard. She licked the salty taste from her lips, enjoying the sight of her husband in his sleeveless white tank. Wow, but his upper body was buff!

An acute burning spasm gripped her with no warning. It ricocheted through her abdomen and settled in her lower back with a throbbing intensity. The muscles in her belly went rock hard for several seconds. She cried out in fear, clutching her middle and trying to breathe through the pain.

Good heavens, but it seemed that Race Calcagni

had a mind of his own already. If her suspicions were correct, he'd decided to make an early appearance.

"Jacey!" Luca dashed across the yard in a fresh shirt and took the gazebo stairs two at a time to bend over her. "What's going on?"

She tried to speak, coughed, and had to clear her throat. "It's time." Her voice shook.

"Are you sure? Your due date is still two weeks away."

"I know, but I think someone forgot to inform Race." Her laugh held a tinge of hysteria.

Luca yanked his phone from his pocket, dropped it, and retrieved it while running a hand through his hair. She'd never seen him so distressed. "Don! Bring the car around back. Looks like the baby's coming. We need to get Jacey to the hospital ASAP!"

The next twenty minutes passed in a blur of black leather seats, excruciating pain, and anxious voices as they sped for the medical center emergency room.

She experienced a blinding flash of cramps and a gush of warmth. Despite the fact Jacey was sitting on a thick blanket, she was mortified at the thought of making a mess in Luca's car.

"I think my water just broke." Her voice shook.

Her husband nodded and continued to hold her, crooning encouragement and assurances in her ear.

She held his hand as if her life depended on it,

squeezing it mercilessly through the worst of the pain.

Don brought the limousine to a halt, threw open the door, and she was transferred to a stretcher. Luca walked beside her, never letting go of her hand, and they were joined at the entrance by Waverly, Rhys, and Knox. No sooner had the paramedics rolled Jacey's stretcher through the double doors did Race make his screaming arrival.

It was a chaotic and messy, but joyous, ride up the elevator to the mother-baby wing of the hospital. They were escorted by an emergency room doctor and a nurse who monitored Jacey's vitals every step of the way. They allowed her to hold her infant son until they turned her over to the OB-GYN staff. There Race was whisked away for his first bath. The nurse returned with him in minutes to lay him back in Jacey's arms.

She couldn't tear her eyes from his cherubim features and plump cheeks. Mercy, but she was drunk with love for him. He was an absolute angel, and he was hers to keep. Hers and Luca's, that is.

Luca bent over her bed to kiss her tenderly in front of everyone present. "Thank you, Jacey. He's an incredible addition to our family."

Bitterness flooded her chest at his words. *Of course.* Today wasn't about her. Or Luca and her. Or Luca, her, and Race. It was only about expanding the Calcagni dynasty. Jacey forced a smile to her lips, suddenly feeling like a third wheel in her own hospital room.

Waverly took her tearful turn at holding Race, and Rhys and Knox hovered over her shoulders, beaming and awaiting their turns to hold their precious nephew.

Yep. I'm invisible. No more than a surrogate who'd lent her womb to their precious blood line. Jacey was an outsider again now that Race had arrived.

CHAPTER 24: CONCERT TOUR

JACEY

At first, the monotonous beeping of Jacey's alarm made her want to fling the contraption across the room. In the next moment, she wanted to kiss it for booting her groggy self from the world of dreams. She'd never been much of a morning person, but she'd settled into the habit of waking early enough on Monday mornings to spend an hour with Race before flying to the studio in Nashville. She typically stayed three nights, recorded two full days, and returned the following Thursday evening. It was painful to spend so much time away from her newborn son each week, but it couldn't be helped. It would be far worse being away from him for two full months during her upcoming tour with Lady Rock.

Luca was already at work, of course. He wasn't happy with her new work schedule, though he didn't openly complain about it. He'd gone silent again on the whole topic of her career, which was driving her crazy. Did he think she was a bad parent for putting in such long hours away from Race?

Like she had much choice. Her new practice schedule with Lady Rock's back-up band involved spending two full days a week in Nashville. If it weren't for Don and the co-pilot Luca had hired to commute her in his private jet, she wouldn't have been able to come home every weekend. She was wildly grateful for her husband's pricey intervention in her scheduling dilemma. She just wished he seemed more contented with the arrangement, but no! He seemed to be more worried about her than ever — fussing over every pound she'd lost since delivering Race and dickering endlessly with Colette to tweak her diet.

Jacey wished she could figure out a way to make the man happy. Period. A foolish wish, but there it was. She was a woman wildly in love with her own husband. A man who'd married her out of duty. A man who didn't have a history of seeking out emotional attachments with the women he'd dated. At the end of the day, he was a man driven to grow the Genesis & Sons empire and to carry on the Calcagni legacy. Nothing more and nothing less.

Thank God, Jacey had never been one to give up easily. After a few sleepless nights in a row, she came up with a plan to win her husband's heart. Step one required staying an extra hour after practice once per week in Nashville. She stressed about how she was going to explain it to Don, but he didn't ask questions. He adjusted their flight schedule without so much as a comment. *Fortunately!* The last thing she needed was for him to pry into her secret appointments at one of the poshest clubs in town.

Jacey hurriedly dressed for the day and skipped breakfast, dashing down the hall in the hopes Colette wouldn't waylay her on the way and guilt her into taking a detour to the dining room. It had only been seven weeks since Jacey's delivery, but she already had her trim figure back. She had no intention of allowing Colette and Luca to conspire to put any unnecessary weight on her right before the Lady Rock World Tour.

Race's whimper had her bursting through the nursery door. "Oh, sweetheart! I'm right here." She scooped him up, despite their new nanny's sound of protest.

"I'm sorry he's not dressed, ma'am." Britt held out her arms with a rueful expression on her fair, rounded features. "He needs to be bathed and changed. Little guy was sleeping in and I hated to disturb him." She was a young college student taking online classes in multiple foreign languages. Her long-term goal was to become a linguist.

Jacey laughed and pressed a dozen kisses to the face of the squirming infant in her arms. "You mean I actually arrived in time for his bath? Bonus!"

Britt tucked her long blonde hair behind her ears as she walked to the nursery bathroom. She filled Race's mini-tub with warm water and returned to the nursery to prop it on his changing table. Next to it, she laid out bottles of baby shampoo, lotion, and powder. "Are you sure, ma'am?"

"I couldn't be happier, Britt. Really." It was the perfect start to Jacey's day.

The visit to the nursery flew past too quickly. Two hours later, Jacey was back on the airplane and headed to Nashville.

The following morning, she perched at the breakfast bar in the studio lounge with Lady Rock's extended band. She idly scooted the food around on the plate Colette had sent with her. She wasn't nervous so much as anxious to make a good first impression. Lady Rock was en route with her premium band members. They would arrive any minute. Today was the day the entire crew would finally meet up in person.

Being immersed in the world of pop music was like living in a dream. It was beyond exciting to practice with a real band, work with a ridiculously fawning agent, and occasionally sign t-shirts and other paraphernalia for the groupies who thronged the doors of their studio.

Jacey loved every minute of it, from the excitement in the air to the flurry of preparations for her opening number in the upcoming concert tour. Her first mini-tour!

"J.C. Crew?"

Jacey raised her head to take in the energetic stride of the tiny fairy-like woman striding toward her. It was Lady Rock in person. A sensation on stage, she appeared to glide more than walk across the room in her glittering red pantsuit and platform heels. Her arms were outstretched in welcome.

Jacey unfolded herself from her stool and reached for Lady Rock's hand, but Lady Rock kept moving and drew Jacey into a perfumed bear hug.

"Thank you for joining my tour." The pop sensation drew Jacey at an arm's length and flipped aside a wave of her long, brunette hair to regard her protege more closely.

"Thank you for asking me." Jacey's apprehension vanished beneath the approving glint in Lady Rock's gaze. The woman's eyes swept Jacey's filmy white body suit with its flowing sleeves.

"Oh, honey! When my tour director first heard Chance Biggers raving about you, he was sold. After he watched your sample recording, he was completing lost. It was only a matter of working out the numbers with Chance after that."

It was high praise, not idle flattery, and Jacey knew it. She grinned. "We've tweaked the beginning of my sequence a few times and added some dance moves. I hope you like it."

Lady Rock waved an unconcerned hand, glimmering with gems. "It's fine. Serge runs everything past me." He was her lead drummer. He stood, and they embraced with a kiss that lasted awhile.

So that was the way the wind blew in this studio.

Lady Rock remained the rest of the morning, observing Jacey's routine and making a few small changes. By lunch time, Lady Rock pronounced that it was perfect, which was a relief since the beginning of the tour was only days away.

LEAVING Race behind to begin the concert tour was monumentally harder than Jacey expected. It was like ripping her heart from her body, one heartstring at a time, to say goodbye to him. She departed home in a dazed funk.

As usual, Don served as her chauffeur. He dutifully commuted her and her impressive pile of luggage to Chicago for the opening night concert. With her first performance in less than twenty-four hours, sleep was out of the question. Jacey laid awake in bed, experiencing a thousand mini-strokes of stress while the hours ticked all too quickly past. The next morning she was wildly grateful for the skilled team of makeup artists who quickly masked the effects of her sleepless night.

Lady Rock popped her head in the door of

Jacey's dressing room minutes before her first performance. "Good luck, sugar." She blew her a kiss and disappeared.

Jacey didn't need luck. She needed a miracle! She had her husband's heart to win, and tonight was step two in her plan. Through some clever negotiating, Chance had arranged for her performance to be live-streamed on a private channel straight to Luca's personal computer. She intended to sing straight to him this evening and could only hope and pray he was watching her.

Jacey drew every ounce of excitement and energy possible from her audience and sang directly into the rolling cameras pointed at her from a half dozen angles. In her heart, she sang for Luca. To Luca. Because of Luca.

The applause was thunderous. When it refused to die down, Serge pounded through the notes for an encore. Jacey delivered the encore, blew more kisses, and jogged from the stage while they continued to cheer. The frenzy of the fans only increased when Lady Rock made her appearance.

The opening concert was a tremendous success. It took a team of bodyguards to keep the rabid fans at bay long enough for Jacey and Lady Rock to board their respective tour buses. Jacey hadn't realized how late it was, or how exhausted she was, until she clapped the door shut to her room on wheels and leaned against it. Her mouth dropped open in surprise. An enormous bouquet awaited her on the credenza across from her bed. There had to be nearly a hundred red roses in the fat crystal vase.

Mystified, she plucked the card from its holder and nearly stopped breathing as she read.

To J.C. Crew. The most beautiful, talented, and enchanting singer, songwriter, wife, and mother. Luca & Race

She stood there in her black leather pants and stage makeup, clutching the card against her chest. She would have preferred a declaration of love, but she would take what she could get from her husband. For now, at least. The flowers were romantic. They were progress.

Three more days passed with no further communication from Luca, and Jacey's hopes in his direction took a dive. But her melancholy only added to her success. A slightly pale face and the glint of mist in her eyes made the words of *Without You* resonate with genuine emotion. Tabloid after tabloid commented on her incredible stage presence. Sales on her first single shot through the roof.

CHAPTER 25: PLAYING FOR KEEPS
LUCA

Luca wasn't a patient man, but now wasn't the time to pressure Jacey. She was a free spirit. Best to let her savor her first taste of stardom. She'd earned it. He just didn't intend to let her revel in it too long without thinking about him.

He sent flowers to her at every tour stop as well as a steady stream of candid photos. They were primarily of Race, a dimpled, wriggling mass of child whose expressive features seemed designed for the camera.

Britt didn't mind helping pose the happy babe. "I never saw a father more obsessed with capturing the perfect picture." That was because most fathers weren't so determined on capturing the hearts of their wives.

As if sensing the magnitude of what was at stake,

Race gurgled in his crib and smiled into the camera lens, waving his fists.

It was his first smile!

By some miracle, Luca's finger had depressed the camera's burst button, not missing a single nuance of the beautiful moment. Seventeen photos in all. He replayed them in slow motion. His heartbeat thudded as he watched Race's smile take shape again. *Oh, yes! This one was a winner. One no heart could resist.* Especially not the heart of Race's mother.

He and Britt finished their photo shoot with a picture of Race sleeping soundly on his bare chest. He wasn't normally one for taking I-love-me photos, but he'd worked hard over the years to keep his body in shape. If Jacey saw something else in the photo to enjoy besides their son, well, he wasn't above getting his hands dirty in the quest to win the heart of his own wife.

CHAPTER 26: JEALOUSY

JACEY

Jacey stared bitterly at the photos, pressing the button over and over again to replay Race's smile in slow motion. She should have been there for it. She'd missed a moment in her son's life that could never be retrieved, except on camera. Being there in person would have been so much better.

She refused to look at the last two photos in the shoot again, but she couldn't help thinking of them. One was a picture of Britt holding Race over her head — a classic mother-baby pose — and the other one was of Race resting on Luca's chest. Obviously, Britt and her husband were getting pretty chummy in her absence.

Such were the dangers of hiring a young and attractive Dutch nanny. Jacey's insides incinerated into black pools of jealousy and fear. Her marriage to

Luca was one of convenience. They hadn't yet been together in the marital sense. What if, in her absence, he decided to — no. She couldn't go there in her head. She just couldn't.

Thank God for makeup artists and her own professional acting skills. It was all Jacey could do to fake her smiles through the next two nights of concerts.

CHAPTER 27: CRASH VISIT
LUCA

When two whole days passed without Jacey responding to the photos of Race's first smile, Luca's gut twisted with worry. Something was wrong.

What if she was enjoying her time on the road so much that coming home would feel like a letdown? There were no adoring crowds waiting for her in his mansion. No flashing stage lights. No screaming fans. Only him and Race, along with Don, Merl, Colette, and Britt. They all missed her, but she was a free spirit and only twenty-five. She hadn't planned her pregnancy. On the concert tour with Lady Rock, she was free from all the responsibilities that came with being a mother. And from being his wife, a role Luca had rather pridefully manipulated her into.

He'd been a fool to think he could sway her heart with pictures of Race. She was already head over heels in love with her son. What he should have been doing was planning something extra special from *yours truly* for her birthday in a week. As of yet, he'd made no plans.

Don drove Luca home from work, jogging around the front of the limousine to open his boss's door.

"Was she happy the last time you saw her?" Luca snarled without thinking. He leaped from the car and faced his driver, his fist clenched around the handle of his briefcase

Don shot him a shuttered look. "As far as I could tell."

"You'll have to do better than that to convince me. You were the one flying her to and from Nashville. You witnessed her moods every morning and every afternoon for an entire month."

"Guess I was hoping you wouldn't ask, sir."

What? Luca glared at his friend. "What's that supposed to mean?" If the man had something he needed to say, what in the world was holding him back?

"It's none of my business, sir."

"I made it your business when I assigned you to be my wife's pilot. What are you not telling me?"

"This, sir." His movements sluggish with reluctance, Don punched a few buttons on his phone and held it up.

Luca's lungs constricted as he recognized his

wife in the snapshot and the building in the background. It was an exclusive club for the wealthiest patrons in Nashville. What could she possibly be doing alone at such an upscale dining and dancing establishment other than meeting someone? It was the only logical explanation. Luca couldn't believe this was the first time he was hearing about it.

All feeling left his chest. His lips moved mechanically. "Did she go inside, Don?"

"Yes, sir. I'm sorry, sir."

"More than once?"

"Once per week at the same time like clockwork."

"And you didn't think to mention this before?"

"I didn't know what to do, sir. I know what it looks like, but it doesn't add up. She's in love with you."

Right. If only. The lie was staring them in the face.

Don sighed and pocketed his phone.

Jacey had cuckolded them both.

"Thank you, Don. That will be all for the evening." Luca strode blindly into his home, for once bypassing the nursery. He went straight to his office and slammed the door. It took him several eternal minutes to compose himself enough to dial his wife.

She answered with a laugh in her voice. "Hi, Luca!"

He closed his eyes against the pain. *My beautiful traitorous wife.*

There was a chatter of voices and a pounding burst of drums in the background. "Is everything okay with Race?"

Her subterfuge knew no boundaries. Pretending concern when she couldn't be bothered to acknowledge the pictures of their son's first smile. "Race is fine. Didn't you receive my pictures?"

Some of the laughter ebbed from her voice. "I did. They were amazing. I'm sorry I haven't texted you back yet." She drew a long, shuddery-sounding breath. "It was just hard seeing —" A shout of laughter rose from the background. "I'm so sorry to cut this short, Luca, but I have to go. I'll call back in a few hours if that's okay? We're about to start our next rehearsal."

"J.C., darlin'!" a man called. "I need you over here."

Luca's blood boiled. J.C. was *his* darling, thank you very much. *He* was the one who needed her! "Do I have any choice?" he groused.

"Not really." Her chuckle held an apologetic, almost breakable note.

Luca hated himself for the way it wrenched through his chest. She didn't deserve his sympathy.

"I'll catch you later."

He doubted she would call back, and he was

right. She texted a brief apology, instead, many hours later.

It was the last slap. Luca dialed a hotel in the town where his wife would be staying the upcoming weekend. He secured a block of rooms for himself and the key members of his household. If his wife thought she was going to be left to party and do God-knows-what with her secret crush on the night of her own birthday, she had a big ugly surprise in store — *him*. She was going to spend her birthday with him whether she liked it or not. If she didn't like it, she could come clean and demand a divorce like an honest woman. As his brother's widow, she at least owed him that.

Ironically, the bridal suite was still available, and it wasn't cheap. Luca reserved it for reasons he couldn't quite define, and reserved the two adjoining rooms, as well. Don would stay in one, and Britt and Race would stay in the other.

He flew his family entourage to Houston without spilling one word of their plans to Jacey. They didn't make it in time for the concert, but Chance managed to secure tickets for him and Don to attend her exclusive late-night celebration afterward. The party was in full roar when he arrived, but Jacey wasn't anywhere in sight.

Puzzled, he asked around but only received a few shrugs. "She never stays long," one band member noted with a grimace. "I hear she just had a baby or something and isn't feeling too well."

Or a secret lover. Luca's heartbeat pounded halfway up his throat. He summoned Don, and they roared away from the party in their rented limo, arriving in record speed at the gated section of the convention center's parking lot where Jacey's tour bus was parked.

Don flashed his security pass, and the gate guard let them through. Luca didn't bother to ask where he'd secured the pass. He didn't care. All that mattered was reaching and confronting Jacey.

It took several minutes of knocking before she cracked open the door of her tour bus. The deadbolt was still in place.

"Luca?" Her voice rose to an incredulous trill of surprise.

"Happy birthday, *princesa*," he announced coldly. "May I come in?"

"Of course!" Her fingers trembled as she fumbled with the bolt.

He leaned closer, craning for any sound of movement in the room behind her, any sign of another visitor's presence besides him. Silence greeted him as she stood in the doorway, pale-faced with shock.

It appeared she was alone.

He and Don exchanged a dark glance. Don looked away first. "I'll wait for you in the car, sir." He strode away, hands jammed in his pockets.

Luca entered his wife's home away from home, and one thing was immediately apparent. The paparazzi photos had lied. Jacey was a crumpled version of her stage self. Barefoot and wearing black yoga pants with a red tank top that accentuated her paleness. Her hair was tousled as if he'd awakened her from a nap, and there were shadows under her eyes.

Luca kicked the door shut behind him. "What's going on? Are you sick?" All her baby weight was gone. Her figure was as thin as ever. Too thin.

Anger tightened her features. "Well, hello to you, too. I was trying to sleep. Where's Race?"

"In the hotel I reserved for us this weekend. I wanted to surprise you at the back-stage celebration, but you weren't there."

She made a sound that was a half-scream, half-sob. "Race is here? In town? How far away?" She reached for him, fingernails sinking into his upper arms.

He glanced down in surprise at the vehemence of his wife's grip, and she withdrew her hands. "I'm sorry." She left him to snatch on her shoes and run her fingers through her hair. "I'm ready. Please take me to him."

Luca's doubts about Jacey turned to puzzled speculation when they arrived at the hotel. Britt entered the room with the sleeping Race in her arms.

His wife blindly reached for their son, her blue eyes glazed with emotion.

"Race." She kissed his downy head like she was never going to stop. Tears streaked her cheeks and dripped all over his face. It was a long while before she acknowledged their nanny. "Hi, Britt," she said coolly.

"Hello, ma'am." With a startled look, Britt quietly tiptoed back to her room and shut the door.

Race puckered his lips and made a sound of protest.

"Oh no, sweetheart. Please don't cry. Mommy is so happy to see you. I'm just a little overwhelmed; that's all." Jacey kissed his cheeks, fingers, toes, and belly until he crowed with pleasure.

She held him and crooned over him until he fell asleep against her shoulder. "Luca," she murmured, lifting her gaze to his in wonder. "How can I ever thank you? This is the best birthday present ever."

Her color was back, eyes sparkling across the room at him. He stood at the bar, pouring two glasses of sparkling water while he studied her.

"We need to talk." He lifted a glass to her. "If you'd like, Britt can give you a break and put Race down for the night."

Jacey flushed slightly and her lips trembled, but she nodded. She was nervous. *Good.* It was past time for their confrontation.

He paged Britt, and she rushed in the room to stand expectantly before his wife.

"Thank you, Britt," Jacey said firmly. "For everything you've done in my absence." Her voice held a curious note of warning. "You've obviously taken good care of him."

Their nanny's wide, friendly face twisted in apprehension. "My pleasure, ma'am." Her Dutch accent added charm to the simple words. She hastily tossed a hank of golden blonde hair behind her shoulder. "I think he's out for the night. If you'd like, I'll tuck him in."

Only when Jacey nodded did she reach for Race.

When they were alone again, Luca handed Jacey the glass of bubbling water he'd poured. "She's an excellent nanny. We are fortunate to have found her."

Jacey raised her glass and drained it before responding. "Are we speaking of Race's needs or yours?"

You've got to be kidding! Luca's fist tightened around the stem of his glass, knuckles turning white. "Are you accusing me of something, Mrs. Calcagni?"

"Should I be, Mr. Calcagni? I presume someone besides you took the picture of Race sleeping on your bare chest."

He slammed his glass down on the bar, shattering the stem, and strode to stand before her. "I can't believe what you're implying! You know as well as I do there are security cameras embedded all over the nursery. You may examine them for yourself when you come home. *If* you ever plan on returning."

"Why wouldn't I?" Her chin came up.

"That's an interesting question coming from a woman who made more than ten trips to one of the most exclusive dining and dancing clubs in Nashville. Alone."

She slammed her own glass down on the nightstand. "Are you accusing me of something, Mr. Calcagni?" She mimicked his tone, lips twisting bitterly.

Two could dance with words. "Should I be, Mrs. Calcagni?"

She turned from him and bent to scribble something on a notepad on his nightstand. Ripping the page from its pad, she stabbed the air with it as she held it out to him. "I was filming an exclusive piece of footage with the Rodeo Girls and their band. You can either call and ask them exactly what we were doing, or you can wait until Christmas like a good boy and open your gift then."

Desperate hope warred with Luca's anger. He was probably the world's worst fool for wanting to believe such a lame story, but he couldn't resist Jacey's challenge. Ignoring the paper she held out to him, he reached for her and sealed his mouth over hers in a punishing kiss.

A strangled sound escaped her, but all she did was twine her arms around his neck and pull him closer. There was a desperateness to her touch, a bite to her kiss. And for the life of him, Luca was powerless to resist her.

He wanted to weep with the relief of discovering his wife had missed him. She was holding him and kissing him like she was never going to let him go. Though they were many hundreds of miles from Anchorage, he experienced a sudden sense of coming home.

CHAPTER 28: MORNING AFTER

JACEY

Jacey awoke to the scent of fresh-brewed coffee with a hint of vanilla beans. "Mmm," she mumbled into the sheets, rolling to her back and stretching languorously.

"Morning, beautiful." Luca raised his mug, gorgeous as usual in a black t-shirt and distressed jeans. He wore one of his intense, hard-to-read looks.

How could he be so deadpan when every organ inside her body was blushing at the memory of the night they'd spent together?

She stretched again. "What time is it?"

"Almost nine."

That late?

She sat up with a cry of dismay. "You shouldn't have let me sleep so long. I have to be at rehearsals by 10:00."

"You were exhausted, *cara*." He treated her to

one of his maddening self-satisfied smiles. They both knew he was part of the reason she'd been so exhausted last night.

She threw off the covers and bounded to her bare feet, refusing to be baited. "I'm a horrible person for sleeping in. Poor Race. He hardly knows his mother. I should be spending every possible moment with him."

Luca's dark eyes glinted with pleasure and approval. "And you will. Over breakfast, *carina*."

Jacey gritted her teeth, dashing for the bathroom. *Easy for you to make light of the time. You get to see him every day.* "I just need to zip through the shower and dress. Oh!" She clutched her head. "I forgot. My clothes are on the tour bus. I'm doomed!"

"Was," Luca supplied smoothly. "I had them brought up a few minutes ago."

"You are the best!" As maddening as her husband could be sometimes, she had to hand it to him. He thought of everything.

"I know." He hooked an arm around her waist and kissed her thoroughly.

Fifteen minutes later, she was sitting on the leather sofa in their private lounge area and had the chubby Race clutched against her shoulder.

"You're an armful, sweet stuff!" she exclaimed. "Such a sturdy little thing."

"Built like a linebacker," Luca agreed. There was

a satisfied sound to his voice that was nearly lost in Jacey's squeal.

"Look at these dimples. Oh, my gosh, Luca! He even has dimples on the tops of his feet."

"You can thank Colette for that. Britt caught her sneaking a few teaspoons of rice cereal into his bottle a couple of weeks ago, and *'Voila!'* as she likes to say. He is more content than ever and sleeps through the night now."

"Oh, my little angel." Jacey bent her head to kiss Race's belly. "Don't grow up too fast. Save a little bit of it for me to see, will you?"

Bless his heart! Her son was the only reason she and Luca were together. She couldn't afford to have the years fly by too quickly. Not before she had the chance to make her husband fall as hard for her as she had for him.

Her gut told her they'd made more than a little progress last night. At least, she hoped so.

"You're very quiet over there," Luca observed, parking himself on an ottoman in front of her.

"Just thinking." She pressed her lips to Race's silky spray of hair. He smelled of lotion, baby powder, and preciousness.

"About?" he probed, caressing her knee through her leather pants.

How much I love you. How much I wish you loved me in return.

The alarm on her watch sounded, giving her an

excuse to avoid a direct answer. "I have to head to rehearsals. We'll only get a short break before the concert tonight, so there's no point in hanging around. I know you need to get back home for work."

"Unfortunately."

It was a single word, and she was probably reading way too much into it, but Jacey's heart lightened at the knowledge he wasn't in a hurry to depart.

She stood. "Thank you again for coming and bringing Race."

"You're welcome." They stood at the same time. He kissed the top of Race's head first then caught Jacey's mouth in a lingering kiss. "We will see you again in two weeks."

Two weeks. Her heart sank. It sounded like an eternity.

Jacey found herself counting not just the days, but the hours, until she could return home to Luca and Race. Everyone remarked on the change in her. Lady Rock, the band members, even Chance Biggers who called her the following evening.

"You sound happy, love," he crowed. "And I have some news that's going to make you even happier."

Jacey was only half listening as she scrolled through the latest pictures of Race on her electronic tablet. Luca had sent them only minutes earlier.

"Lady Rock is extending your segment of the tour. They've enjoyed above-average attendance in the Central U.S. and she credits it to your opening number."

Extending the tour! Her agent's words finally permeated her thoughts. Her fingers froze on the electronic tablet. "How much longer?"

"Three more weeks. Not nearly long enough. I was hoping she would include you in the northeastern segment of the tour, but she hasn't responded to my inquiries."

"How long would that be?" Jacey's heart continued to sink.

"Another eight weeks after the afore-mentioned three."

Absolutely not. "I can't," she declared quickly, firmly.

"Why not?"

"I need to get home."

"Is that CEO husband of yours missing his lovely Maddox bride?"

She caught her breath sharply. Chance had all but called her a trophy wife. Was her ugly secret that obvious to a man who barely knew her? "I just had a baby," she pointed out. "I miss my son."

"Of course you do, love, but he's in excellent hands. That's what nannies are for, right?"

It was how Jacey had been raised, that's for sure. Anger churned in her gut. "No. It's what mothers are for. I will agree to the three-week extension, but I will not be joining Lady Rock for the northeastern segment of her tour. Please do not book me for anything more than standalone concerts for the rest of the year."

"You're making a terrible mistake," Chance exploded. "I know what I'm talking about."

"I trust that you do, but I know my limits, too, and I ask that you respect them."

"Your husband supports the tour, Jacey, if that's what is worrying you. It's natural to become homesick on these long road trips, but there's no need to worry about things on the home front. I assure you that Luca Calcagni is proud of his superstar wife. He bragged all about it on a local television station this morning."

"Really?" Jacey was aghast. Luca normally avoided the paparazzi like the plague. "Which one?"

"Channel three. I'll send you the replay. He's proud of the chance he took on hiring you. Proud of what you've made of yourself. Proud of you landing your first concert tour so soon after delivering a baby. He said he wouldn't change one thing."

Not one thing? Not even her long absence from home? Chance's words sucked the wind out of Jacey's lungs.

"You pay me good money to advise you on this stuff, and I'm telling you this is your big break, J.C. Crew, overnight superstar extraordinaire. Opportunities like these don't happen to everyone."

Jacey had said the very same thing to Luca a few

months ago. At the time, she hadn't realized the enormous consequences of getting what she wanted. Or the personal cost.

She was living her dreams, but she wasn't nearly as happy as she imagined she would be. She wasn't sure if she had what it took to survive three additional weeks away from the two people in the world she loved the most, much less the other eight weeks Chance was demanding she consider. But if her singing career made Luca as proud and as happy as Chance claimed, she would make the best of her circumstances or go down trying.

CHAPTER 29: RUNNING INTERFERENCE

LUCA

Luca frowned at the number flashing on his phone. It was Chance Biggers. As thrilled as he was with the man's success in launching Jacey's career, he was really starting to despise the guy who'd taken his wife away from him. It was petty and unfair to feel that way, but that didn't alter the sentiment broiling through Luca's gut. Apparently he wasn't beyond being petty, selfish and a thousand other uncomplimentary adjectives where the proximity of his wife was concerned.

He connected the line with a suppressed snarl. "Calcagni speaking."

"Mr. Calcagni! It's Chance Biggers down in Nashville, the luckiest agent in the world to be representing J.C. Crew."

Luca's first concern was for his wife. "Is everything okay with her?"

Chance gave one of his jarring, too-loud laughs. "Is everything okay? You tell me. You're the one with the amazingly talented wife who's shining with the stars tonight. I'm just the one who negotiates the contracts, the big advances, and all the other minor details." His voice clearly indicated those details were anything but minor. "And I'm about to make your night with the latest news I have to share."

I seriously doubt it, but lay it on me, champ. "I'm listening." His tone was more terse than he intended.

"Everybody in Lady Rock's entourage loves J.C. Crew. No surprise there, sir. And the two of them have grown close during the tour. A beautiful friendship that I foresee opening up a lot more opportunities."

Chance seemed to be expecting some sort of response.

"Like what?" Luca's voice was dry.

"Lady Rock wants to extend Jacey's tour another three weeks, and your wife was delighted to accept. She couldn't believe it. For her, it's all about the music. But between us businessmen, we know that means more money, more exposure, and a broader listening base for her amazing songs."

Luca settled deeper in his leather swivel chair behind his home office desk, too stunned to respond right away. Jacey wasn't coming home for an additional three weeks. By choice. And she hadn't even bothered calling home to discuss it with him first.

Breathe through it, man. It was a shot in the chest. One that left a gaping hole.

He mustered up his voice. "I appreciate all you're doing for her, Chance. She deserves every bit of her success."

"Yes, she does. She's an incredibly special woman. The kind most agents only dream of finding. It's an honor to represent her, sir. A true honor."

Luca was only half listening while staring up at his bamboo ceiling. His mind was already leaping ahead to his next move.

He must have been wrong again. Though exhausted and rundown from her recent baby delivery and hectic schedule, Jacey was happy enough on the road to extend her tour another three whole weeks. The homesickness he thought he saw in her was no more than wishful thinking on his part. He was losing his wife. Plain and simple. Losing her — not to another man as he originally feared — but to her career.

"Mr. Calcagni? Are you still on the line, sir?"

"I'm here. Is there anything else?"

"Isn't that enough?"

"Good point. Thank you for the call." He disconnected the line before the agent could say anything else.

Weaker men would give up in the face of such odds, but it simply wasn't in Luca's DNA. He never gave up anything worth having without a rip-roaring fight, and he didn't plan to this time — no matter what it cost him or how badly he might lose in the end.

He hadn't gotten to where he was as the CEO of a Fortune 500 company at age thirty-four by being a pushover. He had at least one last card in his deck to play, and he intended to play it well. His entire future and happiness was at stake.

He cornered his secretary the next morning in her office. "I need you to clear my schedule starting this Friday."

LeAnne tossed her lunch sack in the mini fridge on a low cabinet between her desk and the wall. "For how long, sir?"

"Fourteen days."

Her back straightened. "That won't be easy, sir."

"No, it won't, and I wouldn't ask it of you if it wasn't important and completely necessary."

"Very well, sir."

"If there is anyone you don't feel comfortable rescheduling, feel free to put them through to me."

"I appreciate that, sir, but I hope I don't have to trouble you."

"It's no trouble. Our clients are worth it." So was Jacey. She was more important than all of them put together.

Don, Colette, and Britt were shocked to hear they would all be present for the final three weeks of Jacey's tour. Race would be coming, too. The way

Luca saw it? They were Jacey's home team. Not him, alone. She needed to see how much everyone in his household loved, adored, and supported her collectively.

Only Merl would remain behind. She would oversee the commencement of the construction on Jacey's new music studio, a soundproof room complete with recording capabilities. He couldn't wait to unveil it to her.

But first, he had to convince his wife to come home.

CHAPTER 30: PAID IN FULL

JACEY

Jacey took the stage on Friday, the first night of her extended tour, unsure how much longer she could endure the constant grind of celebrity life. The stage lights were giving her the start of a headache, and her lack of sleep the night before was making her lightheaded.

As she cast what she hoped was an adoring smile on her screaming fans, her heart skipped a few beats. Standing in the front row directly below the stage stretched a line of familiar faces — Don, Colette, Britt, and Luca who was beaming one of his challenging smiles up at her.

She swayed in her heels as a wave of dizziness shook her. *I must be dreaming.* But no. They were real. For whatever reason, her family was here in the flesh. They'd travelled all the way from Anchorage to Colorado Springs to watch her perform!

Jacey wasn't about to let them down. Digging deep inside herself, she forced her mind back to the performance and took a long breath.

She closed her eyes and let the opening notes of *Without You* transport her into the song. She sang of hopes and dreams, ambitions, and young love. She reminded her audience of what it felt like to be nineteen again. Invincible. Standing beneath a sky with no limits. Then she transitioned into the verse about broken dreams, bruised hearts, and decisions that came with consequences. She sang of atonement, redemption, and second chances.

With a quick spin on her platform heels, she signaled the band to follow her lead. Serge nodded grimly, but he complied and pounded through a preparatory sequence.

She smiled her thanks at him as she began the lines to a new verse. Bits and pieces of it had been floating through her head for days. She hadn't taken the time to write them down, but she'd hummed through them enough to memorize them. This time she sang about love springing out of nowhere, like a blade of grass pushing its way through the sidewalk. Of new beginnings rising from the ashes like a phoenix.

The words flowed through her, unedited yet perfect for the moment.

She sang directly to her husband; and for the

space of several heartbeats, they were the only two people in the room.

So what if her love showed through her music? She was done playing games. From now on, he was taking all of her or none of her. She could no longer compartmentalize her feelings for him and play at being married part-time. She'd tried on that pair of shoes, and they didn't fit her. She would either be free to love him with her entire heart, or she was walking away. For good, this time.

The audience was already on their feet, but their response to the new verse was immediate and tangible. They jumped up and down, waving in a frenzy as recognition dawned that they were being treated to a whole new verse of her number one hit song.

Jacey blew kisses to them at the end of her sequence and ran laughing and joyful from the stage, more exhilarated than she'd ever been while performing. She'd given tonight's performance her absolute best. She'd poured the very essence of who she was into the song, confessing to the world she was a woman in love. It was both humbling and liberating.

Lady Rock winked at her and kissed her cheek as she whirled past her in a flash of silver sequins and vanilla perfume. "That was amazing," she purred.

Jacey fled to her dressing room, too excited to feel the ground beneath her feet. She slammed the door shut and leaned against it, panting with her eyes closed and a hand pressed to her heart.

"Jacey."

It was her husband's voice. She would recognize it any time, anywhere.

Her eyelids flew open to scan the dimly lit room. Luca rose from her makeup chair and approached to stand in front of her.

"Luca? What are you doing here? When I saw you and Don and the others were down there —"

"I couldn't stay away. Not a single day longer."

There was no mistaking the urgency in her husband's voice, or the adoration. Jacey hardly dared to breathe. Or hope.

"I am sorry if this comes as an inconvenience to your new career, but you deserve to know I'm in love with you." She could hardly believe the vulnerability she saw in Luca's face or the uncertainty she heard in his voice. Most of all, she couldn't believe what he was saying.

He loved her? It was her highest castle-in-the-clouds dream come true.

"Luca!" she gasped, wanting to believe him more than anything she'd ever wanted in her life. The hand she held to her chest crept to her throat.

"I'm hoping it's something you can accept. Something we can work out despite the feelings you have for my brother."

Her feelings for whom? Jacey's brain couldn't register anything Luca was saying beyond the part about loving her. *He loves me.* She slumped against the door, dazed.

He took her hand and pressed it to his cheek. The vanity lights twinkled behind his head like stars. "I know I haven't always been the easiest man to live with, and that's probably not going to change. All I can promise is to love you with every part of me. Forever and always."

She was still too stunned to speak.

"I asked you a few months ago to be mine for the next eighteen years. Well, I have a different request to make tonight. Be mine, Mrs. Calcagni. For the rest of our lives."

She clapped a hand over her mouth, tears prickling behind her lids.

"Don't cry, sweetheart. I can't bear it."

"They're happy tears," she choked, flinging herself into his arms at last.

They closed around her, and his triumphant chuckle sounded in her ear. "Does that mean you're willing to renegotiate the terms of our original agreement?"

She couldn't believe how anxious he sounded. "I can't believe you feel the need to ask."

"I'm a businessman. I like to make things official."

"Oh, Luca! I fell for you the first time you kissed me. I've spent every day since then trying to hide it from you, because I didn't think you felt the same way."

His hand was in her hair, drawing her closer until her face rested against his heart. "And here I was worried I was going to have to spend the rest of my life competing with a ghost. Or your career."

"That's plain crazy." But was it? She herself had been jealous of sweet little Britt not too long ago. "I'm yours, Luca. I've been yours since the day you married me."

"For me, it was nine years ago," he confessed. "I fell for your smile and your laugh out there on the beach and vowed to teach you a lesson for being such a heartless tease."

"I was completely shameless, wasn't I?" Her tone was rueful.

"You still are," he assured with a chuckle.

"Then let's be shameless together." She slid her hands up his chest and tugged his head down to hers.

"I like the way you negotiate, Mrs. Calcagni." His mouth moved over hers, less hurried and less desperate than the last time they'd come together, but no less potent. It was a kiss teaming with hope and promise. A kiss that sparked with the same hopeless yearning for each other that had been between them from the start.

"I will always love you, *mi princesa*," he declared huskily between kisses.

Jacey was in no hurry to leave the dressing room, but her ringing phone transported the two of them back to reality all too soon.

It was Waverly. "I don't suppose you know something about the whereabouts of the CEO of Genesis & Sons?"

Jacey smiled. "He and I are engaged in, er, a negotiation here in Colorado Springs."

"I like the sound of that." Her husband's grandmother laughed in delight, sounding woefully unashamed of whatever it was she had interrupted. "As soon as the two of you come to an agreement with that, ahem, negotiation of yours, I'd be tickled to death if you would attend a little after-hours celebration with us."

"You're in town, too?" Jacey thought she might die of happiness right then and there.

"These old bones don't enjoy traveling the way they used to, but Edric and I weren't about to miss out on the chance to hear our daughter-in-law sing on tour."

Our daughter-in-law. They'd traveled hundreds of miles for her! Not Race and not Luca this time. *Her!* She should have known better. The Calcagnis weren't like the Maddoxes. Though she'd misjudged them way too many times, they were here as living proof of that fact.

Waverly and Edric had done more than make dinner reservations. They'd rented a cozy little Irish pub to celebrate Jacey's successful tour. The whole restaurant, as it turned out. Rhys and Knox were there, too, as well as Greyson and Alora.

It was a perfect end to a perfect evening, made even more perfect by the fact Luca never once left her side. He and Jacey entered the pub with their hands intertwined. He didn't let go of her hand even when they were eating. When they stepped onto the rustic dance floor together, he brazenly sealed his mouth over hers, branding her as his own in front of every family member and employee present.

Jacey kissed him back, no longer caring who discovered how much she was in love with her husband. She'd earned his love and his trust and considered every ounce of the blood, sweat, and tears it had taken to be worth it.

And she was secure in the knowledge that her debt to his family had finally been paid.

Like this book? Leave a review now!

Want to read about Don Kappelman's slightly crazy search for his own happily ever after? Keep turning for a peek at
Black Tie Billionaires #2:

HER BILLIONAIRE BODYGUARD
Available in eBook and paperback on Amazon + free in Kindle Unlimited!

Much love,
Jo

SNEAK PREVIEW: HER BILLIONAIRE BODYGUARD

Don Kappelman was the kind of guy people tended to notice. A guy who stood six feet, three inches tall could hardly expect to hide in a crowd. Plus, he possessed the shoulders, chest, and arms of a bodybuilder, though he'd never pursued that line of work.

He was also the kind of guy people kept their distance from. No doubt it had something to do with his no-nonsense appearance — the closely shaved sides of his head, a throwback from his Special Forces days, though recently he'd been letting the top grow out. People also tended to be a little put off by the faint scar that ran from the corner of his left eyelid to his ear. Oh, and the few folks he associated with claimed he rarely smiled. Or made small talk. His come-no-closer image suited him just fine, though. The way he saw it, guys like him made the world a safer place so that others could live in peace and happiness with their loved ones.

As the right-hand man of CEO Luca Calcagni, he wasn't looking to make a large circle of friends. Mr. Calcagni paid well, and the job offered plenty of opportunities to fly, which allowed Don to maintain his coveted pilot's license. Additionally, it left him with the time he needed to pick up private security gigs on weekends and holidays.

Like the one he was working tonight...

He scanned the crowded ballroom of the Gjoa Haven Conference Center from his second-story balcony post. The hip-high railings were made of glass reinforced with tiny steel rods to unhamper the breathtaking view of the center's three-story hanging gardens and cleverly crafted water features.

It was the annual Christmas charity ball, and nearly all the poshest families in Anchorage were in attendance. As Don watched the festive couples twirling their way across the dance floor, he didn't envy the men wearing long-tailed tuxedo jackets, bow ties, and cummerbunds. Though he typically wore a black suit to events like this, his choice of clothing possessed much more useful accoutrements like a tie pin that contained a hidden camera and inner jacket pockets roomy enough to hold a pair of pistols.

The voice of his co-worker, Grant Whitlock, wafted in clipped tones through his concealed earpiece. "Check your two o'clock. Tall brunette. Killer red dress. Can't get a good angle on the cameraman behind her. Seems to be hovering a little too close."

Don's new earpiece wasn't as snug of a fit as he liked. He tapped it to seat it better inside his ear canal. "Got 'em." His blood boiled at what he saw. The chucklehead with the camera was using a second lens with an extension rod in the attempt to get close enough to peek under the woman's hem. "Looks like we have ourselves a peeper." After more than ten years of service as a soldier and another six years working security, Don had met his fair share of bad hombres. In his opinion, peepers ranked down there at the lowest level of scum.

Grant made a snarling noise. "You want me to bounce him?"

"Nah. I'll do it." Don was already moving in the direction of the escalator. The cold weather had been making his bum knee ache, keeping him in a funk all afternoon. Feeling more than ready to pummel someone who was deserving of it, he took the rolling stairs two at a time.

People assumed he worked the extra hours at jobs like this for the money, but that wasn't the case. With no wife or children, he'd been able to save the lion's share of his paychecks over the years. His desire to serve and protect stemmed from an entirely different reason — a failure, actually. The failure to protect his high school girlfriend from a pair of driveby shooters the night of their homecoming dance. It was seventeen years ago, but it still haunted him. And defined him. And drove him.

The shooters had never been caught, but Don had been serving and protecting others ever since.

Trying to mask his limp, he drew nearer to the brunette in the red dress. She glanced up and looked directly at him. That's when her identity hit him. She was Bailey Maddox, one of the two sisters of Jacey Maddox Calcagni, his boss's wife.

Don couldn't have been more surprised. Bailey Maddox was like a well-kept secret, one of those uber-wealthy women who were rarely seen in public. She lived and breathed behind tinted glass windows, security gates, and a bevy of bodyguards. Such were the risks of being raised as the daughter of billionaires — always having to live in fear of being snatched up for ransom.

His gaze narrowed on her as he strode in her direction. Her normal entourage of bodyguards was notably absent. What was she thinking to come alone to an event like this? Putting herself on such display? Allowing herself to be so exposed? Clearly, one scumbag in particular was taking severe advantage of the opportunity she presented, but there were far worse dangers to a lady in her designer shoes than peepers. Though Don had never made the woman's acquaintance, she was a

VIP at tonight's charity event which made her failure to travel with proper protection his responsibility.

Bailey's dark eyes glistened with curiosity and interest at Don's approach, which utterly intrigued him. Most women would have backed away a few steps at his grimmer-than-usual expression he'd purposefully plastered on to intimidate her stalker. To her credit, she gave a hasty glance around her as if trying to determine who he was really eyeballing.

He reached the young beauty and stepped neatly around her. Pretending to lose his balance, he reached out and caught the cameraman's extension stick. At the same time, he brought his large shoe solidly down on the lens that was resting half-under Bailey Maddox's red skirts.

She whirled around and yanked the red silk away from the two men. "Excuse me. I, ah...oh!" she breathed in mortification as her gaze fell on the destroyed camera lens.

Don clamped a hand on the man's arm. "If you'll come this way, sir." He none-too-gently pivoted the creep in the direction of the entrance doors where the North Cove Security (NCS) team was tracking everyone who entered and exited the ballroom.

A bead of sweat broke out on the balding man's brow. He attempted to brush Don's hand from his arm. "You broke my camera!" When he failed to loosen Don's grip, he paled a few degrees. "I don't know who you are, but I think there's been a terrible misunderstanding here."

Don pinned him with a look that tended to make most people tremble. The man visibly shrank within the confines of his too-tight brown suit. "I work for NCS, and I will be most happy to let you explain the misunderstanding to the authorities."

"There's no reason to manhandle me this way," the man blustered, still trying to wriggle loose from Don's grasp. He was unsuccessful. "I have rights, you know."

Don swung his head back in Bailey Maddox's direction. "I'll ensure all camera data is confiscated and all unauthorized images destroyed, ma'am." He hated the fact she'd been subjected to such ill treatment at an event that was supposed to be focused on altruism. Is that what had brought her here this evening? Philanthropy? It was a noble cause, one that his billionaire boss, Mr. Calcagni, was certainly heavily invested in.

Her porcelain complexion turned chalky, making her red-lacquered lips stand out in stark contrast. "I, ah...thank you." Her voice shook a little.

He quickly scanned the room around her and again failed to detect the presence of any bodyguards, which didn't add up. "Just doing my job, ma'am." He made a mental note to check on her after he ensured the bozo in his grasp was removed from the premises. It was the least he could do for the sister of his boss's wife. Mr. Calcagni himself would expect no less if he found out about it.

Their gazes clashed and held, and he was struck by the sweetness and vulnerability he read there. Her expression wasn't at all like the one her queenly oldest sister, Alora Maddox, wore; nor did it contain the confidence and charisma of her pop-singing-sensation of a youngest sister, Jacey Maddox Calcagni, also known by her celebrity handle as J.C. Crew. If Don had to sum up Bailey Maddox in two words, it would be *demure* and *ladylike*. Not that he was an expert on women. He hadn't been in a serious relationship since he'd lost his highschool sweetheart.

Ignoring the blustering cameraman's tirade of lame excuses, Don swiftly steered him to the NCS security checkpoint. By the time Don and his co-workers turned the man and his equipment over to the authorities, however, Bailey Maddox had left the ballroom.

Squashing an unaccountable burst of disappointment, Don returned to his post on the second-floor balcony to give him a better vantage point. He rocked from his heels to his toes, stretching out the aching tendons in his left knee. The pain was a reminder of the crushing set of injuries he'd endured on his last mission in the Special Forces. It was also a reminder that he was one of the lucky ones who'd survived the explosion. They'd made a difference that night, he and his comrades. Ultimately, they'd rescued nearly thirty Americans who were being held hostage by a ring of drug lords. Don had no regrets. Even if he'd known ahead of time that the injuries he would sustain that night would end his military career, he would have volunteered all over again for the mission. Some things in life were simply worth it.

A voice crackled across his earpiece. It was Grant, again. "Your priestly presence is needed at the front desk."

Don snorted at Grant's reference to his lack of a social life. His solitary existence was one of choice. "Heading there now. Want to tell me what's going on?"

Grant chuckled. "Not in a million years. I do, however, want to borrow those lucky socks you must be wearing tonight."

Shaking his head, Don returned to the main floor and carefully maneuvered his way across the busy ballroom. To his surprise, none other than Bailey Maddox was waiting for him. She was tapping one expensive-looking blood-red sandal against the black and white floor tiles.

"Mr. Kappelman?" Her voice was gracious and musical as she finished spinning around to face him. It was also a bit on the regal side, not quite queenly like her oldest sister, rather like a younger, sweeter princess greeting her subjects.

He nodded to acknowledge her address. "May I help you, ma'am?"

"I sure hope so," she sighed. Worry flitted across her classically lovely features. "As the new Vice President of Marketing at DRAW Corporation, I've been at my wits end the last few days, interviewing candidates and trying to get the right people in the right places on my team."

Don wasn't interested in a tête-à-tête with a socialite, not even one as stunningly attractive as Bailey Maddox. As far as he was concerned, she could trade gossip with her girlfriends over tea. He had a ballroom full of guests to get back to protecting. "Ma'am, if this doesn't involve security—"

"It does," she assured hastily. "I'm sorry if I'm rambling. I was just trying to give you a little background as to why I am short of a security detail this evening. Or was," she pierced him with a hopeful look, "until you showed up."

He inclined his head. "You are welcome, ma'am."

"I'd like to hire you in a more permanent capacity," she announced in a breathless voice.

Though he should be wary of anyone bearing the last name of Maddox, her nervous tone had the effect of rousing his protective instincts. "Have you contacted NCS, ma'am?" He spread his hands, preparing to explain in the kindest terms possible that he wasn't in the market for a new job — certainly not one that would require him to serve a rising executive full-time. "They're the ones who contracted me to pull security at tonight's event. Although I enjoy doing my part to ensure public safety, working these gigs is nothing more than a side hustle."

"Don't worry, Mr. Kappelman. I am well aware of your arrangement with Mr. Calcagni and your loyalty to him and my sister."

Really? Don's brows shot up. That was news to him, considering Bailey Maddox hadn't made it to her youngest sister's wedding or her subsequent baby delivery. Or to any of Jacey's singing performances, for that matter, during her recent concert tour with Lady Rock. Why would the woman standing before him pretend any devotion to her estranged sister for his benefit?

Watching his expression, she sighed. "No doubt you've heard nothing good about me, considering my family's reputation and their ongoing feud with the Calcagnis." Bailey Maddox's dark hazel eyes searched his features, as if trying to peel her way layer-by-layer to some sort of revelation from him. "The truth is, I love my sisters. And, despite the unfortunate feud we inherited, I think I have the right to have a relationship with them if I want to," she grimaced, "which I do."

Not sure why you're telling me all this, but okay. Don inclined his head again to acknowledge Bailey's point, wondering how any of this concerned him.

"And there lies the problem, Mr. Kappelman. Every time I attempt to contact Jacey, I run into...interference."

"What sort of interference?" he asked, his suspicions churning. He had no interest in playing the part of a go-between in their ongoing family drama.

"Anonymous phone threats, online hacks, vehicle malfunctions, you name it. At first, I chalked it up to bad luck or a series of coincidences that were keeping me from my youngest sister, but..." She paused to glance around them, fiddling idly with her skirts.

Threats? Don didn't like the sound of that. "Coincidences don't come in series." He shook his head doubtfully and studied the dark-haired beauty more closely, hoping she wasn't playing some sort of game.

"Exactly," she rejoined with the wave of one perfectly manicured hand. "Something, or someone, is trying to keep me from contacting my sister. I am sure of it!" She sounded genuinely incensed and more than a little alarmed.

If it was a game Bailey Maddox was playing, it was one she was very, very good at it; because, for the life of him, Don's raw instincts were shouting that she was telling the truth. Which contradicted what little he knew about her so far.

Fact. The Maddox and Calcagni dynasties were engaged in a decades-old feud that extended to their competing DRAW and Genesis & Sons mega corporations. Fact. Bailey Maddox had solidly thrown her cards in with the Maddoxes, as evidenced by her recent promotion to VP as well as her five-year estrangement from her youngest sister.

None of which explained why she was attending a Christmas charity event this evening without a bodyguard. A sudden thought struck Don. "Do you think you are in any immediate danger, Miss Maddox?" He kept his voice coolly detached. Though Bailey was in no way his responsibility outside of tonight's event, Mr. Calcagni and his wife might feel differently when they learned about this exchange. Don had best find out as much as he could about Bailey's troubles, so he could report back to them.

"Immediate? No. Danger? Yes." Bailey reached for his arm. "Will you take a stroll with me around the ballroom to discuss my offer of employment, Mr. Kappelman?"

Don's internal radar had kicked into high alert the moment she claimed she was in danger. He was already scanning the vicinity, looking for anything amiss. "It would be my pleasure," he returned in a much blander voice than he was feeling. He glanced down at the delicate fingers Bailey Maddox had wrapped around his forearm, feeling a bit awed that a woman of her social status didn't mind being seen with a regular joe like him. It made no sense, yet he'd be lying if he didn't admit it felt...nice.

A delightful pink color spread across her well-defined cheekbones. She stepped closer to him and wrapped her other hand around his arm. "This is how we would look if I hired you."

He raised a brow at her as they began their promenade around the busy ballroom. "You wish for me to serve as your escort?" That seemed more than a little odd. A beauty like her would have no trouble securing a date for any event he could think of. A real date, not some hired substitute.

"Yes. For an occasional event like tonight's ball. You would need to wear a tuxedo, of course." She scanned his practical, more comfortable suit with critical eyes.

"I'm not much of a fan of tuxedos."

"It would be part of your job. In case you're wondering, Mr. Kappelman, I would cover the expenses of your wardrobe for the duration of the assignment." Her fingers exerted the mildest bit of pressure on his arm as if to offer reassurance.

Her offer amused him. He could well afford a tuxedo, if that's what the job demanded. "Just tell me what you want me to wear. I'm sure I can manage."

"You don't have access to the label I would need you to wear. Trust me."

"Oh?" Don was mildly annoyed at Bailey's

assumptions about what he could and could not afford.

"Yes, it's a by-appointment-only, custom line of clothing called Black Tie."

Why am I not surprised? Don resisted the urge to roll his eyes. He'd seen that label on a few of Luca Calcagni's expensive-looking blazers. Don had never thought much about it, thinking it was yet another indulgence of the rich and famous. "Never heard of them," he lied, more curious than ever about this particular brand.

"Of course you haven't." Bailey sounded aghast. "They're not so much a clothing label as they are," she dropped her voice and glanced around them again, "an exclusive club for billionaires. I imagine Luca Calcagni has told you all about them."

Don's boss had, in fact, *not* told him any such thing. Then again, Luca Calcagni had never spared much time for socializing. That was something they had in common. The man had always been too busy running Genesis & Sons. "If I agree to this arrangement," though Don definitely had his reservations about working for a Maddox, "how soon would you need me to get started?" The first person he'd run the proposition past would be Mr. Calgani. The second person would be his wife. They deserved to know that Jacey's next older sister was trying to contract the services of a member of their household staff, and Don's loyalties were to Calcagnis first — always.

"How does tonight sound?" Bailey looked anxious. "As in right now?"

Don frowned in speculation. "Does this have something to do with the danger you mentioned you are in?" In which case, he would have no choice but to assist her first and inform the Calcagnis afterward.

"Yes." Without any warning, Bailey halted their progress and stepped directly in front of him to slide her arms around his neck.

"What are you doing?" He was immediately assailed with her jasmine scent and the warmth of her touch. It was a novel experience, considering how long it had been since he'd been on his last date. Something told him things were about to get complicated. Correction. He was dealing with a Maddox. Things were already complicated.

"Giving our new arrangement a test run. You'll be appropriately compensated, of course." She stretched on her tiptoes and tipped her porcelain perfect face up to meet his stunned expression. Her ruby lips swayed closer. "Believe me when I say my safety tonight very much depends on how convincing you are with what comes next."

"Why? What exactly do you want from me, Miss Maddox?" Though a thousand red flags were waving inside his head, Don felt powerless to resist the siren pleading in her soulful eyes.

"Just one little kiss, Mr. Kappelman."

I hope you enjoyed this excerpt from
Her Billionaire Bodyguard
*Available in eBook and paperback on Amazon +
FREE to Kindle Unlimited subscribers!*

Complete series — read them all!
**Her Billionaire Boss
Her Billionaire Bodyguard
Her Billionaire Secret Admirer
Her Billionaire Best Friend
Her Billionaire Geek
Her Billionaire Double Date**

*Much love,
Jo*

NOTE FROM JO

Guess what? I have some Bonus Content to share with everyone who joins my mailing list. You'll receive a special bonus scene for each book I write.

You'll also hear about my next new book as soon as it's out (*plus you get a free sweet romance story just for signing up*). Woohoo!

As always, thank you for reading and loving my books!

JOIN CUPPA JO READERS!

If you're on Facebook, please join my group, Cuppa Jo Readers. Don't miss out on the giveaways + all the sweet and swoon-worthy cowboys!

https://www.facebook.com/groups/CuppaJoReaders

FREE BOOK!

Don't forget to join my mailing list for new releases, freebies, special discounts, and Bonus Content. Plus, you get a FREE sweet romance book for signing up!

https://BookHip.com/JNNHTK

SNEAK PREVIEW: WINDS OF CHANGE

***G**etting hired as a high school principal in her hometown is her biggest dream come true, except for one small detail — her ex is the new head of security.*

Ten years ago, Hope Remington graduated with honors from Heart Lake High, while Josh Hawling was...well, bad news on the south side of town. And now she's returning to unite their two rival high schools under one roof. She can't figure out how a guy who spent more time in the principal's office than in class during his teen years managed to convince the school board he can eliminate the student gang problem while coaching a bunch of farm boys into a football team that'll make the playoffs.

Though Hope discovers she feels safer having

Josh on their crime-ridden campus, she's still not looking forward to her daily encounters with the cocky head of security. Or being socked in the heart all over again by his devastating smile. Or having to finally face her unwanted attraction to him that might have kindled into a lot more if she'd never left Texas in the first place.

Grab your copy of
HEART LAKE #1: Winds of Change
Available in eBook, paperback, and hard cover on Amazon + FREE in Kindle Unlimited!

Read them all!
Winds of Change
Song of Nightingales
Perils of Starlight
Return of Miracles
Thousands of Gifts
Race of Champions
Storm of Secrets
Season of Angels
Clash of Hearts
Mountain of Fire
Mountain of Mercy

Much love,
Jo

SNEAK PREVIEW: MR. NOT RIGHT FOR HER

A scarred ranch manager is determined to remain single, but the lovely klutz he hires trips up his carefully laid plans in this sweet, grumpy-sunshine romance.

Asher Cassidy hasn't dated since the freak fire that scarred one side of his face, something his interfering family refuses to accept. They're always on the lookout for his perfect match. Fortunately, their newest ranch hand agrees to pose as his fake girlfriend at the upcoming hoedown to provide a much-needed buffer between him and their latest matchmaking attempts.

Landing a summer job in the country was supposed to give Bella Johnson a much-needed break from teaching. However, ranching ends up being a bigger challenge than expected for a klutz like her.

She's constantly tripping into her sarcastic cowboy boss, which somehow lands her a fake date with him. Falling for him in the process is *not* supposed to happen, leaving her with two choices — either find a way to un-fall in love with him...or convince him to make their fake relationship a real one.

Grab your copy of
Mr. Right But She Doesn't Know It
Available in eBook and paperback on Amazon + free in Kindle Unlimited!

Read them all!
Mr. Not Right for Her
Mr. Maybe Right for Her
Mr. Right But She Doesn't Know It
Mr. Right Again for Her
Mr. Yeah, Right. As If...

Much love,
Jo

SNEAK PREVIEW: ACCIDENTAL HERO

Matt Romero was single again, and this time he planned to stay that way.

Feeling like the world's biggest fool, he gripped the steering wheel of his white Ford F-150, cruising up the sunny interstate toward Amarillo. He had an interview in the morning, so he was arriving a day early to get the lay of the land. That, and he was anxious to put as many miles as possible between him and his ex.

It was one thing to have allowed himself to become blinded by love. It was another thing entirely to have fallen for the stupidest line in a cheater's handbook.

Cat sitting. I actually allowed her to talk me into cat sitting! Plus, he'd collected his fiancée's mail and carried her latest batch of Amazon deliveries into her condo.

It wasn't that he minded helping out the woman he planned to spend the rest of his life with. What he minded was that she wasn't in New York City on business like she'd claimed. *Nope.* As it turned out, she was nowhere near the Big Apple. It had simply been her cover story for cheating on him, the first lie in a long series of lies.

To make matters worse, she'd recently talked Matt into leaving the Army for her, a decision he'd probably regret for the rest of his life now that she'd broken their engagement and moved on with someone else.

Leaving me single, jobless, and —

The scream of sirens jolted Matt back to the present. A glance in his rearview mirror confirmed his suspicions. He was getting pulled over. *For what?* A scowl down at his speedometer revealed he was cruising at no less than 95 mph. *Whoa!* It was a good twenty miles over the posted speed limit. *Okay, this is bad.* He'd be lucky if he didn't lose his license over this — his fault entirely for driving distracted without his cruise control on. *My day just keeps getting better.*

Slowing and pulling his truck over to the shoulder, he coasted to a stop and waited. And waited. And waited some more. A peek in his side mirror showed the cop was still sitting in his car and talking on his phone.

Oh, come on! Just give me my ticket already.

To stop the pounding between his temples, Matt reached for the red cooler he'd propped on the passenger seat and pulled out a can of soda. He popped the tab and tipped it up to chug down a shot of caffeine. He hadn't slept much the last couple of nights.

Before he could take a second sip, movement in the rearview mirror caught his attention. He watched as the police officer finally opened his door, unfolded his large frame from the front seat of his black SUV, and stood. However, he continued talking on his phone instead of walking Matt's way.

Are you kidding me? Matt swallowed a dry chuckle and took another swig of his soda. It was a good thing he'd hit the road the day before his interview at the Pantex nuclear plant. At the rate his day was going, it might take the rest of the afternoon to collect his speeding ticket.

He'd reached the outskirts of Amarillo, only about twenty to thirty miles from his final destination. The exit sign for Hereford was up ahead. Or the Beef Capital of the World, as the small farm town was often called.

He reached across the dashboard to open his glove compartment and fish out his registration card and proof of insurance. His gut told him there wasn't going to be any talking his way out of this one. As a general rule, men in blue didn't sympathize with folks going twenty miles or more over the speed limit.

Digging for his wallet, he pulled out his driver's license. Out of sheer habit, he reached inside the slot where he normally kept his military ID and found it empty. *Right.* He no longer possessed one, which left him with an oddly empty feeling.

He took another gulp of soda and watched as the officer pocketed his cell phone. *Finally! Guess that means it's time to get this party started.* Matt chunked his soda can into the nearest cup holder and stuck his driver's license, truck registration, and insurance card between two fingers. Hitting an automatic button on the door, he lowered his window a few inches and waited.

The guy strode up to Matt's truck window with a bit of a swagger. His tan Stetson was pulled low over his eyes. "License and registration, soldier."

Guess you noticed the Ranger tab on my license plate. Matt wordlessly poked the requested items through the window opening.

"Any reason you're in such a hurry this morning?" the officer mused curiously as he scanned Matt's identification. He was so tall, he had to stoop to peer through the window. Like Matt, he had a dark tan, brown hair, and a goatee. The two of them could've passed as cousins or something.

"Nothing worth hearing, officer." *My problem. Not yours. Don't want to talk about it.* Matt squinted through the glaring sun to read the guy's name on his tag. *McCarty.*

"That's too bad, because I always have plenty of time to chat when I'm writing up such a hefty ticket." Officer McCarty's tone was mildly sympathetic, though it was impossible to read his expression behind his sunglasses. "I clocked you going twenty-two miles over the posted limit, Mr. Romero."

Twenty-two miles? Yeah, that's not good. Not good at all. Matt's jaw tightened, and he could feel the veins in his temples throbbing. It looked like he was going to have to share his story, after all. Maybe, just maybe, the trooper would feel so sorry for him that he'd give him a warning instead of a ticket. It was worth a try, anyway. *If nothing else, it'll give you something to laugh about during your next coffee break.*

"Today was supposed to be my wedding day." He spoke through stiff lips, finding a strange sort of relief in confessing that sorry fact to a perfect stranger. Fortunately, they'd never have to see each other again.

"I'm sorry for your loss." Officer McCarty glanced up from Matt's license to give him what felt like a piercing once over. He was probably trying to gauge if he was telling the truth or not.

"Oh, she's still alive," Matt muttered. "Found somebody else, that's all." He gripped the steering wheel and drummed his thumbs against it. *I'm just the poor fool she cheated on.*

He was so done with dating. At the moment

couldn't imagine ever again putting his heart on the chopping block of love. *Better to be lonely than to let another person destroy you like that.* She'd taken everything from him that mattered — his pride, his dignity, even his career.

"Ouch," Officer McCarty sighed. "Well, here comes the tough part about my job. Despite your reasons for speeding, you were putting lives at risk. Your own included."

"Can't disagree with that." Matt stared straight ahead, past the small spidery nick in his windshield. He'd gotten hit by a rock earlier while passing a semi tractor trailer. It really hadn't been his day. Or his week. Or his year, for that matter. It didn't mean he was going to grovel, though. He'd tried to appeal to the guy's sympathy and failed. The sooner he gave him his ticket, the sooner they could both be on their way.

A massive dump truck on the oncoming side of the highway abruptly swerved into the narrow, grassy median. It was a few hundred yards away, but the front left tire dipped down, *way* down, making the truck pitch heavily to one side.

"Whoa!" Matt shouted, pointing to get Officer McCarty's attention. "That guy looks like he's in trouble!"

Two vehicles on Matt's side of the road passed him in quick succession — a rusty blue van pulling a fifth wheel and a shiny red Dodge Ram.

When Officer McCarty didn't respond, Matt laid on his horn to warn the two drivers, just as the dump truck started to roll. It was like watching a horror movie in slow motion, knowing something bad was about to happen while being helpless to stop it.

The dump truck slammed onto its side and skidded noisily across Matt's lane. The blue van whipped to the right shoulder in a vain attempt to avoid the collision. Matt winced as the van's bumper caught the hood of the skidding dump truck nearly head on, then jack-knifed into the air.

The driver of the red truck was only a few car lengths behind, jamming so hard on its brakes that it left two dark smoking lines of rubber on the pavement. Seconds later, it careened into the median and flipped on its side. It wasn't immediately clear if the red pickup had collided with any part of the dump truck. However, an ominous swirl of smoke seeped from beneath its hood.

For a split second, Matt and Officer McCarty stared in shock at each other. Then the officer shoved Matt's license and registration back through the opening in the window. "Looks like I've got more important things to do than give you a ticket." He sprinted toward his SUV, leaped inside, and gunned it toward the scene of the accident with his lights flashing and sirens blaring. He only drove a short distance before stopping his vehicle and canting it across both lanes to form a makeshift blockade.

Though Matt was no longer in the military, his defend-and-protect instincts kicked in. There was no telling how long it would take the emergency vehicles to arrive, and he didn't like the way the red pickup was smoking. The driver hadn't climbed out of the cab yet, either, which wasn't a good sign.

Officer McCarty reached the blue van first, probably because it was the closest, and assisted a dazed man from one of the back passenger seats. He led him to the side of the road, helped him get seated on a small incline, then jogged back to help the driver exit the van. Unfortunately, the officer was only one man, and this was much bigger than a one-man job.

Following his gut instincts, Matt disengaged his emergency brake and gunned his way up the shoulder, pausing beside the officer's vehicle. Turning off his motor, he leaped from his truck and jogged across the highway to the red pickup. The motor was still running, and the smoke was rising more thickly now.

Whoever was behind the wheel needed to get out immediately before the thing caught fire or exploded. Matt took a flying leap to hop on top of the cab and crawl to the driver's door. It was locked.

Pounding on the window, he shouted at the driver, "You okay in there?"

There was no answer and no movement. Peering closer, he could make out the unmoving figure of a woman. Blonde, pale, and curled to one side. The only thing holding her in place was the strap of a seatbelt around her waist. A trickle of red ran across one cheek.

Matt's survival training kicked in. Crouching over the side of the truck, he quickly assessed the undamaged windshield and decided it wasn't the best entry point. *Too bad.* Because his only other option was to shower the driver with glass. *Sorry, lady!* Swinging a leg, he jabbed the heel of his boot into the section of window nearest the lock. By some miracle, he managed to pop a fist-sized hole instead of shattering the entire pane.

Reaching inside, he unlocked the door and pulled it open. The next part was a little trickier, since he had to reach down, *way* down, to unbuckle the woman and catch her weight before she fell. It would've been easier if she were conscious and able to follow his instructions.

Guess I'll have to do it without any help. An ominous hiss of steam and smoke from beneath the hood stiffened his resolve and made him move faster.

"Come on, lady," he muttered, releasing her seatbelt and catching her slender frame before she fell. With a grunt of exertion, he hefted her free of the mangled cab. Then he half-slid, half hopped back to the ground with her in his arms. As soon as his boots hit the pavement, he took off at a jog.

She was lighter than he'd been expecting. Her upper arm, that his left hand was cupped around, felt desperately thin despite her baggy pink and pla shirt. One long, strawberry blonde braid dangled over her shoulder, and a sprinkle of freckles stood out in stark relief against her pale cheeks.

She didn't so much as twitch as he ran with her, telling him that she was still out cold. He hoped it didn't mean she'd hit her head too hard on impact. Visions of traumatic brain injuries and their long list of complications swarmed through his mind, along with the possibility that he might've just finished moving a woman with a broken neck or back. *Please don't let that be the case, Lord.*

He carried her to the far right shoulder and up a grassy knoll where Officer McCarty was depositing the other injured victims. A dry wind gusted, sending a layer of fine dust in their direction. One prickly, rolling tumbleweed followed. On the other side of the knoll was a rocky canyon wall that went straight up, underscoring the fact that there really hadn't been any way for the hapless van and pickup drivers to avoid the collision. They'd literally been trapped between the canyon and oncoming traffic.

An explosion ricocheted through the air, shaking the ground beneath Matt's feet. On pure instinct, he dove for the grass, using his body to shield the woman in his arms. He used one hand to cradle her head against his chest and his other hand to break their fall as best he could.

A few of the other injured drivers and passengers cried out in fear as smoke billowed around them and blanketed the scene. For the next few minutes, it was difficult to see much, though the wave of ensuing heat had a suffocating feel to it. The woman beneath Matt remained motionless, though he thought he heard her mumble something at one point. He continued to crouch over her, keeping her head cradled beneath his hand. He rubbed his thumb beneath her nose and determined she was still breathing. However, she remained unconscious. He debated what to do next.

A fire engine howled in the distance, making his shoulders slump in relief. Help had finally arrived. More sirens blared, and the area was soon crawling with fire engines, ambulances, and paramedics with stretchers. One walked determinedly in his direction.

"Hi! My name is Star, and I'm here to help you. What's your name, sir?" the EMT worker inquired in a calm, even tone. Her chin-length dark hair was blowing nearly sideways in the wind. She shook her head to knock it away, revealing a pair of snapping dark eyes swimming with concern.

"I'm Sergeant Matt Romero," he informed her out of sheer habit. *Well, maybe no longer the sergeant part.* "Don't worry about me. I'm fine. This woman is not. I don't know her name. She was unconscious when I pulled her out of her truck."

As the curvy EMT stepped closer, Matt could read her name tag. *Corrigan.* "Like I said, I'm here do everything I can to help." Her forehead wrinkled in alarm as she caught sight of the injured woman's face. "Omigosh! Bree?" Tossing her red medical bag on the ground, she slid to her knees beside the two of them. "Oh, Bree, honey!" she sighed, reaching for her pulse.

"I-I..." The woman stirred. Her lashes fluttered a few times against her cheeks. Then they snapped open, revealing two pools of the deepest blue Matt had ever seen. Though glazed with pain, her gaze latched anxiously onto him. "Don't leave me," she pleaded with a hitch in her voice.

There was something oddly personal about the request. Though he was sure they'd never met before, she spoke as if she recognized him. Her confusion tugged at every one of his heartstrings, making him long to grant her request.

"I won't," he promised huskily, hardly knowing what he was saying. In that moment, he probably would have said anything to make the desperate look in her eyes go away.

"I'm not liking her heart rate." Star produced a penlight and flipped it on. Shining it in one of her friend's eyes, then the other, she cried urgently, "Bree? It's me, Star. Can you tell me what happened, hon?"

A shiver worked its way through Bree's too-thin frame. "Don't leave me," she whispered again to Matt, before her eyelids fluttered closed. Another shiver worked its way through her, despite the fact that she was no longer conscious.

"She's going into shock." Star glanced worriedly over her shoulder. "Need a stretcher over here," she called sharply. One was swiftly rolled their way.

Matt helped the EMT lift and deposit their precious burden on it.

"Can you make it to the hospital?" Star asked as he helped push the stretcher toward the nearest ambulance. "Bree seemed pretty insistent about you sticking around."

Matt's eyebrows shot upward in surprise. He hadn't been expecting yet another person he'd never met before to ask him to stick around. "Uh, sure." In her delirium, the injured woman had probably mistaken him for someone else. However, he didn't mind helping out. *Who knows?* Maybe he could give the attending physician some information about her rescue that might prove useful in her treatment.

Or maybe he was just drawn to the fragile-looking Bree for reasons he couldn't explain. Whatever the case, Matt suddenly wasn't feeling in a terrible hurry to hit the road again. Fortunately, he had plenty of extra time built into his schedule before his interview tomorrow. The only real task he had left for the day was finding a hotel room once he reached Amarillo.

"I just need to let Officer McCarty know I'm leaving the scene of the accident." Matt shook head sheepishly. "I kinda hate to admit this, but he had me pulled over for speeding before everything went down here." He waved a hand at the carnage around them. It was a dismal scene, punctuated by twisted metal and scorched pavement. All three mangled vehicles looked like they were totaled.

Star snickered, then seemed to catch herself. "Sorry. That was inappropriate laughter. Very inappropriate laughter."

He shrugged, not the least bit offended. A lot of people laughed when they were nervous or upset, which Star clearly had been since the moment she'd discovered the unconscious woman was a friend. "It was pretty stupid of me to be driving these long, empty stretches of highway without my cruise control on." Especially with the way he'd been brooding non-stop for the past seventy-two hours.

Star shot him a sympathetic look. "Believe me, I'm not judging. Far from it." She reached out to pat Officer McCarty's arm as they passed by him with the stretcher. "The only reason a bunch of us in Hereford don't have a lot more points on our licenses is because we grew up with this sweet guy."

"Oh, no! Is that Bree?" Officer McCarty groaned. He pulled his sunglasses down to take a closer look over the top of his lenses. His stoic expression was gone. In its place was one etched with worry. The personal kind. Like Star, he knew the victim.

"Yeah." Star's pink glossy lips twisted. "She and her brother can't catch a break, can they?"

Since two more paramedics converged on them to help lift Bree's stretcher into the ambulance, Matt paused to face the trooper who'd pulled him over.

"Any issues with me following them to the hospital, officer? Star asked me if I would." Unfortunately, it would give the guy more time and opportunity to ticket Matt, but that couldn't be helped.

"Emmitt," Officer McCarty corrected. "The name is Emmitt, alright? I think you more than worked off your ticket back there."

Sucking in a breath of relief, Matt held out a hand. "Thanks, man. I really appreciate it." It was a huge concession. The guy could've taken his license if he'd wanted to.

They soberly shook hands, eyeing each other.

"You need me to come by the PD to file a witness report or anything before I boogie out of town this evening?" Matt pressed.

"Nah. Just give me a call, and we'll take care of it over the phone." Emmitt produced a business card and handed it over. "Not sure if we'll need your story, since I saw it go down, but we should probably still cross every T."

"Roger that." Matt stuffed the card in the back pocket of his jeans.

"Where are you headed, anyway?"

"Amarillo. Got an interview at Pantex tomorrow."

"Nice! It's a solid company." Emmitt nodded. "I've got several friends who work there."

Star leaned out from the back of the ambulance. "You coming or what?" she called impatiently to Matt.

He nodded vigorously. "I'll follow you," he called back and jogged back to his truck. Since the ambulance was on the opposite side of the highway, he turned on his blinker and put his oversized tires to good use while traversing the median. He had to spin his wheels a bit in the center of the median to get his tires to grab the sandy incline leading to the other side. He was grateful all over again that he'd splurged on a few upgrades for his truck to make it fit for off-roading.

He followed the ambulance north and found himself driving the final twenty minutes or so to Amarillo, probably because it boasted a much bigger hospital than any of the smaller surrounding towns — more than one, actually. Due to another vehicle leaving the parking lot as he was entering it, Matt was able to grab a decently close parking spot. He jogged into the waiting room, dropped Star Corrigan's name a few times, and tried to make it sound like he was a close friend of the patient.

Looking doubtful, the receptionist made him wait while she paged Star, who appeared a short time later to escort him into the emergency room. "Bree's in Bay 6," she informed him in a strained voice, reaching for his arm and practically dragging him behind the curtain.

If anything, Bree looked even thinner and more fragile than she had outside on the highway. A nurse was stooped over her, inserting an I.V. into her arm.

"She still hasn't woken up." Star's voice was soft, barely above a whisper. "They're pretty sure she has a concussion. Sounds like they're gonna run a full battery of tests to figure out what's going on."

Matt nodded, not knowing what to say.

The lovely EMT's pager went off. She snatched it up and scowled at it. "I just got another call. It's a busy day out there for motorists." She texted a message on her cell phone, then cast him a sideways glance. "Any chance you'll be able to stick around until Bree's brother gets here?"

That's when it hit Matt that this had been the EMT's real goal all along — to ensure that her friend wasn't left alone. She'd known she could get called away to the next job at any second.

"Not a problem." He offered what he hoped was a reassuring smile. Amarillo was where he'd been heading, so he'd already reached his final destination. "I wasn't planning on going far, anyway. Got an interview at Pantex in the morning."

"No kidding! Well, good luck with that," she

returned with a curious, searching look. "A lot of my friends moved up this way for jobs after high school."

Officer Emmitt McCarty had said something similar. "Hey, ah..." Matt hated detaining the EMT any longer than necessary, but it might not hurt to know a few more details about the unconscious woman, since he was about to be alone with her. "Mind telling me Bree's last name?"

"Anderson. Her brother is Brody. Brody Anderson. They run a ranch about halfway between here and Hereford, so it'll take him a good twenty to thirty minutes to get here."

"It's alright. I can stay. It was nice meeting you, by the way." His gaze landed on Bree's left hand, which was resting limply atop the white blankets on her bed. She wasn't wearing a wedding ring. *Not that it matters. I'm a complete idiot for looking.* He forced his gaze back to the EMT. "Sorry about the circumstances, of course."

"Me, too." She shot another worried look at her friend and dropped her voice conspiratorially. "Hey, you're really not supposed to be back here since you're not family, but I sorta begged and they sorta agreed to overlook the rules until Brody gets here." She eyed him worriedly.

"Don't worry." He could tell she hated the necessity of leaving. "I'll stick around until her brother gets here, even if I get booted out to the waiting room with the regular Joes."

"Thanks! Really." She whipped out her cell phone. "Here's my number in case you need to reach me for anything."

Wow! Matt had not been expecting the beautiful EMT to offer him her phone number. Not that he was complaining. It was a boost to his sorely damaged ego. He dug for his phone. "I'm ready when you're ready."

She rattled off her number, and he quickly texted her back so she would have his.

"Take care of her for me, will you, Matt?" she pleaded anxiously.

On second thought, there was nothing flirtatious about Star's demeanor. It was entirely possible that their exchange of phone numbers was exactly what she'd claimed it was — a means of staying in touch about the status of her friend's condition. Giving her a reassuring look, Matt fist-bumped her.

Looking grateful, she pushed aside the curtain and was gone. The nurse followed, presumably to report Bree's vitals to the doctor on duty.

Matt moved to the foot of the hospital bed. "So, who do you think I am, Bree?" *And why did you beg me not to leave you?*

Her long blonde lashes remained motionless against her cheeks. It looked like he was going to have to stick around for a while if he wanted answers.

Hope you enjoyed this excerpt from
Accidental Hero.
Available in eBook, paperback, hard cover large print, and Kindle Unlimited!

Read them all!
A - Accidental Hero
B - Best Friend Hero
C - Celebrity Hero
D - Damaged Hero
E - Enemies to Hero
F - Forbidden Hero
G - Guardian Hero
H - Hunk and Hero
I - Instantly Her Hero
J - Jilted Hero
K - Kissable Hero
L - Long Distance Hero
M - Mistaken Hero
N - Not Good Enough Hero
O - Opposites Attract Hero

Much love,
Jo

ALSO BY JO GRAFFORD

For the most up-to-date printable list of my sweet contemporary romance books:

Click here

or go to:

https://www.JoGrafford.com/books

For the most up-to-date printable list of books by Jo Grafford, writing sweet historical romance books as Jovie Grace:

Click here

or go to:

https://www.jografford.com/joviegracebooks

ABOUT JO

Jo is an Amazon bestselling author of sweet Christian romance books full of faith, hope, love, family drama, and a few Texas-sized detours into humor.

1.) Follow on Amazon!
amazon.com/author/jografford

2.) Join Cuppa Jo Readers!
https://www.facebook.com/groups/CuppaJoReaders

3.) Follow on Bookbub!
https://www.bookbub.com/authors/jo-grafford

4.) Follow on Instagram!
https://www.instagram.com/jografford/

5.) Follow on YouTube
https://www.youtube.com/channel/
UC3R1at97Qso6BXiBIxCjQ5w

- amazon.com/authors/jo-grafford
- bookbub.com/authors/jo-grafford
- facebook.com/jografford

Made in the USA
Las Vegas, NV
22 November 2024